Dark of the Moon

Jim Hewitt has earned his living as a vampire hunter his whole adult life, until one fateful night when the hunter becomes the hunted. Now a fledgling vampire trying to accept his new life, he changes his name to Travis Black and moves to Susandale, a small town with a secret.

In an effort to avoid marrying the man her wealthy parents have chosen for her, Sara Winters makes a deal with her father—if she can't provide for herself for one year, she will agree to marry Dilworth Young III. To that end, she moves to Susandale and opens a bath boutique.

Travis and Sara would likely have never met if Travis hadn't chosen her as his prey. Was it mere coincidence that brought the two of them to the same sleepy little town? Or a happy twist of Fate?

BOOKS BY AMANDA ASHLEY

"Born of the Night" in Stroke of Midnight
"Midnight Pleasures" in Darkfest
"Music of the Night" in Mammoth
Book of Vampire Romance
A Darker Dream
A Fire in the Blood
A Whisper of Eternity
After Sundown
As Twilight Falls
Beauty's Beast
Beneath a Midnight Moon
Bound by Blood
Bound by Night
Dark of the Moon
Dead Perfect
Dead Sexy
Deeper Than the Night
Desire After Dark
Desire the Night
Donovan's Woman
Embrace the Night
Everlasting Desire
Everlasting Embrace
Everlasting Kiss
His Dark Embrace

Immortal Sins
Jessie's Girl
Maiden's Song
Masquerade
Midnight and Moonlight
Midnight Embrace
Night's Kiss
Night's Master
Night's Mistress
Night's Pleasure
Night's Promise
Night's Surrender
Night's Touch
Quinn's Lady
Quinn's Revenge
Sandy's Angel
Seasons of the Night
Shades of Gray
Sunlight Moonlight
The Captive
The Music of the Night
Twilight Desires
Twilight Dreams

Dark of the Moon

Amanda Ashley

Dark of the Moon

This edition published 2020

Cover design by Cynthia Lucas

ISBN: 978-1-68068-209-0

This book is published on behalf of the author by the Ethan Ellenberg Literary Agency.

You can reach the author at:
Email: darkwritr@aol.com
Website: www.amandaashley.net OR www.madelinebaker.net

Dedication

To my readers ~ thank you for your friendship through the years. I appreciate your letters, comments and support.

Table of Contents

PROLOGUE

The dream came every day and it was always the same. And even as it unfolded, never changing, the man who had once been known as Jim Hewitt wished it was just that, nothing but a dream…

He had followed the vampire known as Ronan and the woman, Shannah, home, intent on destroying the one and rescuing the other. And he had come so close. Armed with a bottle of holy water and a sharp wooden stake, he had attacked Ronan as they arrived at his lair. The holy water had done its job, burning the vampire's face, giving Hewitt the window of opportunity he needed to drive the stake into the vampire's back. The scent of fresh hot blood wafted through the night.

He hollered at Shannah to run away while she could.

But Shannah didn't run away. With a scream of rage, she grabbed him by the arm.

Startled, he glanced at her. "What are you doing?"

"Stopping you!" She yanked his hand away from the stake, her fingers curling around his wrist in an iron-like grip.

"Are you crazy?" Hewitt exclaimed. "He's a vampire!"

"Yes!" she hissed, baring her fangs. "And so am I."

Startled, he could only stare at her, and then he lashed out as fear and fury swept through him.

She laughed as he struggled in vain to free himself from her hold. And then she trapped his gaze with hers. "Stop fighting me," she commanded.

Unable to resist the preternatural power in her voice, his arms fell limply to his sides. Helpless to move, he watched her drop to her knees beside Ronan and yank the stake from his back. A torrent of dark red blood flowed from the nasty wound.

And then the vampire sat up and uttered the most chilling words Jim Hewitt had ever heard.

"Bring him to me."

The nightmare grew worse from that point on. Shannah released him from her spell and dragged him effortlessly toward the wounded vampire. Fear spiraled through Hewitt as he gazed into Ronan's blood-red eyes.

"I warned you," the vampire said. "You should have listened."

Hewitt struggled in vain as Ronan sank his fangs into his throat. For a time, he seemed to be drifting between this world and the next. And then, as from far away, he heard the vampire's voice.

"Listen to me. You have only a few minutes to make up your mind. Do you want to live or die?"

Hewitt stared up into the monster's face. How could he be expected to make such a decision? He was a hunter. How could he choose between death or spending the rest of his existence as a vampire?

"Your time is running out," Ronan said curtly. "Make your choice!"

"Live." Hewitt forced the word from the depths of his soul. "I want... to live."

With a feral cry, the vampire bit into his own wrist. "Then drink," he said, and his voice was like sandpaper over steel.

Hewitt grimaced as dark red blood—vampire blood—dripped from the wound in Ronan's wrist into his mouth. He choked down the first taste, hating what he was doing, hating the creature who had brought him to this.

And then, to his amazement, he latched onto Ronan's arm with both hands, drinking eagerly, afraid the vampire would make him stop. How could something so repulsive taste so good?

"Damn you!" he cried hoarsely, and then he pulled the vampire's wrist to his mouth again and took his first step into another life.

Chapter 1

The man who had once been Jim Hewitt jackknifed into a sitting position, the nightmare still vivid in his mind. Not for the first time, he wondered why he had been plagued with the same dream since he'd been turned. He was a vampire now and everyone knew that vampires slept like the dead. Yet the nightmare tormented him night after night.

Jim Hewitt had died that horrible night and the name he'd been born with had died with him. Changing his name had seemed like a wise decision for a number of reasons, but mainly because Jim Hewitt had been a vampire hunter who now preferred to remain incognito. He had considered several alternative names before deciding on Travis Black—Travis for the man who had fathered him. And Black for the monster who had turned him. It had been one of Ronan's aliases. It seemed only fitting to take his vampire sire's name, as well.

"Travis." He murmured it out loud, wondering how long it would take before he answered to it automatically. Of course, it was a moot point at the moment, since he was the only one who knew he had discarded the name he had been born with.

If he lived to be a hundred, he would never forget the horror of waking that first night and realizing it hadn't been a bad dream. Even now, four months later, he often roused from the dark sleep feeling lost and disoriented. He was supposed to track and destroy vampires, not hide from the hunters.

As he did every night on waking, he cursed the vampire who had turned him although, to be honest, he had no one to blame but himself. If he had left the damned, blood-sucking creature and his woman alone, none of this would have happened.

Exasperated, he plowed his fingers through his hair. He had hunted the undead his whole adult life, would have sworn he knew everything there was to know about them. Just proved how wrong a man could be, he thought bitterly, and once again, he cursed Ronan for turning him and then leaving him to fend for himself. A sire was supposed to stay with his fledgling for at least a year to help him adjust to his new life, teach him how to hunt, how to find shelter, how to defend himself, if need be. A sire wasn't supposed to abandon those he turned.

Travis swore under his breath. Sure, he knew about *hunting* vampires. He knew how to find them, how to immobilize them, how to destroy them.

What he didn't know was how to *be* one.

"Dammit!"

He had lost more than his humanity, he thought bleakly. He had lost his family, too, as well as the few friends he'd had back home in Nevada. There was just no way in hell his old acquaintances, mostly hunters, would accept him as he was now. Being a hunter hadn't allowed him the luxury of staying in one place long enough to really get to close to anyone other than hunters, male or female.

From time to time, he had thought about contacting Carl Overstreet. Not that he and Carl had been friends, exactly, but they had shared some wildly hairy moments together and survived.

He had met the man while shadowing Ronan and Shannah. Overstreet, who had been a freelance reporter at the time, had written a series of articles titled *Vampires Among Us ~ Truth or Legend?* for a national magazine. Travis, still known as Hewitt back then, had met Overstreet in a bar late one night where they had struck up an alliance of sorts. They had both been after the same thing, though for vastly different reasons. Travis had wanted to destroy a monster. Overstreet had wanted to interview one. Travis had failed in his quest. The writer had succeeded and then quit the field.

Travis shook his head. If only he had done the same. Hunting sure as hell hadn't paid much, but he hadn't been qualified to do anything else. Still, he had been thinking about looking for a more lucrative line of work when he'd gotten a hot tip from another hunter that Ronan was holed up in a little town in Northern California. He had followed the vampire and the woman from a discreet distance for a time and then one night he had followed his quarry into a bookstore where he'd learned that Shannah was a published author. It wasn't until later that he discovered it was the vampire who was the writer and that the woman merely pretended to be him, though, at the time, he'd had no idea why.

If only he had stayed in Nevada and found some mundane nine-to-five job, he wouldn't be in this predicament now, a fledgling vampire with less than forty dollars in his pocket and not a single soul he could confide in.

On the bright side, he no longer had to buy groceries. He didn't have to worry about getting sick, so there was no longer any need for health insurance. Maybe dental, if he broke a fang, he mused with wry amusement.

On the dark side, he still had to pay rent since he didn't want to take his rest in the ground. He had tried that once, he recalled with a grimace, and he had no desire to do it again.

As his old grandmother had been fond of saying—there was no use in crying over spilt milk. For once he had to agree with her. He was what he was and there was no going back.

Or was there?

Rising, he began to pace the bedroom floor. He had never heard of a vampire returning to mortality, but that didn't mean it had never happened. But if there was a cure, the vampire community was keeping it under wraps.

So, how was he to find out if one existed?

The Web, of course.

Padding barefoot into the living room of the cottage, he booted up his laptop and Googled vampire cures. Page after page of links came up. The only problem? They all referred to the role-playing game "Oblivion".

He spent another forty minutes searching the Internet. He found numerous sites about vampires, how to become a vampire, how to recognize one, how to kill the monsters, not to mention numerous sites dedicated to the old TV shows, *Dark Shadows* and *Buffy, the Vampire Slayer*, and newer ones like *Moonlight* and *The Vampire Diaries*, as well as the works of Anne Rice. There were fan sites for notorious individual vampires, as well, both real and fictional—Dracula, Lestat, Rylan Saintcrow, Edward Cullen, Mick St. John, Rhys Costain, and Damon Salvatore. But nothing about a cure for actual vampirism.

Muttering an oath, he signed off, then sat there staring into the distance, until a familiar ache started deep inside of him. His tongue brushed his fangs as his need grew stronger. The hunger had become his master, a cruel tyrant he was helpless to resist, an addiction he craved almost as much as he despised it.

Dressing quickly, he left the small rental house. Blending into the shadows of the night, he went in search of prey—and rent money.

CHAPTER 2

Sara Winters closed the door behind her, turned the key in the lock, and let out a sigh. If today wasn't the worst day she'd ever had, sales-wise, since she went into business, it was certainly in the top two. Opening a store of her own had seemed like such a good idea when she'd first arrived in Susandale. Gourmet chocolates and premium bath soaps and salts had seemed like the perfect combination. After all, practically every woman on the planet loved chocolate of one kind or another. And everybody had to bathe. And none of the other stores in town carried anything like what she offered.

Maybe there was a reason for that, she thought glumly. Maybe the women in this part of the country didn't like sweets and never bought fancy scented soaps, bubble bath or lotion. Or maybe they just didn't like her, although that didn't seem likely. She had hardly met any of her neighbors since she moved here three months ago, and those she had met seemed a little, well, eccentric.

Now that she thought about it, the whole town seemed a little odd. Like the fact that she had seen very few children, which might have been understandable in a retirement community, but most of the people she had seen looked to be in their twenties and thirties. She rarely saw anyone on the streets before sunset, except the occasional tourist. Thank goodness for those, few though they might be, because they invariably stopped in to browse. And usually bought a bag of candy, if nothing else.

Strangest of all, most of the other businesses didn't open until after sundown. Which made sense, she guessed, since few people were out and about during the day. She supposed that since Susandale was so small, most of the inhabitants worked out of town, or worked nights and slept days. Odder still was the fact that there was no school. Still, it *was* a small town. The kids were probably bussed to a bigger city nearby.

Brow furrowed, Sara gazed up and down the quiet street. Maybe she would do more business if she kept the same hours as the rest of the town's shops. If she didn't start turning a profit, she was going to have to pack up and go back home. And she really didn't want to do that. This was her one chance to prove she could live on her own, that she could earn her own way. Her father had agreed to give her twelve months to prove she could succeed. If whatever business she started failed within that time, he expected her to return home and marry Dilworth.

It had been the thought of marrying Dilworth Young the Third and settling down into the same Stepford-wife kind of existence that her mother lived that had given Sara the courage to stand up to her overbearing father in the first place and demand that he give her a chance to strike out on her own. Certain she would fail, he had given her the money needed for the first and last month's rent on her house, as well as the first month's rent on her shop.

She had chosen Susandale because it was a small town, as different from her home in Vermont as night from day.

She was beginning to think coming here had been a major mistake.

Feeling the need for some comfort food, she walked down the street to Verna's Bakery—one of the few places that opened early—and bought a buttermilk doughnut and a carton of milk. Then, thinking it was too nice to stay inside, she sat at one of the little tables in front of the bakery and tried to decide what to do about her future while she watched the sun set. She wasn't desperate enough to go back home, at least not yet. Maybe she should just pack up and move to a bigger city, she thought, nibbling on the doughnut. Maybe Boston or Chicago. Or San Francisco. She had always wanted to see the Pacific Ocean.

She shook her head. In spite of everything, she liked it here. It was a pretty little town. She would give it another month or two. Tomorrow, she would change her working hours. Instead of doing business from ten to five, she would open at three in the afternoon and close at nine. And if that didn't work? Well, she'd worry about that later.

She sat there for several minutes, lost in thought. After drinking the last of the milk, she tossed the carton in the trash can beside the door, then walked back to the shop to get her car, which she had left in the parking lot behind the building.

She was about to unlock the door when she realized she wasn't alone. A sliver of icy fear slithered down her spine as a man dressed in black materialized out of the shadows and stepped into a pool of light cast by the streetlamp on the corner.

Sara took a step back, every instinct she possessed warning her to run, to scream, but all she could do was stand there, as if held by some invisible power.

Travis couldn't stop staring at the woman. She was lovely. A riot of sun-gold curls fell over her shoulders. Hazel eyes, as wide and frightened as those of a doe caught by surprise, stared back at him. He could hear the beat of her heart pounding hard and fast in her chest, smell the sweet nectar flowing through her veins, the fear on her skin.

He hadn't meant to frighten her. "I'm sorry," he said, releasing her from his thrall. "I didn't mean to startle you."

Sara blinked at him. He looked harmless. Had she imagined that odd sense of power that had held her spellbound? He wasn't much taller than she was. His hair, thick and blond, brushed his collar, his eyes were a deep, dark brown. She shook her head. "It's all right."

He smiled at her. "Maybe I could buy you a cup of coffee as a peace offering?"

"I don't think so."

"I hope I see you again." A friendly wave of his hand and he walked away.

She waited until he was out of sight, then quickly unlocked her Chevy and slid behind the wheel. Driving home, she had the weirdest feeling that she *would* see him again.

Keeping to the shadows, Travis followed the woman. She lived in a small white house with bright yellow shutters only a few blocks away from where she worked. He watched as she pulled into the driveway and hurried into the house.

She really was a pretty thing, but it was more than her appearance that drew him, though he couldn't have said what it was. As a hunter, he'd had little time for women or serious relationships. As a vampire, he'd had even less. Unsure of himself, afraid of inadvertently doing or saying something that would give him away, he had avoided contact with women—except for those he preyed on. But he didn't want to prey on this one. He just wanted to know her better.

Drawing closer, he opened his senses, nodded when he didn't detect anyone else inside. Since she hadn't worn a wedding ring and there was no lingering scent of a man — or anyone else—on the premises, he assumed she was single and lived alone.

The thought made him smile because he was determined to see her again.

But for now, he needed to hunt.

Shannah rolled onto her side, her fingers tracing random patterns on Ronan's chest. He lay quiet beneath her roving hands, his eyes closed. She loved him with every fiber of her being. He had saved her life, showed her a world she had never dreamed existed. "It's been four months," she remarked. "Do you think he's all right?"

"I really don't give a damn."

"You sired him." Her lips followed the path of her fingertips. "I still think it was terribly cruel to turn him out with no one to guide him."

"He's lucky I didn't kill him."

"But..."

"The man was a hunter," he said irritably. "He knows enough to survive. He'll learn the rest. And if he doesn't..." He twitched one shoulder.

She couldn't really blame her husband for his uncaring attitude. Jim Hewitt had attacked Ronan without provocation, fully intending to destroy him. Still, she couldn't help feeling sorry for the hunter. He had seemed like a nice guy and she felt partly responsible for what had happened to him. Believing that Ronan was a danger to her, Hewitt had tried to warn her off. Poor man. No doubt he was feeling lost and alone as he tried to adjust to being a vampire. It couldn't be easy, being cut off from family and friends, forced by circumstances to learn how to navigate his new life on his own. She frequently wondered where he was and how he was doing. "Is he still alive?"

Ronan turned onto his side and studied her through fathomless eyes as black as midnight. "Why do you care?"

"I don't know. I just do."

With a huff of impatience, he opened the blood link that bound the fledgling to him, a link that could be broken only by death.

"You can stop worrying," he said curtly. "He's alive."

Travis's head jerked up, the woman in his arms momentarily forgotten as he felt the blood link open between himself and his sire. Why now, he thought, after all this time? But before he could put the question to words, the link was gone.

Frowning, he turned back to his prey. The urge to take it all, to glut himself with his prey's blood, was a constant temptation. Thus far, he had managed to keep his seemingly insatiable lust for blood under control—forcing himself to take only what he needed and not what he wanted. He knew, on some deep, instinctive level, that it would be easier to control his hunger if his sire had stayed with him, to guide him. Not that he could blame the vampire for abandoning him. He had tried to destroy Ronan, after all.

Travis grinned ruefully. He had done what hunters do. He supposed he should be grateful the vampire hadn't killed him. But tonight, with the craving for blood burning hot and strong within him, he didn't feel grateful at all.

Chapter 3

Sara slept late the next morning. Now that she had decided to open at three in the afternoon instead of ten a.m., there was no rush to get ready for the day. She took a long, leisurely shower, washed her hair, painted her nails. Instead of a quick glass of orange juice and a bagel for breakfast, she fixed French toast and sausage, lingered over a second cup of coffee. And a third.

Throughout the day, whenever she wasn't preoccupied with anything else, she found herself thinking about the man she had met, however briefly, the night before. Should she have let him buy her a cup of coffee? She could have met him somewhere. What harm could there be in meeting him in a public place? He had been nice looking and seemed like an easy-going guy. He hadn't made any untoward moves, had accepted her decision without getting angry.

She should have said yes. She hadn't had anything resembling a date since she moved here. Maybe if she saw him again, she would agree to that cup of coffee.

To her surprise, Sara had more people stop by that day than she'd had in the last three months. Mostly women, of course. All young and attractive. A few were friendly, most were somewhat reserved. Even more surprising, they didn't just come in to look around, but to buy.

"Another week like this," Sara mused, "and I'll have to restock a few things." Not that she was complaining!

At seven, she closed for a dinner break.

Travis stood in the shadows, his attention focused on *Sara's Sweets & Salts Shoppe.* A warm wind blew down Main Street, carrying with it the myriad fragrances of sugar and soap and perfume from the store across the street. He was still trying to summon the nerve to go in and say hello when she stepped outside and hung a *Closed* sign on the door.

Curious, he followed her down the sidewalk to the small café. on the corner. He waited ten minutes, then followed her inside.

Sara looked up as the bell over the entrance signaled a new customer. It was him, the man she had met the night before. She smiled tentatively when his gaze met hers. Her smile faded around the edges when he came striding toward her. Was he stalking her? Maybe she'd been right to refuse his invitation.

Sara glanced around the café, reassured by the presence of a handful of other diners. Her heartbeat quickened with trepidation when he stopped by her table.

"We meet again," he said with a friendly smile. "I'm Travis."

She didn't want to tell him her name, but it seemed rude not to. "Sara."

"Nice to meet you, Sara. Enjoy your dinner."

"You, too, Mr…?" Best not to be on a first name basis with a total stranger.

"Black."

She watched him move down the aisle to another table. He took a chair facing her so that every time she looked up, she saw him. Had he done that on purpose?

Sara ordered spaghetti, garlic bread, and a soda. Conscious of Travis watching her, she pulled a paperback book from her handbag and pretended to be reading so she didn't have to look at him.

It didn't help. She was all too aware of his presence. For some reason she couldn't explain, she felt drawn to him.

Taking a deep breath, she put the novel aside and gestured for him to join her.

"Thanks," he said, taking the chair across from hers. "I hate eating alone."

"Me, too."

He gestured at her book, a mystery by New York Times bestselling author Claire Ebon. "You like her writing style?"

"Yes. Do you?"

He shrugged one shoulder. "I've never read one, but I know the author." Claire Ebon was another pseudonym used by Ronan, who also wrote in other genres under the names Eva Black and Stella Raven.

"I'd love to meet her," Sara said, eyes sparkling with interest. "Do you think you could introduce me?"

"Believe me," he said dryly, "that wouldn't be a good idea."

"Really? Why not?"

"Trust me, it would be a big mistake. You're new in town, aren't you?" he said, eager to change the subject.

"Yes. I've only been here a few months. Have you lived here long?"

"About five months," he said. "I'm originally from Nevada."

"Oh? Why did you leave?"

He hesitated a moment, then said, "I needed to get away for a while." This place had seemed perfect for a guy like him. "What brought you here?"

She laughed softly. "Like you, I needed to get away. My father had my whole life planned out for me. Only I didn't like his road map."

Travis nodded. "My life isn't turning out quite the way I thought it would, either."

She didn't miss the faint note of bitterness in his voice. "I'm sorry."

"Not your fault," he said with a wry grin. "The choice was mine and I have to live with it, but believe me, it's not a decision I ever thought I'd have to make."

"I'm sorry you're so unhappy about it."

"What's done is done. There's no going back. No changing my mind."

Sara frowned. She couldn't help wondering what kind of choice he'd had to make. There were only a few decisions she could think of that were irreversible. "I guess you'll just have to learn to live with it then."

"Yeah, that's what my grandmother used to say."

The waitress arrived with Sara's dinner and a glass of red wine for Travis.

"Is that all you're having?" Sara asked.

"I... uh, dined earlier. To tell you the truth, I only came in here because I saw you through the window and..." He shrugged. "I haven't made any friends in town and I just wanted someone to talk to. I should probably go. I'm sorry I bothered you."

"You didn't. I don't know anyone in town, either. To tell *you* the truth, I'm grateful for your company."

He smiled at her, the first truly genuine smile she had seen. It did funny things in the pit of her stomach. She gestured at her plate. "Would you like some? There's plenty."

"No, but thank you."

The next forty minutes seemed to fly by. Sara didn't remember ever being so comfortable around anyone else so quickly, which was odd, because they were strangers, but he had a ready smile and a wry sense of humor.

"I'd like to see you again," Travis said as she was finishing dessert. "Would you mind if I called you sometime?"

"Not at all." Reaching into her bag, she withdrew one of her business cards and handed it to him.

Sara paid for her meal with her credit card. He paid cash for his wine and they left the restaurant together.

"Thanks for this evening," he said. "Be careful going home."

"I will. Good night, Mr. Black."

He watched her get into her car and drive away. Then, whistling softly, he strolled down the street. He didn't know how or why she had picked this town. He couldn't say for certain, of course, but he was pretty sure she didn't know what kind of people resided in Susandale.

But her being here suddenly made everything look brighter.

Although he had fed earlier, it hadn't satisfied his thirst. It was said older vampires didn't need to feed as often. He hoped like hell that was true, because even though he didn't find the taste of blood repulsive, he hated what he had to do to get it.

Hunting within the town limits was forbidden, so he went to the next city, which was about ten miles away. It still amazed him that he could outrun a moving train.

He had spent the first few weeks after he'd been turned trying to learn how to use the preternatural powers that were now his, but he'd had little success so far. He knew vampires had the ability to transport themselves from one location to another merely by thinking about it, and that they could dissolve into mist, both talents he had yet to master. It was mostly fear that kept him from trying to dissolve into mist. What if he got caught halfway between vapor and solid form? Or if he turned into mist and got stuck there?

Now and then, when he was holed up in his lair before the dark sleep claimed him, he thought about all the vampires he had destroyed in the past. As a hunter, he had never thought of them as people. They were monsters, the enemy, nothing more. He had hunted them and killed them without a qualm. Now, he wondered how many had chosen to be turned out of a desperate desire to cheat death. And how many of them had been turned against their will. Most likely all of them. Surely no one in their right mind *asked* to be a vampire.

He grunted softly. Some *had* been monsters, preying on men, women, and even children without mercy or remorse. Somewhere along the way, they had lost their humanity so that they no longer considered themselves part of the human family at all. The thought that he might someday become one of them frightened him as nothing else had.

Pushing such thoughts aside, Travis found his prey on the next street. In what had become second nature, he mesmerized the woman with a look, took what he needed to survive, and released her from his thrall, hoping, as he did so, that he would never turn into the kind of monsters he had once hunted. That he would never lose his humanity. Or his immortal soul.

Back in his lair, he stretched out on the sofa and clasped his hands behind his head. From out of nowhere, he found himself wondering what Carl Overstreet was doing these days.

Suddenly curious, he grabbed his cell phone and Googled Overstreet's name. Links to several articles penned by Overstreet popped up, including the series Carl had written about Ronan. Travis scrolled down to the last page.

And so, dear reader, we come at last to the end of our tale. I searched for a vampire, and I found one. You may not believe me, but I swear by everything I hold dear that they do exist. I spoke to him briefly, under conditions I would rather not repeat or remember. He told me that he had been a vampire for five hundred and thirteen years and admitted that he had killed "a few hundred people, maybe more" in that time.

He said he was made a vampire against his will, that there were many vampires here, in the United States, and many others throughout the world. "More than you want to know" were his exact words.

He said there had been vampires since the beginning of time. When questioned, he said he didn't know where the first vampire had come from, though there were some who believed that Vlad the Impaler was the father of the Undead. Whoever the first vampire had been, it's believed that he made a deal with the Devil, trading his soul for immortality.

Our vampire said he had never turned another into a vampire but he knew how it was done.

Travis snorted. Never turned another? That might have been true when Overstreet wrote the article, but not any longer. He, himself, was proof of that. And so was Shannah. With a shake of his head, he continued reading.

Indeed, he even offered to show me. You may be sure that I quickly declined.

I told him I had heard several versions of how one became a vampire and asked if he knew how it was done. He admitted that he did and even offered to show me. You may be sure that I quickly declined.

At this point, he grew impatient with my questions and the interview was over.

As for me, I hope never to see him again.

Someone once said, "Ignorance is bliss."

Oh, how I long to be ignorant again.

Travis remembered reading the series of articles in one of the national magazines. He had read it twice, then thrown the publication against the wall.

A further search of the Net turned up a short article saying Carl Overstreet had retired shortly after the series was published.

Travis grunted softly, wondering what the writer would say if he knew his former accomplice had become what they had once hunted.

Thinking about Overstreet naturally led to thoughts of Ronan and Shannah and the last time he'd seen them. It had been like a nightmare come true. He had staked Ronan, been about to deliver the killing blow when Shannah came to the vampire's rescue. He could still remember his shock when he'd realized that she, too, was a vampire. He had looked death in the face that night. It was a horror he would never forget. He might hate what he had become but, like he'd told Sara, he had no one to blame but himself.

He shut down his phone as he felt dawn's approach. It was an odd feeling and decidedly unpleasant—a sort of burning sensation, as if all the blood in his body was on fire.

In his room, he undressed, then stretched out on the bed, hands folded behind his head as he stared at the narrow crack in the ceiling.

But it was Sara's face that followed him into oblivion—a wealth of sun-gold waves framing a heart-shaped face, warm hazel eyes beneath gently arched brows, pink lips curved in an innocent come-hither smile.

He murmured her name as the darkness engulfed him and carried him away.

The next afternoon at work, Sara couldn't help noticing again that all the women who came into the shop were lovely and well-dressed. Their skin seemed to glow with good health. She also noticed that they all seemed to be on a first-name basis. Of course, it was a small town, so maybe that wasn't so strange. Still, it made Sara feel like an outsider, and it had nothing to do with the fact that she was new in town. No, it had to do with some kind of underlying camaraderie that she didn't understand, almost as if they all shared a secret she didn't know.

Or like they were Stepford wives.

The thought sent an icy chill down her spine. Of all the horror movies she had ever seen, that one had scared her the most.

At seven, she closed the store. She was deciding whether to go home and make dinner or eat out again when her phone rang. She felt a tingle of anticipation as she answered. Could it be him? "Hello?"

"Hey, Sara. It's me. Travis. Am I calling at a bad time?"

At the sound of his voice, she felt her smile stretch from ear to ear. All day, she had hoped he would call. "No, it's fine." She couldn't keep the excitement out of her voice. "How are you?"

"Doing good. I was planning to wait until tomorrow night to give you call so you wouldn't think I was too anxious, but I guess I blew it."

"I'm glad."

"Are you busy after work? I know you get off late, but I thought maybe we could go out for a drink."

"I'd like that."

"Great. Where would you like to go?"

"How about Teddy's? It's a nightclub over in South Port. Do you know it?"

"No. What time should I pick you up?"

"How about if I meet you there? Around ten? It'll give me time to go home and change."

"Sounds good. See you then."

Smiling, Sara ended the call. She had a date!

Smart girl, not wanting him to know where she lived, Travis thought as he slipped his phone into his pocket. But it didn't matter. He felt better than he had since he'd been turned. He showered and dressed, then headed for Mamie's Manse, a known hangout for the undead. Owned by a middle-aged woman who was addicted to vampire blood, the nightclub was located in the basement of an abandoned warehouse at the end of a long, dirt road five miles west of Susandale.

Candlelight illuminated the basement, casting dancing shadows on the dark gray walls and cement floor. The patrons were predominately vampires, with a few humans who were either addicted to vampire blood or just got a kick out of letting the undead feed on them. There were two house rules strictly enforced by the biggest man-turned-vampire Travis had ever seen. At nearly seven feet tall, the

Hun had been a wrestler in his former life. Travis had no doubt the guy could rip a vampire's head off without breaking a sweat. The first law of the house was that no vampire was allowed to feed on an unwilling human. The second was that any vampire who inflicted death on a patron, mortal or immortal, would forfeit his life.

Travis recognized a few of the vampires as residents of Susandale.

Another thing he had learned was that all the women who lived in town belonged to the vampires—some by choice. Some by compulsion.

Though he had just met Sara, he intended to make sure she didn't become one of them.

Chapter 4

Sara hurried home from work, changed into a white skirt and a pink sweater, ran a comb through her hair and drove to Teddy's. She hoped Travis hadn't been offended when she offered to meet him at the club, but she had only known him a few days and in this day and age, she preferred to err on the side of caution.

After leaving her car with the valet, she took a deep, calming breath and entered the club. Round tables covered with crisp white cloths took up one side of the dance floor, booths the other. A large mahogany bar was located in the back of the room. Shelves made of teak held glasses of all shapes and sizes. A tall, good-looking man with a clipped mustache tended bar.

It was Friday night and the place was crowded with couples laughing, talking, and generally having a good time. A three-piece band provided music for dancing.

Sara threaded her way to the bar and ordered a Cosmopolitan.

Travis came up beside her just as her drink arrived. "Hey, sorry I'm late," he said.

"I was early."

"Shall we get a table?"

"If you can find one." Drink in hand, she followed him around the edge of the dance floor. As luck would have it, they spied a middle-aged couple just getting up from a table nearby.

Sara draped her coat over the back of one of the chairs before sitting down. "How was your day?"

"Quiet as a tomb." He signaled a passing waiter and ordered a glass of red wine. "How was yours?"

"Terrific! Tomorrow morning I'll be ordering a ton of supplies." She shook her head. "It's funny. The first few days I was there, I had maybe three customers. The last few days, business has really picked up. I guess changing my hours was a good idea. It's odd, though, that so few people are out and about during the day." She frowned. "You know, I don't think I've seen more than one or two men on the streets before dark."

"There's aren't many employment opportunities in Susandale," Travis pointed out. "I'm sure they all work out of town."

Sara nodded. She had thought the very same thing. "I guess you're right, although I've never see any of them come home, either."

He could have explained it to her but, all things considered, it didn't seem like the right time. But then, he doubted there would ever be a right time.

Following her gaze to the dance floor, he said, "Shall we?"

"All right." Lifting her glass, Sara finished her drink, then let him lead her onto the floor. She felt a rush of mingled anticipation and apprehension as he took her in his arms. A first dance was like a first kiss. Sometimes magic happened.

And sometimes it didn't.

But this time it definitely did. There was no denying the quick rush of attraction that arced between them as soon as he took her in his arms. Sara had no trouble following his lead. It was almost as if they had danced together many times before. He wasn't much taller than she, but she detected a strength in him she hadn't expected. A kind of... of... restrained power. He was incredibly light on his feet, making it seem as if he was floating just above the floor.

When she glanced up, she found him gazing down at her. His eyes were a dark, dark brown, fathomless, hypnotic, filled with an emotion she didn't recognize. She felt suddenly weightless, as if she were drifting through crimson clouds. When he lowered his head to her neck, she closed her eyes, sighed as a wave of almost sensual pleasure washed over her. Was she dreaming?

She looked up when Travis murmured her name.

Feeling a little disoriented, she blinked several times, trying to clear her head. What had just happened? Why did she feel so strange?

"The music's stopped."

Sara glanced around. Couples were leaving the floor. "I... I think I must have finished my drink too quickly," she said, feeling her cheeks grow hot. "It seems to have gone right to my head."

"It happens. Nothing to be embarrassed about. Are you game to go again?" he asked when the band began to play something soft and slow.

"I guess so."

Taking her in his arms, he twirled her around the floor until she burst out laughing.

"What do you do for a living?" Sara asked when they returned to their table.

"I'm unemployed at the moment."

"Oh. What kind of work *did* you do?"

Travis hesitated a moment. He could hardly tell her the truth. A partial lie would have to suffice. "I was a bounty hunter."

"Seriously? Like in the Old West?"

"Sort of. I found people and collected the bounty on their heads."

"What kind of people?"

"Oh, you know," he said, making it up as he went along. "Fathers who were behind on their alimony payments. People who skipped out on bail bonds. Felons." *Vampires.*

"Sounds dangerous."

"It can be."

"Why did you quit?"

"Circumstances change. I decided it was time to get out of the business. So, have you always wanted to have your own store?"

"Not really. This is my first real job. I saw an ad in the paper for the shop and…" She shrugged. "I like it so far. I do love being my own boss, setting my own hours, having no one to answer to." Like her bossy mother or her domineering father.

Reaching across the table for her hand, he said, "I'm glad you're here."

Warmth suffused her at his touch. "So am I."

They talked and danced for hours, slowly getting to know each other. It was near one a.m. when Sara yawned behind her napkin. "Sorry."

"It's late," he said, although it was still early for him. "We should probably go."

"I had a good time."

"Me, too. Any chance of seeing you again tomorrow night?"

"I think that can be arranged."

Travis left enough money on the table to cover their drinks and a tip for the waitress, held Sara's coat for her, then walked her to her car. "Goodnight, Sara."

"Goodnight, Mr... Travis."

His gaze searched hers and then, giving her time to refuse, he slipped his arm around her waist and kissed her lightly.

At the touch of his lips on hers, Sara's toes curled inside her shoes. First dance, first kiss, on the same night. And both were earth-shattering.

She couldn't stop smiling as she drove through the dark, deserted streets of the city toward Susandale—until her car died three blocks from home, right in the middle of a construction zone.

Rummaging in her evening bag, Sara reached for her cell phone, gasped when her door was wrenched open and a man in a long black coat reached inside. He ripped her seatbelt in half as if it was made of paper, grabbed a handful of her hair, and yanked her out of the car.

Fear trapped the scream in her throat, but it didn't keep her from fighting back. She gouged and kicked for all she was worth, but her attacker only laughed in her face as he backed her up against the front fender.

Terror took over when she looked into his eyes—glowing red eyes that shone in the dark, like a cat's. Her blood ran cold when his lips pulled back in a feral grin, revealing a pair of fangs.

Fangs!

The strength went out of her legs. The world around her seemed to be getting smaller, darker, as he pushed her hair behind her ear. Then, just when Sara thought she was going to die, her attacker was gone.

Shaking from head to foot, she glanced around, grimaced when she saw the body sprawled face-down on the street, a stout wooden stake embedded in its back.

The world began to spin out of focus when, suddenly, Travis was there, his arms wrapping around her, holding her tight.

"It's all right now," he murmured. "You're safe with me."

She collapsed against him, her body wracked by tremors, tears welling in her eyes and dripping down her cheeks.

Patting her back, he murmured, "Relax, Sara. You're out of danger. Come on, I'll take you home."

He settled her in the front seat of his car, then retrieved her beaded bag and keys from the passenger seat of her Chevy. After shoving her things into his jacket pocket, he slid behind the wheel of his car. "Where do you live?" He already knew the answer, but he didn't want her to know he'd been keeping an eye on her.

Voice quivering, she gave him her address, then huddled against the door.

She was still trembling when he pulled into her driveway twenty minutes later. After shutting off the ignition, he opened her door and carried her up the steps to the narrow porch that fronted the house.

"Are you going to be all right?" he asked as he set her on her feet.

"I don't think I'll ever be all right again."

"Take a warm bath. Have a cup of hot tea. It'll calm you down."

"I don't think so." She paused a moment, then said, "Will you come in for a few minutes? I... I don't want to be alone right now."

"Sure." He pulled her bag and keys out of his jacket pocket, then, noting how shaky her hands were, he unlocked the door and followed her inside. He figured she was far too upset to notice the odd vibration in the air when he stepped across the threshold.

Sara quickly turned on a light and shrugged out of her coat, then collapsed on the sofa.

"Can I get you that cup of tea?" he asked. "Or maybe something stronger, if you've got it?"

"I think there's a bottle of wine in the cupboard. Over the sink."

With a nod, he went into the kitchen. He turned on the light, because she would expect it, found the wine in the cupboard. He filled two glasses and carried them into the living room. After handing her one, he sat in the overstuffed chair across from the sofa.

"Thank you. And thank you for saving me from that... that..." Her voice trailed off and her eyes narrowed. "What *was* that thing? And how did you happen to be there?"

"It was late," he said quietly. "I decided to follow you to make sure you got home safely."

She considered that, then nodded. "You... you stabbed him with a wooden stake."

He shrugged. "I didn't have a gun."

"Why did you have a wooden stake?"

Well, damn, he thought, taking a drink of wine to give himself time to fabricate a lie. He should have expected a question like that. He was about to make something up when he decided against it. If she was going to stay in Susandale, she needed to know the truth. Or at least part of it.

Setting his glass aside, he said, "I wasn't completely honest with you earlier, when I said I was a bounty hunter. The truth is, I used to hunt vampires for a living."

Eyes wide, she stared at him. "Are you saying that ... that thing was a *vampire?*"

He nodded.

"That's ridiculous. There's no such thing."

"I'm afraid there is."

"And you hunted them?"

He didn't miss the skepticism in her tone. On the plus side, it seemed to have chased her fears away. "Yes." Even though he no longer hunted them, he still kept the tools of his trade in the trunk of his car. He wasn't sure why. But tonight he'd been damn glad they were there.

"I don't believe you."

"Then how do you explain the man who attacked you? You saw his eyes and his fangs, same as I did."

Suddenly chilled, Sara pulled the afghan from the back of the couch and wrapped it around her shoulders. She would never forget those hell-red eyes or the primal terror that had engulfed her. Hadn't she known, on some deep, instinctive level, that she was facing something inhuman? But a vampire? How was that even possible? She might have thought someone was playing a horrible joke on her but dying for a laugh seemed unlikely. A vampire. She shuddered. If there was one, were there more? And if so, how many?

"You should get some sleep," Travis suggested. "You'll feel better in the morning."

She nodded somewhat doubtfully, certain that sleep would be a long time coming.

Rising, Travis kissed her on the cheek. "Lock up after me."

"A fat lot of good that will do," she muttered, remembering how the monster had ripped the door off her Chevy with no trouble at all.

"Vampires can't enter your home without an invitation."

She recalled hearing that in some old horror movie but had thought it was just a Hollywood myth, like vampires themselves. A rush of panic engulfed her as Travis headed for the door. "Wait! Would you mind staying with me until I fall asleep?"

"Not at all, if that's what you want."

"Maybe you could spend the night? I really don't want to be alone."

Nodding, he locked the front door.

"There's a guestroom..."

"I'll just crash on the sofa if it's all right with you. Good night, Sara."

"Help yourself to a pillow and blankets." Clutching the afghan with one hand and holding her wine glass in the other, she padded out of the room, the afghan trailing on the floor behind her.

Travis stared after her for a moment, then glanced around the room. It was sparsely furnished. The walls, painted a pale yellow, were bare. The floor was hardwood. A flowered sofa and matching chair faced each other across a distressed coffee table. Matching tables stood on either side of the sofa. An assortment of photographs lined the mantel. Most were of Sara at various ages with a tall, austere man with brown hair, and a petite woman with hair the same honey-gold as Sara's. Her parents, he guessed. Above the mantel, a large, wrought-iron clock ticked away the minutes. A braided rug covered the floor in front of the fireplace.

Sinking down on the couch, Travis blew out a sigh. And then he grinned. Hell of a night, he mused. He had saved the world from one more vampire.

Just like the good old days.

Chapter 5

Carl Overstreet drove slowly up Susandale's Main Street, which was wide and several blocks long. He grunted softly as he noticed that most of the shops didn't open until later in the day. There were no schools, no playgrounds. He passed a red brick post office. The sign out front said mail was delivered at 10 a.m. and that the office was open 24 hours a day. Odd, he thought, unless everyone had a post office box.

A grocery store, which appeared to be the largest building in town, occupied the lot next to the post office. It's hours of business were from noon until midnight. He noted the department store across the street didn't open until three.

A small, glass-fronted café. was located on the corner next to the grocery store. Bamboo shades covered the windows. A hand-lettered sign proclaimed Winona's opened at 11 a.m. Oddly, it didn't say when it closed. A store that sold bath products was located a few doors down from the café.

Turning east on First Street, he spied a non-denominational church across the street from a one-story brick hospital. A single ambulance was parked in the lot. There were no other vehicles in sight. The Sheriff's Department took up the end of the block next to the hospital. A single police car was parked on the street.

Carl made a U-Turn at the end of the block and drove west, crossing Main Street again. A gas station stood on the corner. A small, two-story hotel with a "Vacancy" sign out front was located across the street. Two vacant lots separated a drug store from the hotel.

A left turn at the end of First Street took him to the residential section. As expected, there was no activity outside. Every house had heavy curtains drawn against the noonday sun. No dogs barked. No kids played in the streets. There were no mailboxes. And no traffic.

After pulling over to the curb and putting his beat-up Dodge truck in Park, he picked up the small spiral-bound notebook and pencil lying on the passenger seat. Skipping past the first few pages, he wrote, "My informant's info seems to be spot on. I've little doubt Susandale is home to a nest of vampires."

He scanned the hastily scrawled notes on the first few pages. He had been in a seedy bar in New Jersey when he met Joey Cannon. The man had been middle-aged, but he'd looked old and worn out, as if someone had sucked most of the life out of him. As it turned out, that was pretty close to the truth. But he'd had a hell of a story to tell about a little town full of vampires and how he had barely escaped with his life.

Carl had retired from the news game over a year ago, but once a journalist, always a journalist, and Joey Cannon's story begged to be told. So, he'd bought Joey a bottle of bonded bourbon and listened to a tale that seemed too far-fetched to be true, but something in the old drunk's haunted eyes had sent Carl here, to this little town in the middle of nowhere, to uncover the truth.

Always a dangerous game, he thought, remembering the first time he had seen a vampire. It had been Ronan, though Carl hadn't known who it was at the time. He had been in a town outside of Sacramento, sitting in a bar. He'd been more than a little drunk at the time and had slipped out the back door into the alley by mistake. He had come to an abrupt halt when he saw a tall, dark-haired man bending over a woman's neck. At first, he'd thought he had interrupted a romantic encounter—until the man looked up, his eyes red as the fires of hell, his fangs dripping blood.

It was a sight never to be forgotten. Carl had run back into the bar and out the front door as fast as his legs would carry him and he hadn't stopped running until he was back in his hotel room with the door locked and the windows closed.

Remembering that night, Overstreet wondered why on earth he was here, looking for another vampire. But what the hell? He wasn't getting any younger and he didn't have anything better to do.

Except get a late breakfast, he decided, when his stomach growled.

Turning the car around, he headed for Winona's Café.

Chapter 6

Sara woke late after a long and restless night filled with nightmares that had seemed all too real. Her eyes felt gritty from lack of sleep when she peered at the bedside clock. *Ten-thirty!* She shook her head as she threw back the covers and slid her legs over the edge of the mattress. She was late for work, she thought. Good thing she was the boss.

Rising, she pulled on her robe and padded into the living room to ask Travis what he wanted for breakfast. Only he wasn't there.

And then she remembered why she had asked him to stay the night. How could she have forgotten the horrid creature that had attacked her? Had it really happened? In the bright light of day, with sunlight streaming through the window, it seemed impossible. Vampires were supposed to be legendary monsters. They weren't supposed to be real.

But they were. She had seen one with her own eyes.

She wished Travis hadn't left so early. She had questions. So many questions. Who better than a retired hunter to answer them?

Coffee, she thought, shuffling into the kitchen. She needed coffee and lots of it. She smiled when she saw the note on the refrigerator, held in place by one of her Star Wars magnets.

Hey, sleepy head: I'll call you tonight.
Maybe we can take in a movie? Travis

She wondered where he'd gone. It was Saturday. He didn't have a job. Had he gone looking for one? What kind of employment would appeal to a retired vampire hunter?

What he did was really none of her business, she thought. They had just met a few days ago, after all. He didn't owe her any explanations.

She had just filled the coffee pot and was contemplating what to make for breakfast when, on the spur of the moment, she decided to walk to town and eat at the café. It was the only business that opened before noon. But first, she needed to call a repair service to pick up her car, though she didn't know how she'd explain that a vampire had ripped the door off. The truth certainly didn't seem like a good idea. They would probably haul her away instead of her car.

Sara had just ordered French toast, bacon, and orange juice when a heavy-set man wearing brown slacks and a tan sweater over a white dress shirt entered Winona's Café. She'd seen so few men in town, she couldn't help staring. She judged him to be in his late fifties. His hair was dark brown turning gray, his eyes pale brown behind thick glasses, his skin pale, as if he didn't spend much time in the sun.

When his gaze met hers, he looked as surprised to see her as she was to see him. With a nod in her direction, he took the table across the aisle.

Sara acknowledged his greeting with a quick smile, then looked away.

A moment later, Winona came out from behind the counter to take his order. From what Sara had seen, Winona was not only the waitress, but also the cook and the dishwasher. She was a nice-looking woman, with curly brown hair and blue eyes, perhaps forty years old. Sara had tried on several occasions to engage the woman in conversation, but Winona didn't seem inclined to make small talk. Not with Sara, and not with the new customer.

"She isn't very friendly, is she?" the man remarked when the waitress returned to the kitchen. "Are all the people in this town like her?"

"I don't know. I haven't met that many."

"Hmm. Seems like a nice, quiet place."

"It is that. So, what brings you here?"

"I'm a freelance writer."

"Really? Well, if you're after an exciting story, I'm afraid you've come to the wrong place." Or had he? For a moment, she was tempted to tell him about last night's incident, but quickly changed her mind.

"I hope not." Rising, he crossed the aisle and extended his hand. "I'm Carl Overstreet."

"Sara Winters." His hand was cool, his grip firm.

"Pleased to meet you." He shifted from one foot to the other, as if his feet hurt.

She hesitated a moment. Inviting strangers to share her table was becoming a habit, she thought. First Travis Black and now Mr. Overstreet. But then, deciding it would be nice to have someone to talk to, she said, "Won't you join me?"

"Thanks."

He lowered himself carefully onto the chair across from hers and blew out a sigh. "Hell to get old," he said. "I don't recommend it."

"Did you come here to cover a specific story?" Sara asked, although she couldn't imagine that anything worth reporting had ever happened in Susandale.

"I got a hot lead on something that might pan out." He smiled at the waitress as she brought their orders.

Winona didn't smile back. "Can I get either of you anything else?"

Sara shook her head. "Not for me."

"I'm good," Carl said. "Thanks."

With a curt nod, Winona scuffed back to the kitchen.

"I don't know how this place stays in business," Sara remarked, spreading grape jelly on her French toast. "I've never seen more than one or two people in here at a time."

"I'm not surprised," Carl muttered, sprinkling salt and pepper on his eggs.

"Why do you say that?"

"What?" He looked up, as if unaware he'd spoken out loud.

"You said you're not surprised more people don't come in here."

He shrugged. "Oh, you know. Small town. They probably don't get a lot of tourists most of the year."

"I guess so," she agreed. Now that he'd mentioned it, there hadn't been more than a few visitors since she'd been here. Still, the town was off the beaten path. "Would I have read anything you've written?"

"It's possible. I wrote a series of articles on vampires a while back."

"Vampires!" Good Lord. Should she tell him about what had happened last night? she wondered, then decided against it. Just because he wrote about such things didn't mean he believed in them. Or did he? "You don't think they're real, do you?"

"I know they are."

"You've seen one?"

"Two of them. I don't recommend it."

Sara thought again of telling him about the attack last night, but decided it was best not to mention it. She wanted to forget it had ever happened, not share it with a stranger, especially when he was a writer. All she needed was for him to write a story about it that might make its way into a newspaper back home. Her father would be out here to drag her back home before the ink dried.

"So, have you lived here long?" he asked.

"Just a few months."

"What brought you here?"

"I'm trying to prove to my father that I can make it on my own."

"Good luck with that," he said with a wink. "Seen anything unusual since you've been here?" He added two teaspoons of sugar to his coffee.

Sara stared at him, her heart pounding. Once again, she wondered if she should tell him about the incident last night. No doubt he would believe her, but she couldn't bring herself to talk about it, nor did she want to become part of whatever story he might be writing. "Not really."

He nodded, but she had the distinct feeling that he knew she was hiding something.

They finished the rest of the meal in silence. Overstreet insisted on paying the check.

Rising, Sara offered her thanks, then left him sitting at the table, lingering over a second cup of coffee.

As soon as she got home, Sara booted up her computer and searched for his name. And sure enough, a national magazine had published a series of articles titled *Vampires Among us—Truth or Fiction?*

A link took her to the story.

"Vampires. The very word makes your flesh crawl... with terror or titillation, depending on your point of view.

Vampires have been a subject of fascination and horror for countless centuries. Every culture and civilization throughout the known world, both past and present, has their own myths and legends about vampires, be they skeletal creatures who feast on human blood or psychic vampires who prey on the energy of their victims, leaving them exhausted in both body and spirit.

Thanks to the creative imagination of Bram Stoker, Count Dracula is probably the most famous blood-sucker of all time...

Sara read avidly, fear and fascination growing stronger with every word.

So, what do we really know about these creatures of the night? Popular fiction says they sleep by day and hunt by night. They can't be seen in mirrors, they are repelled by crosses, holy water and garlic. Some believe they must sleep in their coffins; others believe they must rest on the earth of their homeland. Some believe vampires are capable of flight, of transforming into bats or wolves and of changing their size and dimension. It is commonly believed that they are able to control animals and the weather and hypnotize mortals to do their will.

But did vampires ever truly exist? Do they exist now? Do vampires walk among us, unseen and unknown? Every year, hundreds of people disappear without a trace, never to be heard from or seen again. Are vampires responsible? During the next few months I'll be traveling the country, digging deeper into the legend and mystique of vampires and other so-called creatures of the night.

The man definitely had a flare for the dramatic, Sara mused as she pulled up the last installment. She read through the lasts few paragraphs quickly until she came to the last few lines.

He said there had been vampires since the beginning of time. When questioned, he said he didn't know where the first vampire had come from, though there were some who believed that Vlad the Impaler was the father of the Undead. Whoever the first vampire was, it's believed that he made a deal with the Devil, trading his soul for immortality.

Our vampire said he had never turned another into a vampire, but that he knew how it was done. Indeed, he even offered to show me. You may be sure that I quickly declined.

At this point, he grew impatient and the interview was over.

As for me, I hope never to see him again.

As someone once said, "Ignorance is bliss."

Oh, how I long to be ignorant again.

Chilled to the marrow of her bones, Sara sat back in her chair, thinking that ignorance was, indeed, bliss. Overstreet had written the most remarkable story since Dracula. After what she'd seen last night, she had no doubt at all that the man had indeed met a vampire face-to-face. Judging from what she'd read, she thought he was lucky to be alive. As was she, having recently encountered one of the creatures herself.

And then she frowned. Had Overstreet come here looking for another vampire? Maybe the one Travis had killed last night?

Travis listened with growing concern as Sara told him about her day.

"... met this man at the café this morning. At first, he just looked like some ordinary old guy, and since we were both alone, I asked him to sit with me. You won't believe this, but he used to be a freelance journalist! When I asked him if he'd written anything I might have read, he told me he'd written a series of articles on vampires. I wouldn't have believed a word of it if I hadn't seen one with my own eyes." She shuddered. "I hope I never see another one."

"Yeah," Travis muttered. "So do I."

"Do you think he came here for another story about those creatures? Maybe he was going to do a series on the one you killed last night."

"Maybe." Travis shifted on the sofa, a horrible suspicion working its way into his mind. "Did you get the guy's name?"

"Overstreet. Carl Overstreet. Have you ever heard of him?"

"I might have." Travis grunted softly, his mind racing. Last he knew, Overstreet had retired. Now he was here, in Susandale. And Travis was afraid he knew why. Damn.

"Travis?"

"What?"

"I asked if you wanted anything."

"Oh, sorry, I didn't hear you."

"So?"

"I'm good."

"You seem distracted. Is something wrong?"

"No." He forced a smile he was far from feeling, careful to keep his fangs out of sight.

"You don't think there are more vampires in town, do you?"

"I hope not." He took her hand and gave it a squeeze. He hated having to lie to her, but he had no choice. It was either keep lying or stop seeing her. And that just wasn't an option. He wanted to know her better, be a part of her life if only for a short time, even though he knew that it was highly unlikely. Still, he enjoyed being with her. Enjoyed pretending he was the same man he had once been.

"I know you said something about going out to a movie, but would you mind if we stayed in tonight?" Sara asked. After last night and reading about vampires today, she was in the mood to stay home.

"It's all right with me."

"We can watch a movie on Netflix."

"Sounds good."

"I'm in the mood for a comedy."

After all she'd been through, he couldn't blame her. She found a romantic comedy starring Cameron Diaz and Jude Law, then sat beside him, her thigh brushing against his. But tonight his mind wasn't on Sara. He was thinking about Overstreet, trying to decide whether to confront the man, or avoid him. A writer nosing around, one who knew the truth, could cause a lot of trouble. The last thing the town needed was for Overstreet to start sniffing around, alerting hunters. If Carl knew what was good for him, he'd get the hell out of Susandale before the wrong people discovered what he was up to.

Travis blew out a sigh. Maybe he *should* go have a talk with him. They had been casual friends not long ago. And if he couldn't convince Overstreet to move on, what then?

Damn. Just when he'd thought his life was looking better, trouble came to town.

There were all kinds of trouble, he thought, running his fingers through the silk of Sara's hair. She had fallen asleep with her head pillowed on his shoulder, one hand resting on his thigh. Her scent surrounded him, warm, womanly, desirable. His gaze moved to the curve of her cheek, down to the pulse throbbing slow and steady in the hollow of her throat. He wanted her. Needed her.

Unable to help himself, he ran his tongue along the side of her neck. Since that night on the dance floor, he had been yearning to taste her again. Just a small taste. What harm could it do? She need never know.

Despising himself for his weakness, he spoke to her mind, willing her to stay asleep until morning as he slipped his arm around her shoulders. After brushing her hair aside, he murmured "Forgive me," and then he took what he so desperately craved.

She stirred in his arms, a soft moan escaping her lips.

Stricken with guilt, he lifted his head. He had to get out of here, now, before his hunger burned out of control.

Cradling her in his arms, he carried her into her room and tucked her into bed. He stood there a moment, gazing down at her, thinking how beautiful she was. How innocent.

How vulnerable.

"I'll keep you safe from the monsters, Sara, I swear I will, no matter what the cost."

In her sleep, she murmured his name.

It was almost his undoing. He brushed a kiss across her cheek, and then fled the house before he broke the vow he had just made.

Chapter 7

Ronan sat in the dark, staring at the flames dancing in the den's fireplace. Shannah slept on the sofa beside him, her head pillowed on his lap. He'd found himself thinking about his fledgling more and more often ever since his darling wife had asked about him. Ronan blew out a sigh. He should have killed the man. Would have done so had it not been for Shannah. She hadn't said anything to stop him, but he had felt her disapproval. It was the one thing he couldn't abide. So, he had given the hunter a choice, never really expecting Hewitt to ask to become what he'd hunted all his life.

He had met Shannah, Hewitt, and Overstreet all within a short period of time and from then on, their lives had been strangely intertwined.

Closing his eyes, he thought back to when it all began...

Dying of some rare blood disease with no known cure, Shannah had come seeking a vampire who might save her life. It had taken a while to convince the girl he wasn't what she was looking for and then, because she had no place else to go, he had taken her into his home. Enchanted by her innocence and her beauty, he had given her a little of his blood while she slept. He didn't have the power to heal her, but his blood had strengthened her and prolonged her life.

About that same time, his publisher began insisting Ronan do book signings and daytime interviews on TV, something he was unable to do. But there was Shannah, young and lovely and literate. He coached her about the books he'd written, bought her an expensive new wardrobe and sent her out into the world as the face of Claire Ebon, Eva Black and Stella Raven.

And then Hewitt and Overstreet had arrived on the scene and his life had taken a dramatic turn. Hewitt wanted his head. Overstreet wanted an interview. Ronan was not inclined to offer either one.

Until the fools kidnapped Shannah.

She had been on the verge of death when he tracked her to where they had taken her. He had demanded they bring her to him. They had refused. And then Overstreet proposed that Ronan give him the interview he coveted in exchange for Shannah. He'd had no other choice but to agree.

When the interview was over, Hewitt refused to surrender Shannah, fearing, and rightly so, that Ronan would kill him and Overstreet both. In the end, Ronan had given his word that he would not harm them that night if they brought Shannah to him before it was too late.

He had brought her across when he got her home. Later, they had wed.

He had never thought to see Jim Hewitt again. Hadn't given the man a second thought since the night he turned him, until Shannah mentioned his name. Now he couldn't think of anything else. Shannah had said abandoning the hunter had been cruel.

And it had been.

Maybe one of these days he would search Hewitt out and see how he was getting along.

And maybe not.

Chapter 8

Sunday was a slow, lazy day. Unlike most cities and towns across the country, Susandale's shops remained closed all day, which was fine with Sara. Her parents hadn't believed in shopping on the Sabbath, a habit that Sara still adhered to.

After making her bed, she fixed breakfast, did the dishes, put in a load of wash.

At loose ends, she called Travis, but the call went directly to voice mail. She wondered if she would see him later. He hadn't said anything about coming over. Still, she had seen him every night since they'd met.

With nothing better to do, she decided to go for a walk. It was a lovely day, the sky a bright clear blue, the air warm, fragrant with the scent of flowers and grass. Susandale might be a small town, but it was immaculate. All the houses were well-tended, the lawns lush and green, the streets free of debris.

She was surprised when she turned the corner and saw a boy and girl playing catch in the middle of the street.

She paused to watch as they tossed a big blue rubber ball back and forth, the boy teasing his little sister when she missed. The two were obviously related. Both had the same build, the same red hair, the same sprinkling of freckles across their cheeks. They stopped playing when they saw her watching them.

Smiling, Sara said, "Hello."

The little girl smiled shyly.

The boy looked at her suspiciously. "Who are you? I've never seen you before."

"I'm new in town. I own Sara's Sweets and Salts Shoppe over on Main Street."

"My mom shops there," the girl said. "Her name's Olivia."

Sara remembered her. Olivia Bowman had the same red hair as her kids. She had been friendlier than Sara's other customers. "And what's your name?"

"Debbie. I'm nine."

"Where do you go to school?"

"Mom teaches us at home," the girl replied.

"That's nice. What does your daddy do?"

Debbie and her brother exchanged glances, their expressions suddenly wary.

"Why do you want to know?" the boy asked, his expression sullen.

"No particular reason," Sara said. "I was just curious."

"He sleeps all day," Debbie said.

"Hush, Debbie," the boy scolded. "You don't need to tell her our business."

Before Sara could think of anything else to say, the front door across the street opened and Olivia stepped out on the narrow porch. "Debbie! Luke! It's time to come in."

"It was nice to meet you," Debbie said. "Bye."

"Goodbye." Sara looked over at Olivia and waved.

The woman hesitated, then waved back.

Sara was hoping to chat for a moment, but as soon as her kids were inside the house, Olivia closed the door.

With a shrug, Sara continued on down the street. She didn't see any more kids, but a few doors down, she saw a woman on her knees, pulling weeds from the flowerbed in her front yard. She looked up, shading her eyes with her hand when Sara stopped on the sidewalk.

"Beautiful day, isn't it?" Sara remarked.

"Yes. You're the woman from the candy shop, aren't you?"

Sara nodded. "I'm sorry, I don't remember your name."

"Deanne. Are you planning to stay in Susandale?"

"Why, yes, I am. Why do you ask?"

"No reason. Most newcomers don't stay long, that's all."

"Why is that, do you think?"

"We're a small, tightly knit town." Rising, Deanne brushed the dirt from the knees of her jeans. "Most people don't think it's a very friendly place."

Sara took a step back. Was the woman telling her to leave? Feeling suddenly chilled, Sara smiled uncertainly and continued on her way. Maybe the town fathers —whoever they were—should change the sign at the town's entrance from "*Welcome*" to "*Susandale isn't a very friendly place.*"

She was almost home when a rather beat-up old green Dodge truck rattled past. The brake lights flashed as the truck slowed, then pulled a U-turn and drove up beside her.

A grinning Carl Overstreet stuck his head out the window. "Morning, Miss Sara."

"Good morning, Mr. Overstreet."

"Just Carl. What's there to do in this burg on a Sunday?"

"Not much. Everything's closed, I'm afraid. Even the café."

"Yeah, I saw that."

"Would you like to come over for lunch?" Sara asked impulsively, then wondered if it was wise, inviting a relative stranger into her house. Still, he seemed harmless enough. And she was lonely.

"That would be great. I was just wondering if I'd have to drive clear to the next town to grab a bite."

"Well, it's not altogether altruistic. I'm tired of my own company. I live in that next house," she said. "And I'm only serving tuna fish sandwiches for lunch."

"Sounds good to me." He parked the car at the curb, then followed her up the flagstone walkway and into the house. At her invitation, he trailed her into kitchen and took a seat at the table.

She worked quickly and efficiently and in no time at all lunch was ready. She added pickles and potato chips to the plates and carried them to the table. "I've got soda, tea, or coffee. Or milk."

"Just water is fine."

She pulled a bottle from the refrigerator for him, grabbed a soda for herself, and then sat across from him. "I read your articles."

"Yeah? I guess you think I made the whole thing up?"

"No. I'm sure you didn't."

He lifted one brow. "Most people don't believe me. If they admit there are vampires, then they have to consider there might be other monsters lurking out there in the dark."

"I was attacked by one Friday night." She hadn't meant to reveal that, but the words poured out of her mouth. "It was horrible! He yanked my car door clean off its hinges. I've never seen anything so frightening or been so scared in my whole life!"

Overstreet's eyes widened in surprise and then narrowed. "Have you seen others?"

'Others?" She shook her head. "Do you think there are more?" Sara put her sandwich aside, her appetite gone.

"It's possible but doubtful. They tend to be solitary creatures, not given to sharing territory." Or prey.

Sara nodded, hoping he knew what he was talking about.

"So, tell me, how did you get away from the vampire who attacked you?"

"A friend of mine came to the rescue. Lucky for me, he used to be a hunter."

Overstreet grunted softly. So much for his story. The vampire was dead. Unless there were indeed others, as Joey Cannon had claimed. Carl finished his sandwich, suddenly eager to explore the town again before the sun set. "Thank you for lunch, Sara. It's much appreciated."

"Thank you for the company. I don't get to do much socializing around here. It's the town's only drawback."

Overstreet nodded. "Well, thanks, again, Sara. It's been a pleasure meeting you. I hope to see you again before I leave town."

"If you're not doing anything for dinner, I'm making fried chicken."

"If that's an offer," he said with a broad smile, "I accept."

"Six o'clock."

A nod and a wave and he left the house.

Sara cleared the table and washed their few dishes. Maybe this wasn't such a quiet little town after all. Vampires. Journalists. Ex-hunters.

What next?

Carl Overstreet drove through one end of Susandale to the other, slower this time that the first, stopping now and then to take notes and photographs. He was aware of unseen eyes watching him from behind drawn curtains. There was a heaviness in the air, an almost palpable tension that hung over the town. He was surprised that Sara hadn't noticed it. He had recognized it for what it was the minute he'd arrived.

He wondered what would happen if he knocked on one of the doors but immediately dismissed the idea. There was always a chance the town housed more than one vampire and he was in no itching hurry to meet another one up close and personal.

He drove down the quiet streets a second time, then parked his truck in the lot behind the hospital. He set his phone to wake him before sundown and settled back for a nap.

Sara had just finished mashing the potatoes when the doorbell rang. She covered the pot, smoothed her hand over her hair and went to admit her guest.

"Hi, Carl." She noticed he had changed his shirt and swapped his baggy sweater for a plaid sports jacket.

"Thanks, again, for the invite."

"You're welcome. How was your day?"

"Uneventful," he said.

"I'm sure. Come on in, dinner's ready." She set the food on the kitchen table, urged him to help himself, and sat down.

"So," he said, selecting a plump drumstick, "how was *your* day?"

"I re-read your articles. It's all just so hard to believe. I don't know how you found the nerve to be in the same room with the vampire. Weren't you afraid?"

"We weren't in the same room. I was inside a house, and he was on the porch."

"How on earth did you get him to talk to you?"

"I was working with this hunter I'd met, Jim Hewitt. We kidnapped the vampire's girlfriend. Long story short, we offered to give her back if the vampire would give me an interview."

"Shades of Anne Rice!" Sara exclaimed. "That's crazy!"

"Yeah, I know that now, but it seemed like a good idea at the time."

"Is the vampire still alive?"

"I imagine so. He was very old and very powerful. And scary as hell."

"What happened to the girl?"

"I don't know. I hightailed it out of town and never looked back. You know what's even more amazing? He wrote romance novels."

Sara burst out laughing. "A vampire writing romance novels? Seriously?"

"Yeah. He had a couple of pseudonyms. Eva Black, Claire Ebon, Stella Raven."

Claire Ebon was a man? And a vampire? And then she frowned as she recalled that Travis had claimed to know her. Or him. How was that possible? Even as the thought crossed her mind, there was a knock at the door. Murmuring excuse me, she went to answer it, her heart skipping a beat when she saw Travis waiting on the porch. "Hi!"

"Hey, I hope it's okay for me to drop by like this. It looks like you've got company."

"I do. Come on in. You'll never guess who it is."

Travis swore under his breath as he caught Overstreet's scent. "Listen, I don't want to intrude. I'll come back later."

"Don't be silly." Grabbing his hand, she pulled him toward the kitchen.

Resigned to his fate, he followed her.

"Carl Overstreet," Sara said, "I want you to meet..."

"Jim Hewitt!" Overstreet pushed away from the table and lurched to his feet. "What the hell are you doing here?"

Confused, Sara glanced from one man to the other. Jim Hewitt had been Overstreet's accomplice in kidnapping the vampire's girlfriend. She looked at Travis, one brow raised as she waited for an explanation.

"Good to see you again, Carl," Travis said. "Although the timing couldn't be worse."

"What's going on?" Sara tugged on Travis' hand. "Why is he calling you Hewitt?"

"It's a long story. Maybe you should sit down." Travis glared at Overstreet. "Both of you."

Sara sank onto her chair, her expression troubled, her hands tightly clenched in her lap.

Overstreet sat down more slowly, his eyes narrowed.

Travis took a deep breath. "I don't know where to start."

"It's been my experience that the beginning is always the best place," Overstreet remarked.

"Yeah. I should have taken your advice and left town," Travis said. "But I didn't. I followed Ronan and Shannah to New York, and I was right behind them when they left. And then I followed them back home." He scrubbed his hand over his jaw. "And that's when my luck ran out. I confronted Ronan and managed to stake him in the back. I told Shannah to make a run for it, that he was a vampire, and then..." He shook his head at the memory. "She yelled that she was a vampire, too, and then mesmerized me so that I couldn't move. I had to stand there, watching, while she pulled the stake out of Ronan's back."

Overstreet nodded. "I always knew he'd turn her, sooner or later."

"Yeah. Well, after she pulled the stake out, she dragged me over to him. I figured I was a dead man for sure. Instead, he gave me a choice. Die or become what I'd hunted my whole life. I should have let him kill me."

"Why would you say that?" Sara exclaimed, even as she tried to process the fact that Travis was a vampire and his real name was Jim.

"Why? I lost everything that was important to me. Friends. Family. My purpose in life. I used to be a hunter and a damn good one! And now? Now I'm just one of the monsters."

"You don't act like one," Sara said quietly. Or look like one, she thought. The thing that had attacked her had *looked* like a monster. "You saved my life from a real monster the other night. You've been nothing but kind to me."

"Looks can be deceiving," Travis muttered.

"Is that how you feel?" Overstreet asked curiously. "Like some blood-thirsty creature with no sense of right and wrong?"

"What? No. But I don't feel like me, either." Travis looked at Sara. "You're a constant temptation," he said. "Your blood smells so good. Sometimes it drives me crazy."

Sara lifted a hand to her throat. He was a vampire. He had spent the night in her house. She had danced with him, let him kiss her.

"You're wondering if I've bitten you," he said, his voice thick with guilt.

She nodded, her eyes wide.

"Sara, I'm sorry. I swear I only took a little. Please believe me, I'd never hurt you."

She stared at him, pity and trepidation warring in her mind. And then to her astonishment, his body took on a strange aura.

A moment later he disappeared from sight.

Overstreet grunted softly. Hewitt had killed vampires. Now he *was* a vampire. How many others resided in this quiet little town?

Chapter 9

Travis went hunting in the next town, which was considerably larger than Susandale. Langston was just a normal American city, full of noise and people going about their business, completely unaware that a monster had entered their domain. He detected no other vampires within the city limits as he prowled the back streets.

He had chosen to reside in Susandale because it was a quiet place, rumored to be a haven for vampires who wanted to live as normal a life as possible. As a rule, vampires were solitary creatures and he'd found that to be more or less true in Susandale. They all lived in the same town, but as far as he knew, there was little socializing among the Undead, although he knew the human spouses—male and female—met often.

He swore under his breath. Why the hell had Overstreet shown up here now? he wondered bleakly. It had ruined everything. Sara would never look at him the same way again. Assuming she ever *wanted* to see him again, which he doubted. Oh, hell, it wasn't going to last, anyway. He was pretty sure that the women who would knowingly date a vampire were few and far between.

And then, thinking about Ronan, he frowned. Shannah had loved that vampire enough to let him turn her. Of course, she had been dying at the time, so maybe it hadn't been much of a choice, but there was no doubt she had been deeply in love with him. And Ronan with her. But how often did that happen?

His incessant hunger clawed at his vitals, driving every other thought from his mind. Pickings were slim on a Sunday night. Only the bars and the movie theaters were open late, and since females on the prowl were apt to be in the night clubs hoping to get lucky, he headed for the nearest one.

Inside, he glanced around, his gaze settling on a woman in her early thirties sitting alone at the end of the bar, nursing a drink. He took the seat beside her and spoke to her mind, assuring her that he meant her no harm as he took her hand and led her outside into the shadows. He fed quickly, then released her from his thrall and sent her on her way. He told himself he wasn't a monster. A monster would have taken it all.

But it didn't help. He knew what he was.

Sara and Overstreet remained at the table after Travis left. She wondered if Carl was as flabbergasted as she was by what she had learned tonight. Travis—no Jim—was a vampire. She never would have guessed. He seemed so ... so normal. Maybe one of the nicest guys she had ever met. Just her rotten luck that he was a vampire, she thought glumly.

"That interview you did," she said, breaking the silence between them. "Was that the vampire who turned Travis, er, Jim?"

Overstreet nodded. "Ronan, yeah. I'm surprised he let Hewitt go. From the little I knew about that vampire, I would have bet my last dollar he would have killed the boy out of hand," he said, and then added, "I guess, technically, he did, since vampires are considered dead by some."

Sara grimaced. "Do you think that's true?"

"I'm not sure. Some think they're stone-cold dead by day, but I've heard some older vampires can be awake when the sun is up, so I guess they're not really dead, at least not in the way we know it." He regarded Sara a long moment. "You're not falling in love with Jim, are you?"

Her gaze slid away from his. "I don't know."

"I wouldn't advise it."

"I don't suppose it matters. After tonight, I'll probably never see him again." She pushed away from the table. "Can I get you anything else?"

"No. Thank you for dinner. It was most... enlightening." Rising, he dropped his napkin on the table. "Be careful, Sara. There might be other vampires in this town. And be careful of Hewitt. He hasn't been a vampire very long. New ones can't always control their hunger, or their urge to kill."

She nodded, then followed him to the door.

He reached for the handle, then turned to face her. "Vampires can only enter a home with an invitation from the owner or the one who has legal residence—like a renter. For your own safety, I would advise you to revoke Hewitt's invitation. And whatever you do, don't invite any strangers into your house, day or night."

"Carl, you're scaring me."

"A little fear is a healthy thing. Good night, Sara. Don't forget to lock up after me."

"Good night." She watched him climb into his battered old truck and drive away, then closed and locked the door. How did one revoke a vampire's invitation? Was it enough just to say the words? Did Travis or Hewitt or whoever he was have to be there when it was done? Feeling somewhat foolish, she murmured, "Travis Black, I revoke your invitation. You are no longer welcome in my home." And then she frowned. "That goes for Jim Hewitt, too."

To her amazement, she felt an ever so subtle shift in the air around the door.

With a shake of her head, she returned to the kitchen to clear the table and load the dishwasher, hoping that doing something so normal would make the night seem less bizarre.

Vampires in America. And in this day and age. Who would believe it?

It was hard to concentrate at work on Monday afternoon. Sara sat at her desk in the small office in the back of the store, filling out order forms, but she kept hearing Travis' voice in her mind, assuring her that he would never hurt her at the same time he admitted he had taken her blood. Why didn't she remember that? It didn't seem like something one would just forget. She recalled the stricken look on his face when he told her what he was. How could she blame him for choosing to live? Wouldn't anyone do the same? Would she?

She stared out the front window, trying to imagine what it had been like to be under Ronan's control, to have to make such a life-changing decision on the spur of the moment. Travis must have been half out of his mind with fear. She certainly would have been.

Overstreet had asked if she was falling love with Travis and she'd said she didn't know. But she wasn't sure that was the truth. What was love, anyway? It was caring for someone, thinking about them when you were apart, wanting to be with them as much as possible, and that was how she felt about Travis. She had enjoyed being with him. It hurt, knowing she might never see him again. She had never felt this way about any of the other men she had met. Certainly not the man her father expected her to marry.

Dilworth Young was a nice-enough guy. She had known him most of her life. He was tall and blond. He came from a wealthy family. They got along well enough. But there were no sparks between them, at least not where she was concerned. She rarely thought about him when they were apart. The few kisses they had shared hadn't made her toes curl the way Travis' did. She had never spent hours daydreaming about Dil. Never got butterflies in her stomach at the sound of his voice.

She looked up as the bell over the door announced a customer. Going out into the shop, she saw Debbie and Luke, the two kids she had met on the street the day before. "Hello. How are you guys today?"

Debbie smiled at her. "We want to buy a present for our Mom," she said, her blue eyes sparkling with excitement. "It's her birthday tomorrow." Then, lowering her voice, she whispered, "She's going to be thirty-five, but don't tell anyone."

"Your secret is safe with me," Sara whispered, biting back a grin. "What were you looking for?"

"She likes bubble bath," the boy, Luke said. "Something that smells like gardenias."

Sara nodded. "I think I have just what you're looking for right over here."

She led the way to a long, low counter that held an assortment of bubble bath in pretty decanters, as well as bath bombs, imported soaps, perfume, and cologne. "How much money do you have?"

"Daddy gave us twenty-five dollars," Debbie exclaimed, hopping from one foot to the other in her excitement.

Reaching into his pocket, Luke said, "And I saved up ten more."

"I'm sure we can find something she'll like. How about this?" Sara held up a tall, cut-glass decanter filled with her best gardenia-scented foaming bubble bath.

"Oh, that's so pretty," Debbie said.

"How much is it?" Luke asked.

"For you? Fifteen dollars. Did you want to spend more than that?"

Debbie nodded.

"Well, then, how about adding some pretty scented soap and maybe a box of premium chocolates?"

"She likes candy," Debbie said, smiling enthusiastically.

"How much is all that gonna cost?" Luke asked.

"Because you're a first-time buyer, I'm going to give you my special discount. I'll let you have it all for thirty dollars." She wouldn't be making much of a profit, but she was charmed by Debbie. She wondered if their father worked nights, or if he was a vampire, and if he was, did his children know? If so, it must be a hard secret for them to keep.

"Okay," Luke agreed. He carefully counted out the right amount and handed it to her.

"Would you like me to gift wrap these for you?" Sara asked as she rang it up.

Debbie nodded, then wandered over to the children's section while Sara wrapped their purchases.

Luke stood at the counter, watching Sara intently.

"How old are you?" she asked.

"Almost twelve."

"Have you lived here very long?"

"Why do you want to know?"

"I was just making polite conversation." She put everything in a flowered bag, added some colorful tissue paper, and tied it with a bright pink bow. "I hope you'll come back again."

Luke nodded. "Debbie, let's go."

The girl sent Sara a toothy grin as she followed her brother outside.

Sara stared after them. She couldn't decide if Luke didn't like her or if he was just suspicious of anyone he didn't know. If his father was a vampire, she guessed she couldn't blame him.

Several other customers came in as the afternoon wore on, including Deanne, the woman Sara had seen pulling weeds.

Smiling, Sara asked, "Can I help you find anything?"

"No, I was just..." Deanne sighed. "I just felt like I needed to get out of the house. Is it okay if I just look around?"

"Of course."

The woman looked troubled, Sara thought, as if she had something on her mind. Eventually, Deanne made her way to the counter.

"I was rude to you the other day," she said, not quite meeting Sara's eyes. "I'm sorry."

"Don't give it another thought." She hesitated a moment, then asked, "Is something wrong?"

"Wrong?" Deanne blinked several times. "I guess I'm just lonely. My husband was kill...er, died a few months back. I miss him."

"Of course you do. I'm so sorry."

"We were together for twenty years," she said with a sigh. "Are you married?"

"I'm trying to avoid it," Sara said.

"Oh?"

"My father has someone in mind for me. But I'm not in love with him."

Deanne nodded. "You should always marry for love," she said wistfully. "Even if everyone you know is against it. After all, the real thing only comes along once in a lifetime. And life is short. So short." She blinked rapidly. "I should go before... I should go." Turning on her heel, she hurried out the door.

"Well, that was odd," Sara murmured. "I wonder what she was going to say."

Carl Overstreet spent the early part of the day re-reading his notes and wondering what he would have done if given the same choice as Hewitt. Would he have chosen life? Unlike Hewitt, who was still a young man, his life was more than half over unless he lived to be a hundred. And given his weight and his health, that was highly improbable. Like a lot of people, death scared him. And it got scarier with ever passing year. Maybe he should talk to Hewitt about becoming a vampire, he mused, because life was always the answer.

At five, he went to the café for lunch. A few minutes later, he saw Sara step through the door. When she met his gaze, he waved her over.

"We've got to stop meeting like this," she remarked with a grin as she slid into the booth across from him. "People will start to talk."

"Let 'em," he said, waggling his eyebrows. "Be good for my image, being seen with a pretty young thing. But seriously, how are you doing, Sara?"

"I'm not sure. I just don't know what to think. I can understand why Travis didn't tell me what he is, but why did he lie to me about his name?"

"That's easy. Think about it. He used to be a hunter. Now he's the hunted. People on both sides of the line would be more than happy to drive a stake through his heart. Better if he just slips off the radar altogether."

"I guess so. I talked to a couple of kids earlier today. They were very secretive about their dad. Do you think he's a..." She bit down on her lower lip when Winona shuffled up to their table.

Overstreet ordered a pastrami sandwich and fries.

Sara had intended to just stop by for a malt but decided on an early dinner instead. "I'll have the turkey club and a side salad," she told Winona. "And a chocolate shake."

Overstreet waited until the waitress went back into kitchen, then whispered, "I wouldn't use that word around here. It's not safe."

Sara stared at him. "What do you mean?"

"I don't think Hewitt's the only one of *those* in town. In fact, I wouldn't be surprised if most of the residents of Susandale were, shall we say, far from ordinary."

"How is that possible? You said they didn't like to share territory."

"That's true. But they aren't hunting here, so there's no competition."

"Am I in danger?"

"I don't think so."

"You don't *think* so?"

"Most of them don't hunt where they live. Too much danger of being caught. And they need some regular people around to run the businesses if they want to keep up the charade that this is just an ordinary town."

"What about the women who live here? None of the ones I've met seem... different."

"The ones who are normal are likely married to the ones who aren't."

"But...Olivia Bowman has kids. How is that possible?"

"Maybe from a previous marriage. Maybe born before he was turned."

Sara sat back in her chair, mind reeling with possibilities. Maybe nothing in this place was as it seemed.

Winona sent Sara a curious look when she brought their lunch. "Everything all right?" she asked. "You look a little pale."

"I'm fine, thank you," Sara murmured. And wondered if she would ever be fine again. When Winona returned to the kitchen, Sara leaned forward. "Are you sure about all this?"

"Not a hundred percent," Carl admitted. "But in cases like this, it's always best to err on the side of caution."

"Do you think that's why Travis came here?" She couldn't think of him as Jim.

"I'd say it's a pretty good bet."

Sara took a bite of her sandwich. If Carl was right, she was living in a den of vampires. A bubble of hysteria rose up within her. Maybe she should change the name of her shop to *Vamps R Us* and start selling bottled blood and custom caskets!

After Sara went back to work, Carl pulled a new notebook out of his coat pocket. He stared out the window for a moment, and then he began to write.

Joey Cannon was just an ordinary guy. Recently divorced, he drove a truck across country for a living. Late one night, he pulled into a little town to grab a few hours sleep. He parked his truck on a quiet side street and woke up in a nightmare.

Chapter 10

Travis woke as soon as the sun began to set. He had learned that one of the so-called "perks" of being turned by an old vampire was the ability to rise a little before full dark. He couldn't go outside as long as the sun was in the sky, but it still gave him a chance to get a glimpse of day-light before it was gone.

Trapped inside, he prowled from room to room, his thoughts churning. What was Sara doing—thinking? He had the ability to read her thoughts but that was like raping her mind, something to be done only if her life depended on it. Where was Overstreet? And what had brought him to town?

Did he dare call Sara? Would she talk to him? Agree to see him again? Or would she hang up the minute she heard his voice?

Damn. Only hours since he had seen her, yet he missed her desperately. He picked up his phone. Put it down. Picked it up again. Took a deep breath and made the call, figuring, nothing ventured, nothing gained.

"Please, Sara," he murmured. "Please pick up."

It rang five times before she answered. "Hello?"

"Sara... it's me. I... I just wanted to hear your voice."

"I have nothing to say."

"Then why did you answer my call?"

"I don't know."

"Any chance you're missing me half as much as I'm missing you?"

He heard the soft exhalation of her breath as she sighed.

"Sara?"

"Travis... I guess I can't call you that now, can I?"

"I wish you would. I don't feel like Jim Hewitt anymore."

"How *do* you feel?"

"Lost. Alone. Trying to figure out what I've become. My whole life has been turned upside down. These days, *I* don't even know who I am."

"I'm sorry, Travis."

He heard the tears in her voice. It made him ache deep inside. "Sara..." Just her name, like a plea. A prayer. He didn't know what else to say.

"Would you...?" A long pause. "Would you... do you want to come over?"

"More than you can imagine. But... are you sure?"

"Not really," she replied candidly. And then she sighed again. "I miss you, too."

And just like that, despair turned to hope.

Travis took a long shower, dressed in his best jeans and a dark blue shirt, and combed his hair, more nervous than he had ever been in his life. He couldn't help feeling that whatever happened tonight would permanently affect their relationship one way or the other.

He pulled on his boots, took a deep breath, and grabbed his keys. Even though he could move with remarkable speed, he liked driving his Mustang. It was the only thing he had left from his former life.—one of the few things that made him feel human.

Sara didn't remember ever being so edgy. Her upbringing had been somewhat sheltered. Both her parents had been overly protective of their only daughter, refusing to allow her to date until she was sixteen, insisting she be home before midnight, carefully screening her boyfriends. And then her father had decided she should marry Dil. It was the last straw. She was a grown woman. She didn't want or need an arranged marriage to a man who would never be more than a good friend. She had been surprised when her father agreed to let her have a year to "find herself," until she realized he was certain she would fail, and that she would come running back home long before that year was up.

She had been just as sure that she wouldn't, until last night. Now, finding herself living in a town that might be inhabited by vampires, home didn't sound so bad.

She almost jumped out of her skin when the doorbell rang. Was she about to open the door to the biggest mistake of her life?

Taking a last glance in the mirror over the mantel, she smoothed her hand over her hair then went to answer the door. "Hi."

"Hey." He heard the tension in her voice, saw the apprehension she couldn't hide in her eyes. "I'll understand if you've changed your mind."

"What? Oh, no, it's just... I guess I'm a little nervous."

"Can't say as I blame you."

Her gaze moved over him, making him wonder what she was looking for, what she saw. "Sara?"

"You just look so normal," she murmured with a shake of her head. "And yet... not."

Travis knew what she meant. Vampires were subtly different from humans. Their hair tended to be thicker, their skin a little paler, their movements more fluid, they were lighter on their feet. Plus they all carried a hint of otherworldly power, although not every mortal picked up on it. Obviously, Sara did. He didn't miss the fact that whatever supernatural power prevented vampires from crossing the threshold into her house uninvited was back in full force. He could feel it now, repelling him like an invisible shield.

He shifted from one foot to the other, waiting for her make up her mind.

After what seemed like forever, she stepped back and said, "Come on in."

"Thank you." There was a familiar ripple in the air as he stepped inside, closed the door, and followed her into the living room.

Sara took a place on the sofa and gestured for him to take the chair opposite.

She didn't want him too close, he thought, as he sat down. "Are you doing okay?"

"I don't know. It's a lot to take in. I mean, it's like the world I knew is gone and everything is possible. If there are vampires, why not zombies? Or aliens from outer space? I guess I'm just having trouble absorbing it all."

"I know how you feel."

"Probably better than I do." Her fingers worried the hem of her sweater. "So, it was the vampire that Overstreet interviewed who... who made you? Is that the right term?"

Travis nodded. "Ronan. I wish to hell I'd never heard of him."

"Is it awful, being what you are?"

"It's not all bad. Just most of it."

"What's the good part?"

"Vampires never get sick. They don't age. If you're thirty when you're turned, you'll always look thirty. They can think themselves wherever they want to go in the blink of an eye, although I haven't mastered that yet. They're incredibly strong and fast."

She noticed he said *they* and not *we*, as if he hadn't yet fully accepted what he was. "But you can't be outside during the day?"

"No. And I can't enjoy a good steak or a bottle of beer. I can't visit my family or my old friends. I can't father a child."

"Have you ...?" She bit down on her lower lip. "Carl's article said Ronan had killed 'a few hundred people, maybe more.'"

"I haven't been a vampire long to kill a hundred people," he said dryly. "But no, I haven't killed anyone yet." He didn't tell her how hard it was to stop feeding before it was too late, how many times he had been tempted to glut himself. Or how badly he wanted to drink from her again.

"Did you come to Susandale because of the other vampires?"

"Yes and no. I don't know any of them. I haven't even met any of them. But I heard this town was a kind of haven for ... for their kind and I was looking for a safe place to stay until I figured out how to live with what I've become."

"Aren't new vampires supposed to stay with the one who made them? Seems I read that in a book somewhere."

"Yeah, well, that didn't happen in my case. There was no love lost between me and my sire."

Love, she thought. Were vampires even capable of it?

"Is there any chance we can still be friends?"

Friends? She stared at him. They had only known each other a short time, but the few nights they had shared had been wonderful. She had felt the attraction between them and hoped it might lead to a lasting relationship. Of course, that had been before she learned that he had been keeping a dreadful secret from her. Not that she could blame him for that. "What does 'being your friend' entail, exactly?"

"You know. Hanging out. Going to the movies." He shrugged. "Pretty much what we've been doing."

The memory of his kisses rose in her mind. But, of course, there'd be no more of that, she thought sadly. Because no one had ever kissed her the way he did or made her toes curl with the sheer pleasure of being in his arms. If only he wasn't a vampire, he would be the perfect guy. "We can give it a try, if you want."

"I won't hurt you, Sara. I swear it on my mother's life."

She nodded, hoping it was a promise he could keep. "Carl said he thought I'd be safe, here in town. That the other vampires wouldn't hurt me because they don't hunt where they live. Is that true?"

"From what I know, I'd say he's probably right."

"So, what would you like to do tonight?"

His gaze moved to her lips, to the pulse throbbing in the hollow of her throat. "Anything you want to do is fine with me."

"We could go to a late movie. They're showing the newest superhero flick over in Langston."

"Sounds good."

"Just let me get a jacket. Oh! My car's in the shop for another week."

"That's okay," he said, glad that he had decided to drive over. "We can take mine."

Travis tried not to stare at Sara as he drove to the theater, tried not to notice how tense she was. Not that he could blame her for being on edge. She had a lot to be nervous about.

He parked in the lot next to the theater. It was late and there was no line. Travis paid for the tickets. Sara bought a candy bar at the concession stand.

It was late on a week day night and the crowd was light. They found two seats in the middle section just as the lights went down.

Travis stared at the screen, acutely aware of the woman beside him. The scent of her skin, the fragrance of the soap she had used earlier in the day, the whisper of the blood flowing through her veins, the rapid beat of her heart. She refused to look at him, but he sensed that she was as aware of him as he was of her.

The movie started after numerous trailers. Gradually, she relaxed enough to nibble on the candy bar. He took heart when her arm brushed his and she didn't pull away. Maybe there was hope for them, after all.

It was after midnight when they left the theater. They talked about the movie on the way home—a nice safe topic of conversation. They both agreed it wasn't as good as the first one, but then, sequels were rarely as good as the original. His favorite superhero was Batman. Hers was Thor.

"What is it with women and Hemsworth?" he asked as he turned onto her street.

"He's gorgeous, for one thing," she said with a dreamy smile. "And sexy with a capital S."

Travis grunted. "If you say so."

Pulling up in front of her house, he shut off the engine, then got out of the car to open her door. Side by side, they walked up the stairs to the front porch. He stood behind her while she unlocked the door.

"Thanks for this evening," he said.

She smiled at him over her shoulder. "I had a good time."

"Would it be okay if I called you tomorrow night?"

Sara nodded. Vampire or not, she enjoyed being with him. "Good night, Travis." She stepped across the threshold, only to be stayed by his voice.

"Sara?"

She turned and looked up at him, felt her heart skip a beat.

"Would it be all right if I kissed you good night?"

"Is that what friends do?"

"I don't know, but I've been wanting to kiss you all night."

It was what she wanted, too. She had felt him watching her during the movie, had hoped he might kiss her, even though she knew she shouldn't. But since he'd asked... She nodded, her eyelids fluttering down as he crossed the threshold to cover her mouth with his.

It was little more than the brush of his lips and yet it unleashed a longing deep within her. When he broke the kiss, he rested his forehead against hers.

Sara blinked against the tears welling in her eyes. She could feel his loneliness, his need to be held, and her heart ached for him. Wanting to help, she put her arms around him, gasped when he wrapped her in his embrace. He held her tightly, as if he was afraid he might lose himself if he let go.

"I'm sorry," he said, taking a step back. "I didn't mean to..."

"It's all right."

He cupped her cheek in his palm, his eyes filled with an emotion she couldn't read. "Good night, sweet Sara."

"Good night." She watched him walk down the path and get in the Mustang. When he drove away, she let the tears come—tears for what he had lost, for what they might have shared if he had never hunted a monster named Ronan.

Sara was about to shut the door when she noticed several men and women strolling along the sidewalk across the street. It was a sight so unexpected she couldn't help staring. It was the first time she had seen any of the men in town. She recognized Olivia by her red hair as she passed under a streetlight. The man beside her was tall, with short, dark hair. And likely one of the vampires.

Sara backed away from the door when he looked in her direction. She felt his gaze burning into her. Oh, lordy, she thought, the last thing she wanted was to draw his attention, or that of any of the others.

Pressing a hand to her heart, she closed the door, and slid the dead-bolt home. Did the vampires come out every night after she had gone to bed?

It seemed that everyone else in Susandale, save Overstreet, was a vampire or linked to one. Unless she was mistaken, she was the only person in town who had come here not knowing what she was getting into. And now that she knew? If she was smart, she would pack up and leave town just as fast as she could. And yet ... she was reluctant to leave Travis. He was so alone. If she left, he'd have no one. Well, Overstreet would still be here, but for how long?

It was too late to make a decision now, she thought as she smothered a yawn. She'd worry about it in the morning.

After brushing her teeth, she went to bed, only to lay there in the dark staring up at the ceiling. Feeling a little foolish, slipped out of bed and turned on the light in the hall before padding into the kitchen and the living room, turning on the lights as she went.

Returning to her room, she left the door open just enough for the light in the hallway to keep the darkness at bay.

Chapter 11

Olivia tugged on her husband's hand as they passed Sara's house. "Do you think she knows about you and the others?"

"Have you said anything?" Jason asked.

"No, of course not!"

"The kids?"

"I don't think so."

"It doesn't matter. She's no danger to any of us. I'm more worried about that fledgling who rented the house on Third and Main. He's made no contact with any of us."

"Have you tried to talk to him?" she asked curiously.

"No, but he seems okay. I'm more interested in that stranger in town."

"Why? He seems harmless. Winona said he hasn't done or said anything the least bit suspicious. She said he seems friendly with Sara. Maybe he's here to see her."

"Maybe."

"But you don't think so?"

"Did Winona get his name?" Jason asked as they returned home.

"Not that I recall." Standing in the entryway, Olivia sighed as he drew her into his arms.

"I need to go out for a while," he said. "I won't be long."

She nodded. "Be careful."

"As always. Tomorrow, I want you to go back to Winona's and see if you can find out anything else about this new guy. And then I want you to go to Sara's shop and see if you can learn anything else about him, like what he's doing here." He ran his tongue along the side of her neck, then kissed her, long and deep. "Will you do that for me, darlin'?"

"You know I will." How could she not? She loved him with every fiber of her being. When her children were a little older and better able to care for themselves, she intended to ask Jason to turn her so they could be together forever.

Chapter 12

"Olivia, good morning," Sara said cheerfully. "What can I do for you today?"

"I just came by to thank you for helping Debbie and Luke pick out my birthday present. I love the bubble bath."

"I was happy to do it. They're great kids."

"Thank you. I think so. I was wondering, do you have any gardenia-scented hand lotion?"

Sara nodded. "Right over here."

Olivia followed her to a shelf on the far side of the room. Jars of face powder and tubes of hand lotion were interspersed with silk plants in a pretty display.

"I think you'll like this one," Sara said. Taking a sample bottle from the shelf, she poured a little in Oliva's hand. "It's my favorite."

"I was talking to Winona the other day," Olivia remarked, rubbing the lotion between her palms. "She said you eat in the café. quite often."

"I do," Sara admitted as she replaced the bottle. "I hate cooking for one. Actually, I hate cooking, period. And the food in the café is pretty good."

"She also said you've been meeting a male friend there. Is it serious?"

Sara frowned. Was she talking about Overstreet?

"I'm sorry," Olivia said quickly. "I shouldn't pry. I mean, I don't know you well enough to ... I should go," she exclaimed, and hurried toward the exit.

"Olivia, wait!"

Olivia paused at the door.

"It's not a secret. I met Mr. Overstreet in Winona's quite by accident. But I do enjoy his company, since he's the only friend I have in town."

Glancing over her shoulder, Olivia ventured a smile. "I hope *we* can be friends."

"I'd like that. Do you still want the hand cream?"

"Yes, it smells wonderful. And I'm really sorry for prying into something that's none of my business."

"Don't give it another thought." Sara rang up the lotion and placed it in a bag, then added a gardenia sachet. "Have a great day."

"Thanks. You, too." At the door, Olivia turned and waved before stepping out on the sidewalk.

Sara stared after her. Why had Olivia asked about Carl? Was everyone in town speculating about the two of them?

Sara mentioned her conversation with Olivia to Travis when he came over that night. "Does it seem odd to you?"

Travis shrugged. "It's a small town. Maybe she's just curious," he said, his expression thoughtful. "Or maybe someone asked her to find out who he is."

"Someone like who? Her husband?"

"I don't know. Maybe."

"I saw them out walking last night after you went home. It's the first time I've seen so many people outside. It seemed odd, somehow. Do you think they all come out late at night?" Like bats, she thought. Or vampires.

"The night belongs to my kind," he said dryly. "Did you see Overstreet today?"

"No." She frowned. "Do you think he left town?"

"I doubt it."

"Maybe you should go look for him? He might be in trouble."

Travis grunted softly. If there was any trouble around, Overstreet was sure to be hip-deep in it. "All right. I'll go have a look. But I'd rather stay here with you."

"I'll still be here when you get back," she said with a wink.

Outside, Travis glanced up and down the street. All was quiet. No whisper of wind stirred the trees. He turned right and started walking. Most of the houses had lights showing behind closed curtains. He detected vampires inside all but one. Farther down the street, a man and woman sat out on the porch. The man tensed when he saw Travis, and then he nodded as he recognized a fellow vampire.

Travis nodded back, then turned right at the corner.

He found Overstreet's old Dodge truck parked four blocks away, in the lot behind the hospital. The cab was empty. There were no other cars in the lot.

Opening his preternatural powers, Travis followed Overstreet's scent into the hospital. He found the writer in one of the private rooms, sitting on a hospital bed, pillows propped behind his back as he scribbled in a notebook.

He looked up, startled, when Travis stepped into the room. "Dammit, man, you scared the crap out of me."

"Sorry." Travis glanced around., noting the empty potato chip bag and three cans of diet soda on the tray table. Several crumpled notebook pages were scattered on the floor. "Looks like you're making yourself at home."

Overstreet shrugged. "There's no one else here. No doctors, nurses, patients. Nobody."

"Why not stay at the hotel? It's probably more comfortable than this."

"Probably. But this isn't costing me anything."

Travis pushed an old newspaper off of the hard, plastic chair next to the bed and sat down. "Do you think you're safe here?"

The journalist lifted a corner of the sheet, revealing a sharp wooden stake.

Travis snorted derisively. "You think that one little stick is gonna protect you from a whole town?"

"I doubt if the hotel would be any safer. Besides, no one's bothered me so far."

"That's because they don't know who you are. Yet. Or what you're doing here."

"And you know?"

"I can guess."

Overstreet arched one bushy brow.

"There's got to be a story involved," Travis remarked. "I'm just not sure what your angle is."

Carl tapped his pencil against his notebook. "Did you ever hear of Joey Cannon?"

"No. Why?"

"I met him in a seedy bar in New Jersey a while back. He'd been drinking heavily but he wasn't drunk. He told me he passed through here a few months ago. Said a couple of vampires imprisoned him in a basement and fed off him for a couple of weeks before he managed to escape. The guy's only thirty but after what they did to him, he looks all used up. Deflated, like."

"So you're writing another exclusive on vampires in America?"

Overstreet shrugged one shoulder. "It's what I do. I tried the retirement route. When I started watching soap operas every day..." He shook his head ruefully. "Joey Cannon's story lit a fire under me. It was just what I needed to get my butt off the couch."

"Yeah, well, I hope you don't get burned. I would have thought you'd have wised up after the last time."

"I'm not the one who went after Ronan."

"Good point."

"So, what are *you* doing here?" Carl asked. "Don't tell me you're worried about me."

"Me? Hell, no. But Sara is."

"Ah. She's a sweet girl. If I was twenty-five years younger, I'd give you a run for your money."

"You'd never catch me, old man. Not these days."

Overstreet nodded. "I guess you do have an edge—what with all that mystical vampire mojo. Tell Sara I appreciate her concern."

With a wave of acknowledgement, Travis left the hospital.

Sara met him at the door. "Did you find him?" she asked.

"Yeah. He's holed up in the hospital."

"The hospital!" she exclaimed. "Is that safe?" Looking worried, she went into the living room and sank down on the sofa.

"No." Travis sat beside her. "But neither is anyplace else."

Sara chewed on her thumbnail. "Maybe I should ask him to stay here," she remarked, and then grinned, thinking that would really give Olivia Bowman something to gossip about.

"I don't think that's a good idea," Travis said.

"No?"

He shook his head, then, rather tentatively, slipped his arm around her shoulders. When she didn't pull away, he said, "Do you think we could start over?" Travis asked. "No secrets between us this time?"

"I honestly don't know." Why did it feel so right, so natural, to have his arm around her? When he was this close, it didn't seem to matter that he was a vampire. All she saw was a man with sad brown eyes who made her feel loved and needed.

"I didn't want to lie to you," he said quietly. "But you must understand why I had to."

"Travis, I just don't know how it could work. I don't want to fall in love with a vampire. What kind of life could we have together? You were a hunter. You know what we'd be up against."

He nodded. So much for being friends, he thought. Although he had hoped for so much more than that.

She felt him withdraw from her even before he lowered his arm and rose to his feet. "I won't bother you anymore."

Before his words had time to sink in, he vanished from the room.

Murmuring, "What have I done?" Sara stared at the place where Travis had stood only moments before.

And then she burst into tears.

⚜ ⚜ ⚜

Travis stood in the shadows, feeling lost, and then he went back to the hospital. He found Overstreet still sitting on the bed, still scribbling in his notebook.

"Damn!" the journalist said. "Can't you make some noise when you enter a room?"

"Sorry. Next time I'll slam the door or knock over a trash can."

"What brings you back here so soon?"

"Like you, I've got nowhere else to go."

"Oh? What happened? Did Sara throw you out?"

"In a way."

"I'm sorry," Overstreet muttered. "I shouldn't have said that."

"I was a fool to think there was a chance for us." Shoulders slumped, Travis dropped into the chair he had occupied earlier.

Overstreet shook his head. Man or vampire, there was nothing worse than unrequited love. "So, what are you going to do now?"

"I don't know. What about you? How's the story going?"

"Nowhere, actually. I haven't seen anything suspicious even though I'm sure this place is crawling with vampires. And I'm beginning to think it was a mistake coming here. I'm pretty sure nobody in town is going to confess to torturing Joey Cannon and equally certain if I found out any of the details or who was involved, I'd be dead before I could get it down on paper."

"I think you're right."

"I just hate like hell to give up and let whoever was responsible go unpunished. If you'd seen Joey..." Overstreet shook his head. "He looked like he'd been through hell and back."

Travis snorted. "What were you planning to do if you found the culprit? Haul him off to the local law? I'd pay money to see that."

Overstreet laughed good-naturedly. "Yeah, me, too!" Putting his notebook aside, he held up a deck of cards. "Gin rummy?"

"Why not? I've got nothing better to do."

Olivia looked up when Jason entered the room. She smiled, thinking this was the best part of the day. The chores were done. Luke and Debbie were in their rooms doing their homework. And she had Jason all to herself until it was time to put the kids to bed.

He kissed her then asked, "Did you find out anything?"

She nodded. "I went to see Winona a little while ago and she told me his name is Carl Overstreet. He's a freelance journalist. I looked him up online and you won't believe this, but last year he published a series of articles about vampires! Do you think he came here looking for another story?"

"I don't know but it makes sense. How about booting up the computer while I go out? I'd like to read his stuff. And then I think we'd better let the others know what's going on."

"Jason, what if that man *is* here to do another story on vampires? That could be dangerous."

"Not to worry, darlin'. I don't intend to let that happen."

Chapter 13

Shannah sighed as she curled up next to Ronan and pillowed her head on his shoulder. She had been wasting away from some rare disease when she tracked him down. Dying and afraid, she had begged him to turn her into a vampire. At first, he had denied what he was. Gradually, they had become friends. And then more than friends, she thought with a smile. Life was certainly strange. She had gone to him seeking the dark trick and then, when he had bestowed it on her, she had hated him for it for a long time. Only now did she realize he had given her a wonderful gift—the gift of life. True, it was as different from her old life as night from day, but she had no complaints. Not when he was here to share it with her.

"Ronan, are you ever going to write any more books?"

"I don't know. Why?"

She shrugged one shoulder. "You're such a good author. I'm sure your avid fans are eagerly awaiting the next one."

He grunted softly. Being a vampire, he had never done interviews, never gone on national book tours or talk shows. It had been easier to flat out refuse than to constantly come up with one excuse after another to explain why he wasn't available for appearances on Sunday morning gab fests or make an appearance at afternoon book signings. And then, just when his publisher declared they were sick and tired of his excuses, Shannah had come into his life. The timing couldn't have been more perfect. He had convinced her to pretend to be him, which had worked well until Overstreet and Hewitt showed up at a book signing and started asking questions.

"I think maybe I'll have to retire," Ronan said, stroking her cheek, "now that you can no longer pretend to be me."

"Oh! I didn't think of that." She tilted her head to the side. "I guess you could go back to being a reclusive author again. Or maybe you could self-publish?"

He nodded. "I suppose that's a possibility, should I suddenly be stricken with inspiration for a new book. Fortunately, we don't need the money."

That was for sure, she thought. He had more money than he could spend in a dozen lifetimes.

Ronan held her close, remembering how desolate he had been when Shannah was on the verge of death. She had told him she didn't want to be what he was, that now, when he was offering it to her, she no longer wanted it. Unable to face a future without her in it, he had turned her against her will. At first, he had been certain he had lost her love forever, but their feelings for one another could not be ignored or denied and, in time, she had forgiven him.

Ronan?"

'Yes, love?"

"I'm worried about Hewitt."

"That again?" He drew back so he could see her face. "Is there something going on between the two of you that I'm not aware of? Something that has you worrying about him night after night?"

"Don't be ridiculous! I just feel guilty for what we did to him, that's all."

"*You* did nothing," he reminded her. "I'm the one who turned him."

"I should have stopped you."

Ronan looked at her, one dark brow arched in amusement. "As if you could have." He had been engulfed with pain and fury that night. The hunter was damn lucky he hadn't been ripped to shreds.

"We could go check on him," Shannah suggested, her voice soft and sultry as she trailed her fingertips over his lower lip. "Think of it as a long over-due vacation."

He laughed softly as she stretched out on top of him, her hair like silken strands of ebony against his bare skin.

"Please, Ronan?"

He rolled onto his side, his gaze burning into hers. "What will you give me?"

Her hands slid over his bare chest, then trailed lower, lower. "I'm sure I can think of something you'd like."

Chapter 14

The Susandale vampire council met in the basement of Jason Bowman's house. It was a large room with block walls painted white and a cement floor covered with a deep green carpet. Three leather sofas were grouped around a large coffee table.

Jason glanced at those present. Six men and one woman. Of the twenty-three vampires in town, these seven had been vampires almost as long as he had. Jason had been turned in his mid-thirties and had been a vampire almost forty years, making him the oldest vampire among them. Jeff Hackett was the youngest of the group, having been turned close to twenty years ago. Destiny Monahan's human husband had been killed in an automobile accident three years ago. The others—Joe Tuck, Rick Payson, Steve Handeland, and Jonah Kidder, were all married. Human spouses were never invited to the meetings.

Those gathered waited for Bowman to speak.

"I called you here tonight because I'm concerned about the two new residents in town. I'm sure you're all aware of them. What you may not know is that the human, Overstreet, is a freelance journalist. He did a series of articles on vampires some time ago. The other one, Travis, is new in the life. Have any of you had any contact with either one of them?"

In turn, each one present shook his head.

"Do you think that writer is here because of us?" Hackett asked, looking worried.

"I can't think of any other reason," Jason said. "Can any of you?"

"Maybe you should talk to him," Tuck suggested.

"Maybe you should talk to that writer *and* the vampire," Handeland said.

"Maybe you should contact Jarick."

Jason stared at Destiny, a muscle twitching in his jaw. Jarick was the master vampire in charge of the town and everything that went on within its limits, a fact Destiny never let Jason forget.

"You're only here on my sufferance," Jason snapped. "And don't you forget it." His gaze rested heavily on each one in the room. "Anything else we need to discuss?"

"What are we going to do if Overstreet is planning another story on vampires?" Payson asked. "Something like that will bring hunters swarming here from miles around."

"Don't worry," Jason said flatly. "If that's the case, he won't live long enough to write it."

CHAPTER 15

Sara heaved a sigh as she rang up the first purchase of the day. If things didn't pick up, she wouldn't be able to pay her rent on the store. Funny, but she didn't really care anymore. Maybe she should just admit defeat and go home. Sure, business had gotten a little better, but not enough to pay the rent on the store *and* her house. She didn't really have any friends in town. She tried to remember why she thought this would be a good place to prove her independence, but all she could think about was Travis.

She sighed again. Truth be told, the only reason she hadn't left town was because of him.

Why did he have to be a vampire? She stretched her arms over her head, then walked from the back of the store to the front and back again.

Why did time pass so slowly at work and so quickly when she was with Travis? And why couldn't she stop thinking about him? And why, even though she knew he was a vampire, did she still find him a hundred times more appealing than Dilworth Everett Young the Third?

If she married Dil, her life would be nothing but a series of political get-togethers, endless fund-raisers, and boring cocktail parties with senators and congressmen. Some women would no doubt find such a life fun and exciting. Not Sara. If she married Dil, she would have to be mindful of every word she said, everything she did, who she associated with, how she dressed, where she shopped.

Just thinking about it made her grimace with distaste.

With business so slow, she decided to walk down to the café and drown her sorrows in a chocolate malt.

She felt her spirits rise when she glanced in the window and saw Carl Overstreet sitting at one of the tables. He was, she thought as she opened the door, rapidly becoming her best friend.

He motioned her over when he saw her. "Hey, Sara. Good to see you. Sometimes it feels like we're the only two people in this whole damn town. Except for Winona, of course."

"I know what you mean." She took the chair opposite his, asked for a chocolate malt and an order of fries when Winona sashayed up to the table.

Overstreet arched an amused brow. "Malt and fries? Sounds like comfort food to me."

"Nothing gets by you," Sara said with a wry grin.

"That's why I'm such a good journalist."

"How's your story coming along?"

"It's not. I haven't talked to anyone except you and Hewitt. And Winona, of course. For all I know, Joey Cannon fabricated the whole incident." He fell silent when Winona brought Sara's order.

Sara smiled at the waitress. She didn't smile back.

"Does that mean you're leaving town?" Sara asked after Winona returned to the kitchen.

"No reason to stay." Head cocked to one side, he asked, "So, what happened between you and Hewitt, now known as Travis?"

"He asked if we could start over." Sara shook her head. "I just don't see how it could work. I mean, we don't have anything in common."

"Except the attraction between you."

She stared at him.

"Hey, a blind man could see it."

"I don't deny it, but that's hardly enough to build a life on."

"You never know until you try. So, he's up nights and sleeps days. So do a lot of regular people who hold night jobs. So he needs blood to survive. Think of it as a dietary restriction."

"What about children?"

Overstreet grunted softly. "Low sperm count?"

Sara laughed in spite of herself.

"I don't mean to make light of the situation," Overstreet said. "But love—the real thing—doesn't come along every day. I've certainly never found it. The funny thing is, the vampire who turned Hewitt—I'll never get used to calling him Travis—seems to have found what the rest of us are still looking for."

"Really?"

Overstreet nodded. "I'm not sure how Shannah and Ronan met, but they seem very happy together."

"Is she a vampire, too?"

"She is now. She wasn't when they met." Carl finished his coffee and wiped his mouth with the back of his hand. "I hope you and Hewitt can work things out. I don't know about you, but he's miserable." Rising, he picked up his check and Sara's. "I've got this."

"Thank you. You'll let me know before you leave town?"

"Sure." Touching a finger to the brim of his Fedora, he left the café.

Sara stared after him. What if he was right? Maybe she should give Travis a chance. What did she have to lose? Silly question, she thought. What, indeed?

Business picked up when the sun went down. By day's end, Sara was happy to see that she'd turned a nice profit. Another few days like this and she could stop worrying. For this month, at least.

It was almost nine-thirty when she stepped out the back door and locked it behind her. She let out a shriek when a dark shape materialized out of the shadows. "Travis! You scared the crap out of me."

"Sorry. I… the truth is, I was going to follow you home to make sure you got there safely."

"Oh?" Her heart skipped a beat. "Am I in danger?"

"Not that I know of. I just…"

"Just what?"

"I just wanted to be near you."

Sara stared at him. In movies, vampires were arrogant, powerful, emotionless creatures with little on their minds but blood and ravaging innocent women. But Travis? He was just a lonely guy forced into a life he didn't want. Vampire or not, her heart went out to him. "I'd be happy to have the company."

"Sara…"

She unlocked the door of her new rental car and slid behind the wheel, then looked up at him. "I missed you, too. Get in, I want to go home and take a shower and change into something more comfortable."

Thirty minutes later, clad in a pair of bright yellow PJ bottoms and a white tee shirt, Sara rummaged around in the refrigerator looking for something to snack on.

Travis stood in the doorway behind her, admiring the view.

Finding nothing, she grabbed her cell phone and ordered a small ham and pineapple pizza. "You must miss eating," she remarked on her way into the living room.

"You have no idea." Trailing behind her, he took the chair while she settled on the sofa.

"What was it like, the first time you... you know?"

The question was inevitable, Travis thought. He was only surprised it had taken her so long to ask. "It was horrible. I woke up disoriented. Scared. And in pain." He shook his head. "You can't imagine what it's like. I knew enough about vampires to know what was wrong with me, but I had no idea how to..." There was only one way to say it. "To hunt. I knew vampires mesmerized their prey, but I didn't really know how. And I was afraid."

"Afraid? Of what?"

"Afraid that I'd bungle it and kill somebody."

Sara bit down on her lower lip.

"It took me days to figure out how to mesmerize my... my prey. By then I was almost out of my mind with thirst. And once I had a woman in my arms, the thought of what I was going to do made me sick to my stomach. But the smell of her blood..." He paused a moment. "Are you sure you want to hear this?"

She nodded, as fascinated as she was repulsed by what he was telling her.

"My fangs were razor sharp. I'd learned that when I ran my tongue over them. I was worried I'd hurt her because by then I was desperate for relief. It took what little self-control I still had to keep from burying my... my fangs in her throat and drinking her dry." He shook his head, his eyes tormented. "I don't know how I stopped.

When I released her, she seemed unhurt, so I sent her on her way."

"And the blood?" She was intrigued in spite of herself.

"I don't know how to describe it. Taking it, drinking it..." Travis shook his head. "It should have been disgusting, but it was..." He made a vague gesture with his hand. "Once you taste it, you really don't want anything else. I guess I've freaked you out, haven't I?"

"A little. Maybe you should tell your story to Carl."

He looked at her as if she had lost her mind. "That's the last thing in the world I'd ever do. And I mean that literally."

"Well, it's one heck of a story. I doubt if very many people have ever heard one like it."

"Well, they won't hear it from me." He wrinkled his nose against the sudden smell of cheese and garlic. "Your pizza's here."

Travis watched her go to the door, heard her laughter as she paid the delivery guy. He had never thought to be this close to her again. Being with Sara made him feel whole, let him forget what he was, at least while he was with her.

She carried the pizza into the kitchen, then poked her head around the door. "Would you like a glass of wine?"

"Yeah, thanks."

She came back a few minutes later carrying a tray laden with a couple slices of pizza on a paper plate, a can of soda, and a goblet. She placed the tray on the coffee table between them, then handed him the glass. She jerked her chin toward the pizza. "Does it bother you? The smell, I mean?" She had eaten in front of him before but at the time, she hadn't known what he was.

"Not really."

"I could eat in the kitchen."

"It isn't necessary." He raised his drink. "Enjoy your dinner, Sara."

She felt a little self-conscious as she nibbled on the first slice. She tried to imagine what it would be like to survive on a warm, liquid diet, to never eat solid food again. Bread and pasta. Fried chicken and cheeseburgers. Decadent chocolate cake. Shrimp and lobster and all of her other favorite dishes. She didn't think even staying young forever would be a fair trade. "How are you able to drink wine?"

"I don't know. But it's a nice change." He smiled at her and she smiled back. It warmed him more than the Merlot.

"Carl's thinking of leaving town," she remarked.

"I'm not surprised."

"I guess whatever story he hoped to write isn't working out."

Travis nodded. "Joey Cannon."

"You know about that?"

"Yeah. Overstreet mentioned him."

"Do you think the man's story is true?"

"I don't know. It very well could be."

Sara finished her dinner and put the plate aside. She didn't know how or why, but suddenly the atmosphere in the room changed. She looked at Travis, felt her heart skip a beat when she saw him staring at her throat.

Vampire.

"Sorry." He lifted his gaze. "The wine's good but it's not very filling, if you know what I mean."

"Who do you ... um ... prey on? Certainly not anyone in town."

"No. That wouldn't be wise."

"How do you choose them"

He shrugged, bemused by her curiosity. "Whoever's handy, I guess. A woman walking alone down a dark street. Sitting alone in a bar. Waiting at a bus stop."

She leaned forward, her whole body tense. "Have you ever wanted to drink from me?"

Damn, there was a loaded question if he'd ever heard one. How the hell was he supposed to answer it? *All the time? I already have? Can I do it again?* "I'm a vampire, Sara. What do you think?"

"What's it like, when you bite someone?"

"For me or for them?"

"Both."

"In most cases, blood is blood." Not in her case, though. It had been spectacularly satisfying. "For those I prey on, I try to make it pleasurable, even though I wipe the memory of it from their minds afterward."

It was the wrong thing to say. He could see the wheels turning, see her wondering if he had bitten her and made her forget. *Damn.* Just when he thought there might be a chance for them.

"How do you do make them forget?"

"It's a form of hypnotism, I guess. I'm not really sure how it works. Only that it does."

Her gaze speared his. "Have you ever done that to me?"

And there it was. "The truth?"

She nodded. "No more lies, remember?"

"I tasted you the night we went dancing."

Her eyes widened. "I don't believe you!"

He shrugged. "I only took a very little."

"And you made me forget it?"

"It seemed like the smart thing to do."

"Is that the only time?"

"No."

A flood of emotions chased themselves across her face.

He held up his hand as if to stave off her protest. "I know, I know, it was a despicable thing to do, but Sara, your blood..." He shook his head. "I've never tasted anything like it. It's warm and sweet and... and I don't know how to describe it exactly, except that after tasting it once, it was all I could think about."

Sara stared at him, wondering if she should be furious because he had stolen her blood or flattered that he liked it so much.

"I won't blame you if you hate me and never want to see me again." He raked his fingers through his hair. "This is all so new to me. I don't know what the hell I'm doing half the time. But I'm crazy about you, Sara. And I don't want to lose you. I know this is gonna sound corny, but I was lost until I met you. If you'll give me a chance, I swear I'll never drink from you again unless you say it's all right." Suddenly out of steam, he huffed a sigh and fell silent.

"You're right," she said, leaning back on the couch. "I should throw you out on your ear right now, but..." She shook her head. "I don't know. Call me crazy, but that's the sweetest thing anyone's ever said to me."

"Sara!" He started to reach for her, then drew back. "Sorry."

Smiling, she grabbed his hand and pulled him toward her. He sank down on the sofa beside her, his arm sliding around her waist to draw her close as his mouth claimed hers.

Sara melted into his embrace, thinking that it felt oh, so right to be in his arms. She moaned softly as his tongue teased her. Vampire or not, the man knew how to kiss!

And, like it or not, she was falling in love with him. She had no idea if such a relationship would lead to a life of happiness or if it might end in sorrow and regret, but she was determined to take a chance and hope for the best.

One kiss led to another, and then another, each one longer and sweeter than the last. They were lying side by side on the sofa now, bodies pressed intimately together. Lost in the magic of his kisses, it took Sara a minute to realize someone was pounding on the front door.

"Leave it," Travis said, his voice husky. "Maybe they'll go away."

"Good idea." She slid her fingers into the hair at his nape, her eyelids fluttering down as he kissed her again, only to let out a whimper of protest when Travis rolled to his feet.

Sara blinked up at him. "Travis? What's wrong?"

"It's Overstreet. Maybe we'd better let him in. He might be in trouble."

Chapter 16

"Carl, this is a surprise," Sara said, smoothing a hand over her hair. "Is something wrong?"

"Is Hewitt here?"

"Yes."

Overstreet stood in the open doorway, his shoulders slumping when he saw Travis.

"What's wrong?" Travis asked. "You look like hell."

"I was at the hospital, looking over my notes... and..." Overstreet scrubbed a hand over his face.

"And what?" Travis asked impatiently. "Spit it out, man."

"Ronan's here."

Travis swore under his breath. "What the hell! Are you sure?"

"Of course I'm sure! He's waiting for you at the hospital."

"I decided not to wait."

Sara let out a shriek as a tall, dark-haired man suddenly appeared on the porch beside Carl.

Overstreet darted across the threshold as if his life depended on it. And maybe it did, Sara thought.

Travis put himself between Ronan and the others, eyes narrowed as he stared at the vampire who had turned him and then abandoned him. "What the hell are you doing here?"

"Shannah's been worried about you," Ronan replied with a negligent shrug. "She insisted we come and make sure you were adjusting to your new lifestyle."

"Is she here, too?"

"Indeed. She's waiting for me at the hospital." Ronan looked his fledgling up and down. "You seem to be doing all right."

"No thanks to you."

Ronan shrugged. "As I frequently remind my wife, you're lucky I didn't kill you."

"Yeah," Travis said bitterly. "Lucky. So, you've seen me. You can tell Shannah to stop worrying about me and go home."

"But you haven't introduced me to this lovely lady."

Travis hesitated a moment before answering. "This is Sara. She's a friend of mine. Sara, remember when you said you wanted to meet Claire Ebon? Well, here she is."

Sara stared at the man standing on the other side of the threshold. Clad all in black, he was tall and broad-shouldered, with hair and eyes the color of ebony. She took a step back when his gaze met hers. Danger emanated from that flint-like stare like the warning rattle of a snake.

"Always pleased to meet a fan," the vampire said, his voice silky soft and smooth.

She nodded, speechless.

The vampire laughed softly, as if her fear greatly amused him.

Sara felt a wave of relief when the vampire turned his attention back to Travis.

Frowning, the vampire said, "You've changed your name."

"Get out of my head!"

"Travis Black? Interesting choice for a last name. Should I be flattered?"

Travis scowled at him.

"When you have time, please come to the hospital." It wasn't a request. "Shannah would like to see you." Ronan sketched a bow in Sara's direction. "Until next time, Miss Winters," he said, and vanished into the darkness.

Sara looked at Travis and frowned. "How did he know my last name?"

"He's a master vampire. He can't only read your mind, but he can compel you to do whatever he wants."

Sara pressed a hand to her heart. That was the scariest thing she'd ever heard.

"Are you going to go the hospital?" Overstreet asked.

"I don't have much choice."

"Do you think that's wise?"

"It doesn't matter what I think. He's my sire. If he commands it, I have to obey. "Why don't you stay here with Sara?"

"Fine with me, if Sara doesn't mind."

"No, please. I'd rather not be alone." She smiled, though it felt a little frayed around the edges.

Carl looked at Travis, his eyes narrowed thoughtfully. "Do you think that's why he's really here?" he asked, frowning. "Because Shannah's worried about you?"

Travis snorted. "I don't know why she would be. After I staked him, she dragged me over to him so he could feed on me and then ruin my life."

Somewhat timidly, Sara took Travis' hand. "I'm glad he didn't kill you."

He looked at her, his anger melting away. "Yeah. Me, too, because I never would have met you. And believe me, darlin', you're the only thing that makes me want to go on living." He kissed her lightly. "I'll be back as soon as I can."

⚜ ⚜ ⚜

Travis found Ronan and Shannah sitting side by side on a faded sofa in the hospital waiting room. In her mid-twenties when Ronan turned her, Shannah was as lovely as he remembered, with a wealth of thick black hair, blue eyes, and a curvy figure.

"So, you wanted to see me and here I am," Travis said flatly. "Is that all?"

Shannah glanced at Ronan.

He shrugged. "I told you he wouldn't be happy to see us."

"Right as always," Shannah murmured as she turned those wide blue eyes on Travis. "I'm sorry for the way things turned out, but you brought it on yourself. You should have left us alone."

"Yeah. Well, silly me, I thought your life was in danger. Little did I know the female was just as deadly as the male."

She stiffened, her chin jutting out. "I guess I don't need to worry about you anymore."

"I guess not." Travis looked at his sire. "Okay if I go now, master?"

"No."

"Why the hell not?"

"There's something strange going on in this town. I'm surprised you haven't noticed."

"What are you talking about?"

"I'm not sure, but I smell treachery in the air."

Travis frowned. "Are you serious? I've only counted maybe forty people in town, counting kids, and twenty-three of them are vampires."

Ronan snorted. "I'd say there were more than fifty vampires living here. Don't you think that's odd?"

"I never thought about it," Travis said, shrugging. "Fifteen or fifty, it seemed like a nice quiet place to hole up."

"Expand your feelings, vampire. What do you smell?"

"I don't know how to do that," Travis retorted, his voice bitter. "The vampire who turned me didn't see fit to stick around long enough to teach me the ins and outs."

What might have been regret passed behind Ronan's eyes and was quickly gone. "It's easy. Just open your senses. It's like opening a door."

Taking several deep breaths, Travis closed his eyes and imagined his senses expanding, reaching outward. An odd sensation came over him, almost as if he was drawing on a power not his own. Sensations slammed into him—not just feelings but the overwhelming emotions of hopelessness and despair, fear, and pain. Old blood. And death.

And over all a stifling air of preternatural power.

Reeling under the assault, he opened his eyes. "What the hell!"

"Now do you see what I mean?" Ronan asked.

"Yeah. Something's definitely wrong here. But what?"

"I suspect the vampires here are selling humans to other vampires, and they're keeping them prisoners, either in their homes or in some sort of containment center nearby."

"That's horrible!" Shannah exclaimed.

"Why would they do that?" Travis asked. "Prey is easy enough to find."

"I have no idea." Ronan took Shannah's hand in his and gave it a squeeze. Rising, he went to the front window and looked out. "It makes no sense. What do you know about the vampires in town?"

"Nothing. I haven't met any of them."

Ronan glanced over his shoulder. "Doesn't that seem odd to you?"

"I don't know. Should it?"

"More than one or two vampires in any town is unusual. This many is unheard of unless there's a master vampire in charge. Someone who can keep the others under control. That's not the case here. The oldest vampire was turned less than forty years ago."

"Why are the rest of them hiding?"

"That's a good question."

Travis sat on the arm of a chair, his brow furrowed. "Joey Cannon," he murmured.

"What?"

"Overstreet met some guy named Joey Cannon. The man claimed he'd been held prisoner for a couple of weeks in some little town called Susandale and that he barely escaped with his life. That's what brought Overstreet here in the first place. He was hoping to get a story out of it."

"Overstreet, yes," Ronan murmured. "I remember him well. I thought he'd retired."

"He did, until the journalist in him suspected Joey might give him one last claim to fame."

"We don't need another titillating tale about vampires in America," Ronan said dryly. "We've spent centuries staying under the radar. I'm not going to let some two-bit reporter ruin it for all of us."

"Well, they've been keeping it a secret, so far. Well, except for Cannon."

"All it takes is one match to set the world on fire." Ronan paced the floor in front of the window. "We're going to find out what the hell is going on and shut it down."

Travis lifted one brow. "We?"

Ronan nodded. "You. Me. and Mr. Overstreet."

"Shouldn't that be four?" Shannah asked.

Ronan smiled at his wife. "Only if we run into trouble that I can't handle, love."

After agreeing to meet with Ronan and Overstreet the following night, Travis returned to Sara's house. He found her and the writer at the kitchen table playing Gin Rummy. "Who's winning?"

"He is!" Sara declared acerbically. "But he cheats!"

Overstreet tossed his cards on the table, then sat back in his chair. "So? Was Shannah happy to see you?"

"Not particularly."

"You were gone for quite a while. What did you talk about?"

Propping his shoulder against the door jamb, Travis folded his arms over his chest. "It seems there's a dark undercurrent in Susandale."

"What are you talking about?" Sara asked.

"Ronan said there's something shady going on in this town." Travis glanced at Overstreet. "From what he said, I gather he thinks there's a master vampire pulling the strings, and that they're selling people to other vampires. I told him about Joey Cannon. Ronan wants to meet with you and me tomorrow night."

"Me?" Overstreet squeaked. "Why does he want me there?"

"I have no idea, but I guess you'll find out." Travis shifted his gaze to Sara. "He thinks there must be fifty vampires in town."

"Fifty!" The color drained from her face. "Do you believe him?"

Travis nodded. Now that he knew how to use his preternatural senses, he had no doubt about it.

"He's very bitter, isn't he?" Shannah remarked, taking Ronan's hand as they strolled down the dark, deserted street.

"What did you expect, my love? A hug and a warm welcome?"

"Of course not. But..." She shook her head. "I thought we were friends."

"Friends? The man was a hunter. He kidnapped you to get to me."

"I know, but he seemed genuinely concerned about me when I got sick. And he did try to save me from you because he thought I was in danger."

"That was his biggest mistake."

"He was only thinking of my safety. He didn't know you'd turned me."

"I fear that's something he's never going to forgive. Or forget."

"I think you're right. And I'm sorry for that. I have so few friends."

Ronan stopped abruptly, his gaze searching hers. "Are you unhappy, Shannah?"

"No! No. It's just that..."

"You don't have to explain. I've changed your whole life. I've been a vampire for so long, I've forgotten what it's like to have friends you can talk to. People you can trust."

"I don't have any regrets, Ronan. I love our life together. I wouldn't change anything."

"But?"

She smiled up at him. He knew her so well. "It's just that he was the last friend I made before you turned me, and even though it was a rocky friendship at best, I guess I was clinging to that. It's silly, I know, but it hurts that he hates me now. Even though I don't blame him."

He drew her into his arms and held her close, one hand lightly stroking her hair. "Do you want to go home?"

"Do you think we should?"

"It's up to you."

"I think we should stay and clean up the town first."

"What are you now, the marshal of Dodge City?"

She laughed at that, as he had hoped she would.

"No, but if the vampires really are selling people... We have to stop them. Not just for their sakes," she said earnestly, "but because it's the right thing to do."

"I hope you never lose that delightful spark of humanity, my love." He said it lightly, but he meant it, just the same.

Chapter 17

Overstreet took his leave soon after Travis returned. Sara walked the journalist to the door, bid him a cordial goodnight, then went into the kitchen to clear the table and tidy up the kitchen.

Travis lingered in the doorway, admiring the sway of Sara's hips as she moved about the room. After listening to Ronan's assessment of what was going on in town, he was reluctant to leave her alone. While it was true that no vampire could enter her house without an invitation, that didn't mean one of the human inhabitants couldn't break in and force her out of the house where she would be vulnerable to the vampires.

Sara glanced at the clock on the stove as she wiped down the counter and dropped the towel over the back of a chair. "It's late," she said, yawning. "I need to get some sleep."

"Yeah." He shoved his hands into his pants' pockets.

"What's wrong?" She felt the tension radiating from him, saw it in the tense set of his shoulders. "Travis? You're scaring me."

"I don't mean to. Sara, listen. I don't think you should be alone tonight."

"Why not?"

"Things have changed. This isn't the sleepy little town I thought it was. Ronan told me how to expand my preternatural senses and it's changed everything. You shouldn't be alone. Not after dark. And not during the day."

"Now you're really scaring me."

"A little fear is a healthy thing."

Funny, she thought, Carl had said the same thing not long ago.

Taking her hand, Travis led her into the living room, then sat on the couch and pulled her down on his lap. "I don't know if the humans who live with the vampires are aware of what's going on, but we need to go on the assumption that they do. Which means you can't trust any of them, either. I think maybe you should close the store for a while."

"I can't afford to do that. I'm barely making ends meet as it is."

"Maybe we can get Overstreet to stay with you during the day," Travis said, thinking out loud. "I'll see about getting him a couple of stakes. And some holy water," he added, remembering how it had burned Ronan's flesh. "I'll relieve him when the sun goes down." Caressing her cheek with his knuckles, he said, "Maybe you should just go home."

"No!" Sara shook her head vehemently. "I won't do that."

"Maybe move to the next town for awhile, then."

"Do you really think I'm in danger? I mean, why now? No one's bothered me before."

"Well, how about taking a few days off and just staying home until we find out what's really going on? Overstreet can keep you company." At the store or here, in Sara's house, Travis intended to see that Overstreet had weapons to repel invaders, human or vampire.

"All right," Sara agreed reluctantly. "If you really think it's necessary."

"I do. Better safe than sorry." He kissed her cheek. "I'm going to spend the night here, if it's all right with you."

"Okay. The bed in the guestroom is made up. Just make yourself at home." Sliding off his lap, she kissed him good night, though she doubted she would get any sleep after this evening's startling revelations.

Travis prowled through the house, his thoughts chaotic as he reviewed what Ronan had said earlier about the town, and as he considered the thrill he'd experienced while expanding his senses. he wondered what other powers he might possess that he was not yet aware of.

But most of all, he thought about Sara. He was determined to protect her, no matter what the cost. She was the best thing in his accursed life. He realized there was a chance that she might never want to see him again after all this was over, but if that was the case, then so be it. Her life meant more to him than his own.

It was near dawn when he went to the window to stare out into what was left of the night. Of course, due to his preternatural vision, he had no trouble seeing in the dark. And what he saw was troubling indeed. A motor home was parked across the street, its door facing Sara's house. Three men—all vampires—stood on the sidewalk. As Travis watched, two of them went into the motor home. The coach rocked violently for a moment, then the two men exited the coach. The first one carried a man over his shoulder. The second, a woman.

The two vampires and their burdens vanished from sight. The third vampire got behind the wheel of the RV, turned on the engine, and sped away.

Travis cursed under his breath when he saw a young boy, perhaps five years old, staring out the back window of the RV, his pale face frightened and streaked with tears.

Shit! Should he go after the boy? Doing so would leave Sara unprotected. Torn, he left the house in pursuit of the motor home. He found it abandoned in a ditch six miles out of town. There was no sign of the boy, his parents, or the vampires.

As desperate as he was to search for the kid, the first painful rays of the rising sun drove Travis back to the shelter of Sara's house. Inside, he went downstairs to the basement and closed the door. The sofa would have been more comfortable than the cement floor, but he needed the darkness.

He had time to make one quick phone call before the dark sleep carried him away.

Sara woke to the sound of someone pounding on the door. She opened one bleary eye and tried to focus on the clock on the nightstand beside the bed. Five-thirty. She groaned as the pounding increased.

Throwing back the covers, she staggered down the hall. A glance into the guestroom show the bed was empty. At the front door, she looked through the peephole. "Carl!" she exclaimed. "What are doing here? Do you know what time it is?"

"Yeah." He sounded as groggy as she felt. "Travis called and told me to haul my lazy butt over here ASAP."

Blinking the sleep from her eyes, she unlocked the door. "What's going on?"

"I don't know." He lumbered inside, still in his pajamas.

Sara closed and locked the door behind him. Scuffing into the living room, she paused when she noticed the sofa was empty. Hadn't Travis said he was spending the night? He wasn't in the guestroom. He wasn't in the living room. Where was he?

"I'm going back to bed," she murmured. "The couch is yours if you want it."

Sara tossed and turned for an hour before she gave it up for a lost cause. Pulling on her robe and slippers, she padded into the kitchen, put on a pot of coffee, then sat at the table, her chin resting on her steepled fingers. Moving here had seemed like such a good idea. Now it seemed like a nightmare.

She looked up as Overstreet shuffled into the kitchen and dropped onto the chair across from hers.

"I should have stayed in New Jersey," he mumbled crossly.

Sara nodded sympathetically. "Coffee?" she asked, rising.

"Sugar, no cream. Thanks."

She filled two cups, added sugar to both, milk to hers, and returned to the table. "Have you noticed things seem to be going from bad to worse?"

"Oh, yeah. I guess you know that Travis asked me to spend the day with you. And to remind you that you're not supposed to go to work."

"We talked about it last night. Maybe you should start spending the night here so we can both sleep later in the morning."

"We'll see." Lifting his cup, he drained it in three long swallows. Pushing away from the table, he refilled his cup.

"Do you have any idea what Ronan and Travis are planning to do?"

"Not a clue. I'm guessing we'll discuss it tonight. Although I don't know why they want me there. I'm no vampire hunter."

"Have you ever thought how ironic it is that Travis was once a hunter and now he's what he hunted? It would make a great novel."

"And I'm going to write it. As soon as I get out of this town."

"Seriously?"

He nodded. "I've got the outline in my head."

"Promise you'll send me a copy when it's published."

"You know I will," he said with a wink. "Maybe I'll dedicate it to you."

"That would be awesome. Just think, I've met two famous authors without even trying."

Sara and Overstreet passed the day watching old movies, napping, and playing endless hands of Gin Rummy.

As the sun went down, Sara found herself glancing at her watch time and again. Travis was usually here by now, so, where was he?

⚜ ⚜ ⚜

Travis met Ronan at the hospital as soon as the sun went down.

"I thought I told you to bring Overstreet," Ronan said.

"I wanted to see you alone first. I want you to teach me how to dissolve into mist and think myself wherever I want to go. And anything else a good master teaches his fledgling."

Irritated and amused, Ronan lifted one brow. "Do you now?"

"I deserve it."

"Really? Why?"

"Because you turned me, dammit."

"It was your decision."

"The lesser of two evils," Travis retorted.

"I admire your grit," Ronan said. "But the truth is, there's nothing to dissolving into mist, or transporting yourself from one place to the other. The power is in you. You just have to believe you can do it, whether it's crawling up the side of a building like a spider or shape-shifting."

"Shape-shifting?"

"I prefer wolves." The words were still in the air when the vampire disappeared, and a large black wolf stood in his place.

Travis stared at the beast. And then he grinned. How awesome was that?

Ronan shifted back to his own form. "Impressed?"

"Where do your clothes go?"

"That," Ronan said with the first real smile Travis had ever seen, "is a mystery no one can answer."

"So, if I want to dissolve into mist, I just have to believe I can do it and it happens?"

"Mind over matter, that's all it is," Ronan said, remembering that he'd said the same words to Shannah not long ago. "You think it, believe it, do it." He chuckled softly. "It can be a little scary the first time."

Travis grunted, unable to believe his sire had ever been afraid of anything. Putting everything else out of his mind, he pictured himself as a thick gray mist floating in the air ... and it happened. And it was scary as hell, just as Ronan had said. He saw the world through a hazy cloud. Sound was muted. He had no sense of touch or smell.

And then he felt himself drifting aimlessly.

Fear shot through him as he floated out the open window. Below him, the hospital grew smaller and smaller. *Shit!* What was he supposed to do now? He tried to concentrate but his mind was frozen with fear as he imagined himself drifting ever upward toward the stars. Disintegrating into nothing.

Concentrate! He imagined himself gradually drifting toward the earth, knew a sense of relief when thought turned to action. He pictured himself back in the hospital and a moment later, he was there. *I want to be me again!*

He blew out a shaky breath when he realized he had form and substance. "Damn! I'm not sure I *ever* want to try that again."

"But you will. And because you were turned by a master vampire, your powers are stronger than most."

"Thanks, Dad."

Ronan glared at him. "You will *not* call me that."

Travis nodded as the vampire's preternatural strength rolled over him. It was like being crushed beneath an overwhelming, invisible weight. He breathed a sigh of relief when Ronan withdrew it.

"Anything else?" his sire asked.

"How do I transport myself from one place to another?"

"The same way you turn into mist. Mind over matter. It's as simple as that. Any more questions?"

When Travis shook his head, Ronan said, "Let's take a walk through the town."

After leaving the hospital, they turned right and headed toward the residential section. It had been dark for about an hour and the streets and sidewalks were deserted.

"These houses are all inhabited by vampires," Ronan remarked as they reached the end of the last street. "All but the one on Hampstead. The vampire who owned the house is dead, but his mate still lives there."

"Did you detect any sign of humans being imprisoned anywhere?"

"No. But the scents of dozens of humans lingers in the air. Many are fresh, which leads me to believe they're still here."

"So, where are they?"

"The only possibility I can think of is that they're being kept somewhere underground."

"Assuming you're right, how do they get their prey to the buyers?"

"A good question. I'm also wondering if they kidnap people from other towns. I can't imagine this place gets that many visitors."

"Last night, two vampires kidnapped a couple from a motor home. A third vampire drove the vehicle away, with a kid still inside."

"Of course. They'd have to dispose of the vehicle."

"What do you think happened to the boy?"

Ronan didn't answer, merely looked at him.

Travis nodded. Either they intended to sell the kid, or the vampires had a fondness for young blood. He shook the thought away. "So, the vampires sleep all day. A few of their mates work the businesses to give the town a look of normalcy, which is why no one has bothered Sara."

Ronan nodded. "She's window dressing, like the other women."

"Are we done here?" Travis asked. "I need to get back to Sara's so Overstreet can take a break."

"Go ahead. I'm going to look around some more."

"Where's Shannah?"

"She went to get a room at the hotel in the next town. I'm going to meet her there later."

"Tired of bedding down in the hospital?"

"Indeed."

With a grin and a wave of his hand, Travis headed for Sara's.

He found her and Overstreet in the living room watching *Frasier* reruns, a large bowl of popcorn between them.

"Sorry I'm late," Travis said, dropping a burlap bag on the floor. "How was your day?"

Overstreet grunted. "Long and—nothing against this lovely lady—boring."

"You can take off now, if you want," Travis said.

"Thanks, I think I will."

"Hang on a minute. Sara, I think it's okay for you to go back to work, as long as Overstreet is there with you." Picking up the bag he'd dropped on the floor, he handed it to the writer. "This stuff's for you."

"And I didn't buy you anything," Carl muttered, peering into the sack. "Damn, are we going to war?"

"Maybe."

"What's in there?" Sara asked.

"A pistol loaded with silver bullets," Travis said with a shrug. "A couple of wooden stakes. Three large spray bottles filled with holy water. And a silver-bladed dagger."

Her eyes widened. "Wow. Where did you find all that stuff?"

"It used to be mine. I had it in the trunk of my car."

Sara bit down on her lower lip. She couldn't begin to imagine how he felt, what he thought, about the-one-hundred-and-eighty degree turn his life had taken.

"Thanks for the weapons," Overstreet said as he tucked one of the stakes into the waistband of his trousers and slipped the pistol into his coat pocket. "I'll see you tomorrow, Sara."

"Goodnight." Sara put the popcorn bowl on the coffee table when Travis came to sit beside her.

Sliding his arm around her shoulders, he said, "I miss you when we're apart."

She smiled up at him. "I miss you, too. I think about you all the time."

"Oh?"

She shrugged. "I keep thinking how hard it must have been for you to go from hunter to hunted," she remarked. And then frowned. "Has anyone hunted *you*?"

"Not yet. I've been keeping a low profile. It's one of the reasons I changed my name. Too many people knew what I was before. The last thing I want is for some old friend to track me down and try to drive a stake in my heart when he realizes what I've become."

She nodded. "Did you see Ronan tonight?"

"Yeah. We walked through the town. He thinks there are definitely people being held here against their will, but he can't locate them, which surprised me. He thinks they're being kept somewhere underground and I think he's probably right. It's the only explanation, unless they're being held somewhere on the outskirts of town."

"It's all just so bizarre," Sara murmured, massaging her temples. "I keep thinking it's a nightmare and I'll wake up. But then I think about you and I'm glad it's not a dream."

"Sara." He cupped her face in his hands and kissed her lightly. "Do you know how amazing you are?"

"What do you mean?"

"Any other woman would be scared out of her wits to know she had a vampire in her house. She'd be running for the hills. And yet here you sit, with my arm around you, as if we're just an ordinary couple. Like I said. Amazing."

Sara laughed. And then she sobered. "Not really. What I am is scared half to death. Oh, not of you," she said quickly. "But that Ronan character scares me right down to my socks."

"He scares me, too. But he taught me how to do some remarkable things tonight."

"Oh? Like what?"

"For one thing, he turned into a wolf in the blink of an eye."

"He did? Now *that* is amazing!" She looked at him quizzically. "Can you do it, too?"

"I haven't tried yet. But he told me that all I have to do to use my supernatural abilities is to believe that I can."

"The power of positive thinking?" she asked with a grin.

"Something like that."

She snuggled against him, thinking of everything he'd said. Why *wasn't* she more afraid? She was in a town filled with vampires. There was one sitting beside her on the sofa. And yet she felt curiously untroubled by it all.

She was still trying to figure it out when she fell asleep.

Late that night, Jason called the vampire council together. They all looked at him askance, since meetings so close together were rare.

"I'll keep this short and to the point," he said. "In case it's escaped your notice, there's a master vampire in town. And it's not Jarick."

Chapter 18

Sara opened the shop the next day. Overstreet sat in the back corner of her office. Armed with holy water, a stout wooden stake and the pistol Travis had given him, he passed the time by writing in his notebook, or just staring out the front window.

The supplies Sara had ordered arrived late that afternoon and she spent a couple of hours restocking the shelves and going over the books.

To her surprise, she had a dozen customers between the time she opened and seven o'clock when she and Overstreet walked down to the café. She remarked on it to Overstreet over dinner.

"You're not complaining about having a lot of business, are you?" he asked with a wry grin.

"Of course not. It just seems odd, that's all. I don't think I've had that many customers in an entire day, let alone in four hours." She nibbled on a piece of fried chicken. "Do you think they're spying on us?"

"More likely on me. I've no doubt they all know why I'm here."

"That could be dangerous for you!" Sara exclaimed.

Carl shrugged. "I'm probably safe enough as long as the sun's up. After dark, I'm depending on Travis and Ronan to keep the bad guys at bay." He took a few bites of his steak, his brow furrowed. "Although I'm not sure I can count on Ronan."

"He's scary as all get out," Sara said. "I wouldn't put it past him to kill all of us."

"Yeah. Well, let's hope it doesn't come to that."

They ate in silence for several moments, then Sara asked, "How's your story coming along?"

"It isn't."

"What do you mean?"

"Well, until something actually happens, there's nothing to tell. I need concrete proof that there's a nest of vampires selling humans to other vampires. All I have now are Joey Cannon's story and my own suspicions and that doesn't cut it."

"Travis and Ronan seem convinced."

"I can't sell a story on speculation, no matter now certain they seem."

Sara pushed her plate away, then picked at the chocolate cake she'd ordered for dessert, while Overstreet wolfed down a large slice of apple pie.

It was dark out when they started back to the store. Sara didn't see anyone on the street, but she couldn't shake the feeling that they were being watched. Grabbing Overstreet's arm, she said, "Let's go home."

When he didn't ask questions, she guessed he had also felt those unseen eyes tracking their every move.

Travis, Ronan, and Shannah were waiting for them on the front porch when they reached Sara's house.

"We went by the store and you weren't there," Travis said, his voice tinged with anxiety. "Did something happen?"

Sara glanced at Overstreet. Now that they were safely home, her fears seemed foolish.

Travis's gaze searched hers. "Sara?"

"I..." She shrugged one shoulder. "I just had the feeling we were being watched and it freaked me out." She unlocked the door and stepped inside.

Travis followed her.

Ronan and Shannah remained on the porch.

Travis tugged on Sara's hand. "You need to invite them in."

Sara stared at him, eyes wide. Inviting the master vampire into her house was the last thing she wanted.

"We can't talk out here," Travis said. "You can rescind the invitation when they leave if it will make you feel better."

Sara glanced over her shoulder. Ronan looked like the angel of death itself. Shannah was lovely, with long black hair and expressive blue eyes. She looked very young, probably in her early 20s. With a sigh of resignation, she said, "Ronan, Shannah, please come in."

Sara stepped back. She felt a strange vibration in the air as the two vampires stepped across the threshold.

Leading the way into the living room, she invited her guests to sit down.

Shannah sat on the chair by the sofa. Ronan stood behind her, his hands resting lightly on her shoulders.

Overstreet dropped heavily into the other chair. Sara and Travis sat side-by-side on the couch.

"You were right to come home," Ronan said.

"So we were being watched." Overstreet said. It wasn't a question.

"Yes. There were a number of vampires lurking in the shadows." Ronan looked pointedly at Sara. "We're very good at that," he added, a note of menace in his tone.

Shannah covered one of his hands with hers. "Ronan, stop it. She's already afraid of you. Don't make it any worse." Looking at Sara, she said, "You'll have to forgive my husband. His social skills are non-existent."

"I can see that." Sara smiled at Shannah, thinking that, in other circumstances, they might have been friends.

"We aren't here to discuss my social skills or lack of them," Ronan growled. "Travis and I are going out to have a look around. If it's all right with you, Miss Winters, Shannah will stay here."

Sara nodded.

"All right then." Leaning forward, he kissed his wife's cheek, then headed for the door.

Squeezing Sara hand, Travis said, "We won't be gone long."

Overstreet glanced at Travis. "Do you want me to come along?"

"Do you want to?"

Overstreet shook his head. "Not really."

Throwing the journalist a grin, Travis followed his sire into the night.

"So, what's your plan?" Travis asked as they lingered in the shadows outside Jason Bowman's house. A single light burned in an upstairs bedroom, but all was quiet.

"I haven't decided whether to just destroy the nest or see if I can talk some sense into their leader."

"You'd kill them? All of them?"

"There are unwritten rules for vampires. The first is tell no one. The second is that you don't leave bodies drained of blood where they can be found. It always alarms mortals, who start seeing vampires everywhere. Sure, there are hunters who know of our existence," he went on. "And a few people who believe. But if humans start disappearing in large numbers, or bodies drained of blood start turning up, then it becomes a problem for all of us."

Travis nodded. Ronan wasn't telling him anything he didn't already know.

"What this coven is doing isn't a secret anymore," Ronan continued. "Not since Joey Cannon escaped. No telling how many people have heard his story by now. Most will ignore it as some drunken fantasy, but a few will pay attention. And then there's Overstreet. He knows vampires exist. He'll either write Cannon's story, or he'll do a full-blown series on this town, the way he did about vampires in general last year."

"Are you going to kill him, too?"

"I'm not sure. It might be too late for that."

"You really are a cold-hearted son-of-a—" His head snapped back when Ronan slapped him hard, twice.

"Call me whatever you want, but don't bad-mouth my mother."

Stunned by the blow he hadn't seen coming, Travis licked the blood from his lip, then muttered, "I'm sorry."

"Don't do it again."

"Don't worry, I… the door's opening. What do we do now?"

"We're going to grab whoever comes out and see what they have to say."

Sara tapped her fingers on the arm of the couch as she searched for something to say, but nothing came to mind.

She glanced at Overstreet. His eyes were closed. Whether he was asleep or just pretending, she had no idea. Either way, no help was coming from that direction. Feeling ill at ease, Sara smiled at Shannah.

"You don't have to be afraid of me," the vampire said. "Or worry about entertaining me. I'm just here to keep you safe."

Sara worried her lower lip between her teeth, then blurted, "Have you been a vampire a long time?"

"No, it's a rather recent event."

"Was it something you wanted?"

"I thought I did. I went looking for a vampire and I found Ronan."

"Why on earth were you looking for a vampire?" Sara shook her head, unable to believe anyone would purposely do such a thing.

"I was dying and desperate. I sought him out hoping he'd change me. Instead, he gave me some of his blood and it strengthened me and prolonged my life for awhile. I lived with him in his house for quite some time. I even pretended to be him at book signings and interviews. But then, when I was on the verge of death, he turned me against my will. I know it's hard to believe, since that's why I went to him in the first place. But after spending time with him, I knew that as much as I loved him, I didn't want that kind of life." She blew out a sigh. "For a while, I hated him for it."

"And now?"

"When I realized what he'd done, I told him I would him never forgive him. Do you know what he said?" Shannah laughed softly at the memory. "He said, 'Then may it be a long and healthy hatred'." I felt so lost and confused, I ran away but I couldn't hide from him. I couldn't shut his thoughts out of my mind. He begged me to come home. At first, I refused, but he was so patient with me, so kind and understanding. Willing to let me make the choice. In the end, I couldn't deny the love between us."

"So you forgave him?"

A faint smile curved her lips. "Love is stronger than hate. He turned me because he felt he couldn't live without me. And now I know I wouldn't want to live without him. So, you see, everything worked out for the best."

"Everything? It doesn't bother you that you can't eat or have children, or go out in the sunlight, or do any of the other mundane things ordinary people take for granted?"

"Of course there are things I miss. But Ronan means more to me than anything else in the world."

Sara nodded pensively. She was falling in love with Travis, a little more every day. But would she ever love him enough to sacrifice everything to stay with him?

It was a troubling question. One for which she had no answer.

"You distract him," Ronan said as Bowman strolled down the street, "and I'll take him down."

Distract him? Travis thought. How the hell do I do that? Stepping out of the shadows, he called, "Hey, Bowman! Are you looking for me?"

Jason stopped on the sidewalk. "As a matter of fact..." The breath whooshed out of his body as Ronan tackled him from behind. They both hit the cement, with Ronan on top, the fingers of one hand biting deep into the other vampire's neck.

"If you try to get away, your wife and children will pay the price," Ronan warned.

Jason froze as all the fight went out of him. "What do you want?"

"Answers," Ronan said. "I'm sure you already know the questions."

"I can't tell you anything."

Ronan dug his fingers a little deeper into the man's neck, drawing blood. "No?"

"He'll destroy me."

"I'll kill your family."

Without knowing how he did it, Travis connected with Ronan's mind. *You wouldn't? Damn you, tell me you wouldn't kill an innocent woman and her kids.*

Ronan glanced over his shoulder to meet Travis' gaze. *Keep your thoughts to yourself!*

"What do you want from me?" Jason asked, his voice hard and flat.

"How many people have you got locked up in this place?"

"Go to hell."

"Travis, go get his wife."

"She doesn't know anything!" Jason said, his voice raw with worry.

"But you do."

Travis took a step closer to his sire. "Ronan, we've got trouble."

"You think I don't know they're there?"

Travis watched as a handful of vampires emerged from the darkness to stand in a loose circle around them. Their eyes gleamed a hideous red in the moonlight.

Ronan looked at each one in turn before he said, "Go home unless you want to watch me rip out his heart."

"You can't fight us all," said the only female in the bunch.

"You think not?" Ronan didn't move, but a wave of preternatural power rolled through the air like an invisible scythe.

Travis moved closer to his sire as, one by one, the vampires surrounding them were driven to their knees. And held there.

"I want to know what's going on in this town," Ronan said. "And I want to know now."

"I'm in charge here," Jason said, grimacing with pain. "But I answer to someone else."

"His name. I want it."

"Jarick."

"He's still alive?" Ronan grunted. "I'm surprised no one's destroyed him yet."

"I don't think anyone can," Jason muttered. "Can I get up now?"

"Are you keeping any people here, now, against their will?"

"A few."

"What are you supposed to do with them?"

"A truck will be by in a few hours to pick them up."

"Where are they?"

"In the cellar beneath the police department."

"As of right now, you're out of business," Ronan said. "What you're doing is dangerous. Sooner or later, a hunter will get word of this and Susandale will be covered in blood. Vampire blood. You understand me?"

"What do I tell Jarick?"

"Tell him to come and find me if he's got a problem," Ronan said, "and I'll explain it to him." Releasing his hold on the other vampire, he stood.

Jason scrambled to his feet, one hand at his throat. "Can we go now?"

With a nod, Ronan released the other vampires from his thrall.

They eyed him warily as they stood and gathered around Bowman.

Travis wondered how long it would take for Jarick to get word of what had happened here and come to town.

And what would happen when the two master vampires confronted each other.

"Nothing good," he muttered, as he followed Ronan down the dark street to the police department. "That's for damn sure."

Chapter 19

There were no lights showing inside the police department and no one on duty. Travis didn't recall ever seeing anyone patrolling the town. They found a narrow set of stairs in the back of a broom closet. The door, made of heavy steel, was locked but it was no match for Ronan, who simply kicked it in.

Travis followed him down the stairs to another door. This one was warded against human intrusion, but not against vampires.

Ronan broke the lock and pushed it open, revealing a rectangular room lit by a couple of wax candles. The air smelled of old sweat and fear. A noxious odor emanated from a bucket in the far corner. Two dozen sleeping bags lined the floor. Nine of them were occupied. Three men. Four women. And two children, who huddled against one of the women. They all cringed when they saw Ronan and Travis standing in the doorway.

Ronan glanced around the basement, his expression filled with disgust, then jerked his thumb toward the door. "Let's go."

They didn't argue. One by one, they rose and shuffled toward the door and climbed the stairs, like sheep on their way to the slaughterhouse.

Travis looked at Ronan. "What are you going to do with them?' he asked, his voice pitched low.

"I'm going to take them home and then wipe the memory of everything that happened from their minds."

"What do you want me to do?"

"Stay here. I can't take them all at once."

Travis nodded as Ronan put his arms around the woman and her children. There was a ripple in the air as the vampire transported them out of the office.

An audible gasp rose from the throats of the remaining people. They stared at Travis, their fear a palpable thing. "Relax," he said quietly. "You're safe now."

As one, they all looked at him, hope in their eyes.

"Trust me," he said. "No one's going to hurt you."

Ronan made three more trips.

"Come on," he said when all the prisoners had been taken home. "Let's get out of here."

Sara couldn't help flinching when Travis and Ronan suddenly appeared in the living room. Overstreet snored softly in his chair.

Shannah smiled at her husband. "How did it go?"

"We found out who's behind the kidnappings."

"Anyone you know?" she asked. Ronan had been a vampire for over five hundred years. He had undoubtedly crossed paths with any number of other vampires.

"His name's Jarick. I've never met him, but I've heard of him. He's known to be totally ruthless."

"Do you think he'll come here?" Sara asked.

"Sooner or later," Ronan said. "Once he realizes exports from Susandale have dried up, I imagine he'll come around."

"Dried up?" Shannah asked. "What do you mean?"

"I told the guy in charge at this end that he was out of business as of tonight."

"And you think he'll listen?"

"If he's smart." Reaching for Shannah's hand, Ronan pulled her to her feet. "Let's go, darlin'." He nodded to Travis and Sara. "We'll be in touch."

Sara blinked as both vampires simply disappeared.

"What did the two of you do tonight?"

"I didn't do much. Ronan persuaded Bowman to tell him where the prisoners were being kept. We went there and Ronan took them all home."

"Bowman!" Sara thought of Olivia and her children. "How did Ronan get them home?"

"He asked the people where they lived, transported them there, and wiped the memory of everything that happened here from their minds."

"That's... unbelievable."

"I know. But he did it. Are you all right?" Travis asked, taking the seat beside her.

"I guess so." She glanced at Overstreet as Travis slid his arm around her.

"Don't worry about him," Travis said. "I think he's out for the night."

With a sigh, Sara snuggled against him. "Do you think things will be better now? Or worse?"

"No way to tell." His gaze met hers, and then he kissed her lightly. A kiss that quickly grew deeper, longer, and more intimate.

Sara melted into him. It was hard to think about anything else when she was with Travis, when he was holding her, kissing her... unbidden came her earlier conversation with Shannah.

"What's wrong?" Travis asked, feeling a subtle change in her.

"You'd never turn me against my will, would you?"

"What?" He drew back so he could see her face. "What are you talking about?"

"Shannah said when she got really sick, Ronan turned her even though she'd told him she didn't want to be a vampire."

"Believe me, Sara, I'd never do that to you. I give you my word."

With a sigh, she pulled his arms around her again, her eyelids fluttering down as his lips reclaimed hers. She didn't know what the future held, but she was young and in love and anything was possible.

Sara woke smiling. She and Travis had kissed and cuddled until the sun came up.

Throwing back the covers as the scent of fresh coffee tickled her nose, she padded into the kitchen where she found Overstreet fixing French toast and bacon.

"'Bout time you woke up," he said, turning the bacon. "Late night?"

"You could say that."

"Did I miss something between then and now?"

"What do you mean?"

He twitched one shoulder. "It's just that things were looking a little grim last night and this morning you're practically bubbling over with happiness." He filled two plates and set them on the table, then poured two cups of coffee.

"I can't help it," she said, settling into one of the chairs.

He arched one brow as he sat across from her. "Sounds like love to me."

"Have you ever been in love?"

He grunted. "Who would ever give their heart to an old reprobate like me?"

"I believe there's someone for everyone."

"And you think your someone is a vampire?"

Sara stared at him, the joy she had felt earlier snuffed out by that one single word. *Vampire.*

"I'm sorry," Overstreet said. "What you do with your life is none of my business. But I've seen vampires up close and personal and believe me, they're not like us."

Sara nodded. "I know." Pushing her plate away, she left the table.

Overstreet huffed a sigh and wished he had never listened to Joey Cannon.

Sara showered and dressed, her heart heavy. Not wanting to sit home and think sad thoughts, she decided to open the shop.

"Not without me," Carl said, grabbing his coat and his notebook.

"I'm sure I'll be fine," she said. "It won't be dark for hours."

"Doesn't matter. I'm not leaving you alone."

"Let's walk. It's a beautiful day."

With a nod, he followed her out the door and down the narrow path to the sidewalk.

Sara frowned. "Do you feel it?" she asked as they made their way down the street.

"Feel what?"

"I'm not sure." She glanced around. Everything looked the same and yet…something was different. It took her a minute to realize what it was. The sense of oppression that had hung in the air was missing. Funny, she had never noticed it until it was gone. For the first time since moving to Susandale, there were people on the street. Neighbors were outside, talking to each other. Luke and Debbie were playing catch. Deanne was watering her yard.

When they turned onto the street where her shop was located, Sara came to an abrupt halt. Several women were gathered in front of the store, looking in the windows and chatting with each other.

They smiled at her when she unlocked the door. Actually smiled.

Overstreet and Sara exchanged glances, then he went to sit in his usual place in the corner while Sara waited on her customers, none of which she had ever seen before.

It was during a mid-afternoon lull when Deanne came into the shop. "Hello, Sara," she said, as friendly as can be. "Do you have any lilac bath salts?"

"Yes. It's right over there."

With a cheery wave of acknowledgement, Deanne went to look at the display.

Sara watched as she picked up a bottle of bath salts and three cakes of lilac-scented soap.

"What's happened?" Sara asked as Deanne placed her selection on the counter. "Something's changed." The woman looked different, relaxed, as if she didn't have a care in the world.

"The vampires have all left town," Deanne said. "We're free."

"Left? Why? Where did they go?"

"I don't know. And I don't care."

"But you didn't go with them."

"The only woman who went with them was Sadie Wentworth. I thought Olivia would go, too, but..." Deanne made a vague gesture with her hand. "She decided to stay, probably because of her kids."

"I don't understand."

"Olivia and Sarah were the only two women, besides myself, who were here by choice. The rest of them were here because the vampires compelled them to stay. This was a nice town before Jason Bowman and the others came. I'm hoping it will be again."

"So, you lived here before the vampires came?"

"Yes. With my husband. Raoul was a vampire, but he never approved of what Jason and the others were doing. We talked about leaving, but..." She shrugged. "We kept putting it off and then, eight months later, he was killed by a hunter."

"Why didn't you leave then?"

"I had nowhere else to go, no family. And by that time, the other women were my friends. We relied on each other."

Sara nodded. Maybe she wouldn't leave town, after all. "Will this be all?"

"Yes, thanks."

Sara rang up the woman's purchases and bid her good day, wondering, as she watched Deanne leave the store, where she got the money to pay for the things she'd bought.

The rest of the day passed quickly and since business had been so good, Sara closed at six. Overstreet decided that he'd imposed on Sara's hospitality long enough and since the vampires were gone, he decided to go back to his room in the hospital.

At home, Sara slipped into a pair of sweat pants and a tee shirt, tied her hair back in a ponytail, then headed for the kitchen to start dinner.

She decided on spaghetti, and while the water boiled, she opened all the windows, something she hadn't done since she discovered there were vampires in the town.

Conscious of the coming night, she wondered if Travis was awake and if he knew the vampires had left. She smiled, thinking that Ronan and Shannah would be able to go home. She would be relieved to see the last of Travis' sire. Being in the same room with him had scared her half to death.

Dinner was over and the dishes done when Travis knocked at her door.

She met him with an enthusiastic, "Hi!"

"Judging by that smile on your face, I'm guessing you heard the vampires have all left town," he said.

She nodded as she tugged him toward the sofa. "Isn't it wonderful? Did you know that most of the women were kept here against their will? I'll bet that's why I rarely saw them. They were probably afraid they'd let something slip."

"I think you're right." He dropped down on the sofa beside her, his hand curling around hers.

He was different, too, Sara thought. More relaxed than he had been in days. She hadn't realized until now that he'd been on edge, too. When his gaze met hers, it seemed like the most natural thing in the world to go into his arms. To raise her head so he could brush her lips with his. So she could wrap her arms around his neck and climb onto his lap and kiss him in return.

She shivered with pleasure as his hand slid up and down her back, then dropped to stroke her thigh.

"Sara." He groaned low in his throat as his rising desire aroused his hunger.

She pulled back a little, her gaze searching his. "Travis? What's wrong?"

"I'm all right."

"You don't sound all right." She frowned, then murmured, "Oh."

"Yeah." He threaded his fingers through her hair. "I should have... ah..." He cleared his throat. "You know, before I came to see you, but I wanted to make sure you'd heard the good news."

"Maybe you should go now and... you know."

He kissed the tip of her nose, then set her on the sofa. "Okay if I come back after?"

Sara nodded. "Hurry."

Like Sara, Travis had noticed the change in the town as soon as he roused from the dark sleep. The aura of danger and oppression and fear was gone.

Not wanting to feed on any of the women in town, he went to the neighboring city. He was strolling along a side street, searching for prey, when he saw Ronan striding toward him. Startled, he came to an abrupt halt, his hands clenching as his sire paused beside him.

"Am I intruding on your hunting ground?" Ronan asked.

"And if you are?"

"Proper etiquette demands that I go elsewhere."

"Is that another rule you failed to teach me?"

Ronan shook his head. "Still waiting for an apology?"

"No. And you don't need my permission to hunt here. Or anywhere else. Bowman and the others left Susandale."

"I know. I can't help wondering why."

"I figured they were afraid of you. They sure as hell aren't afraid of me. Where's Shannah?"

"She went home. I told her I'd join her in a day or so." He jerked his head toward a pair of women coming toward them. "Shall we?"

"Father and son dining together for the first time," Travis said, his lips twitching in amusement. "I'll have to make a note in my diary."

Chapter 20

With the vampires gone, there was a dramatic change in the town. The women spent more time outside. Tourists stayed longer. Sara realized belatedly that visitors hadn't left early of their own free will. The vampires had kidnapped most of them. The very idea made her shudder as she imagined being imprisoned and then sold as prey to hungry vampires. It was worse than slavery, she thought bleakly, and wondered how long a vampire could drink from someone before they died. Or did they keep them like cattle? Thrusting the disquietly image away, she wondered what they had done with the cars, vans, and motor homes left behind.

With the change in the atmosphere, some of the tourists passing through decided to stay. There was no government in the town, so no one objected when Robert Clary, a retired Los Angeles police officer, decided to take on the duties of Sheriff. Or when Leonard Amata, a retired general practitioner, hung up his shingle at the hospital. Without the vampires to heal the women when they got hurt or sick, a doctor was just what Susandale needed to look after the town's inhabitants.

Winona smiled more. She hired a cook who went by the name of Oscar. She also hired his daughter, Mercy, as a waitress.

Within a month, Susandale had turned into a bustling little town.

Four of the women decided to leave town. They sold their homes to a realtor in the neighboring city and moved away. Weeks later, three families with children ranging in age from a few weeks to seventeen moved in. One of the women, Mary Robbins, mother to twin six-year-old girls, was a teacher, who found a vacant building and turned it into a school.

Sara was amazed at the changes. Susandale was like a different place. She knew now that it had been the vampire's influence that had hung over the town like a dark cloud. People who had sensed it had hurried through without stopping. Those unaware had been captured and sold by the vampires.

"Isn't it amazing?" Sara remarked one night while sitting on the front porch swing with Travis. "So many changes in such a short time."

He nodded, thinking how glad he was that he'd come to this town. Since meeting Sara, his life, while still not normal, was a hundred percent better than it had been before. Most amazing of all, since meeting Sara, his nightmares had stopped. Ronan had left town the day after Shannah went home, which was also a bonus as far as Travis was concerned.

They sat in silence for a time and then, needing to touch her, he slipped his arm around Sara's waist. She sighed and snuggled against him as if it was the most natural thing in the world. He didn't know what it was, but there was something about being near her that filled him a sense of peace.

Putting a finger under her chin, he tilted her face up, his gaze meeting hers before he kissed her. Sara clutched at his shirt front when his tongue dipped inside to duel with hers. It lit a fire deep inside her that she felt clear down to her toes.

"Maybe you two should get a room."

Sara's eyes flew open at the sound of Overstreet's voice.

Travis grimaced as the journalist climbed the stairs. "What's up?"

"Nothing. I got bored and decided to take a walk." He groaned softly as he eased his bulk down onto the top step.

"Can I get you something, Carl?" Sara asked. "Soda? A cup of coffee?"

"I don't want to intrude."

"A little late for that, don't you think?" Travis remarked irritably.

Sara sent Travis a quelling glance. "Carl?"

"Coffee would be great if it's not too much trouble."

"No trouble at all," Sara said. "It'll just take a minute."

Travis glared at Overstreet after Sara went inside. "What are you doing here?"

"I told you. I was bored. I can't write *all* the time. I needed a break."

"What are you working on? Your story left town with the vampires."

"Yeah." He huffed a sigh. "Do you think they're gone for good?"

Travis shrugged. "Who knows? I can't think of any reason for them to come back."

"Unless they're holed up somewhere nearby, just waiting for Ronan to move on."

"He already did."

"Oh? I didn't know that. I guess there's nothing to stop Bowman and the others from coming back and taking up where they left off then. Except you."

"Me?" Travis snorted. "I've been a vampire less than a year. I'm no match for any of them."

Overstreet rubbed his hand over his jaw. "I don't know. You were turned by a master vampire. You're probably a lot more powerful than you think."

"Who's more powerful?" Sara asked, stepping out onto the porch.

"Nobody," Travis said.

She handed Carl a mug of hot coffee. "Two sugars, no cream, right?"

"Right, thanks."

Sara resumed her place on the swing beside Travis. "Why are you both looking so glum? Is something going on?"

"No." Travis sent a warning glance at Overstreet. "Everything's fine."

"Really? Why don't I believe you?"

Travis blew out a sigh. "Big mouth here was wondering if I thought the vampires would come back to town now that Ronan's gone."

Sara's eyes widened. "Do you think that's possible?"

Overstreet shrugged. "Anything's possible."

"Where are you staying, now that there's a doctor at the hospital?" Travis asked.

"I took a room over at the hotel. It's not a bad place. It's cheap. And they even have Wi-Fi."

"Are you planning to stay for a while?" Sara asked.

"I haven't decided. Not much point in it. Still, I might hang around for a few weeks. Nowhere else to go, nothing waiting for me when I get there." Carl set his cup aside and slapped his hands on his knees. "Well, I'm off to bed. Sorry for the interruption, you two. Thanks for the coffee, Sara."

"You're welcome."

⚜ ⚜ ⚜

Overstreet shambled down the stairs. He paused at the sidewalk and lifted his hand in a gesture of farewell and continued on down the street.

"He's a lonely guy, isn't he?" Sara remarked.

"Yeah."

"Has he ever been married?"

"Beats me. The subject never came up."

She leaned into him again, one hand on his thigh, content to sit and stare out into the night. Inevitably, her thoughts turned to Travis. And vampires. Sitting beside her, he seemed so normal, as if he was any other guy calling on a girl. But he wasn't like other men. Was she making a mistake, spending so much time with him? It would be so easy to fall head-over-heels in love with him. He was soft-spoken, easy to get along with. Hard to believe he was a vampire. Or that he had once hunted and destroyed them. Did he ever regret that, now that he, himself, was a vampire? Did he feel like a monster?

"You're awfully quiet," Travis remarked. "Are you worrying about Bowman and the others coming back to town?"

"No. Well, yes, but that's not what I was thinking about."

"Want to share your thoughts with me?"

"I don't know. I'm afraid they might make you uncomfortable. Or angry."

"I could never be angry with you."

"I was wondering...I mean, you're a vampire now, but you used to be a hunter. Do you ever regret what you did?"

He took a deep breath, exhaled it in a long, slow sigh. "I try not to think about it too much. I viewed them as less than human. Not fit to live." He shook his head. "I don't know. Maybe now I'm the monster. I mean, I feel different but still the same. Does that make any sense at all?"

"In a way."

"What if they were all just regular guys before they were turned? I never bothered to find out if they'd been turned against their will, or if they wanted the change so they could murder indiscriminately. When I hunted them, all I saw were vampires and I destroyed them without a second thought." He raked his fingers through his hair. "I haven't killed anyone since I was turned. But what if a few years down the road I lose my sense of humanity? What if I start to see people as nothing more than a ready food supply?" He stared into the night and felt the darkness wrap around him as his hunger stirred to life. What if he started to think of Sara as prey? The possibility was like a stake in his gut.

"Travis?"

"You shouldn't be with me," he said, his voice thick with pain. "It isn't safe."

She looked at him, her eyes filled with concern. "I don't believe that."

He groaned low in his throat. "You don't know what it's like to be near you. Hear the beat of your heart, smell the blood flowing through your veins. It's a constant temptation." He surged to his feet. "What if someday I can't control it?" he asked, his back toward her. "What if…?" He swore under his breath when she came up behind him, her arms sliding around his waist. Was she out of her mind? Hadn't she been listening to him?

And yet, her nearness calmed him even as it aroused another desire. Turning in her embrace, he wrapped his arms around her and covered her mouth with his. Holding her, kissing her, left him thinking of nothing but the sweet taste of her lips, the way she leaned into him, her breasts crushed against his chest, the scent of her hair, her skin.

With regret, he let her go and took a step back. "Sara, you'd better go inside before I take you on the porch, right here, right now."

She smiled up at him, her lips bruised from the force of his kisses. "I'll see you tomorrow night, won't I?"

"Try to keep me away."

"Never." She cupped his face in her hands and kissed him ever so gently. Then, with a murmured "Good night," she went inside and closed the door.

Travis waited on the porch until he heard the turn of the lock before he returned to his lair. He spent the rest of the night practicing his vampire powers, doing them over and over again until turning to mist or willing himself from one place to another became second nature.

Most exciting of all was shape-shifting. The first time he succeeded in transforming into a wolf, he let out a victory howl that likely sent chills down the spines of everyone in Susandale still awake to hear it.

Chapter 21

Jason Bowman looked up from the woman he was feeding on, felt an icy ripple of fear when he found himself staring into Jarick's cold gray eyes. Before he could release the woman from his thrall, the master vampire pulled her from Bowman's grasp and sank his fangs deep into her throat. He drank until the woman was pale and on the verge of death, then broke her neck and tossed the body aside.

His steely gaze never left Bowman's. "Let's go. We need to talk."

Feeling like a convict on his way to the gallows, Jason followed the master vampire into the shadows.

CHAPTER 22

Now that the vampires were gone and the women were able to come and go as they pleased, Sara decided to return to her original hours at the shop.

With the coming of summer, tourists arrived more often. The hotel hired three of the local women to work as maids. The Sheriff hired a couple of deputies so that someone was available at the station around the clock.

Business picked up in all the stores. An enterprising young couple from out of town opened a small department store that sold clothing, as well as some household items like towels and dishes, and a small assortment of toys.

The only bad thing about summer was that the days were longer, which meant she didn't get to see Travis until later at night.

Thinking about him, she sighed as she closed the shop on Friday night. She could no longer deny she was in love with him. They had spent every evening together for the last month or so. During the week, they usually stayed in, often watching a movie, sometimes playing gin rummy, sometimes just listening to music while they cuddled together on the sofa.

Weekends they usually went out dancing or to a movie in Langston, or just went for a leisurely stroll through the town.

Sara paused outside the store and then, on the spur of the moment, decided to eat out. She had a date with Travis later, but she had two hours to kill until the sun went down.

She smiled and waved to several people as she walked down the street toward the café. Stepping inside, she came to an abrupt halt when she saw Carl Overstreet sitting in a booth with his arm around Winona.

She was debating whether to go over and say hello when Overstreet caught her eye and waved at her.

"Hey, Sara," he said cheerfully. "I haven't seen you for a while. You know Winona, of course."

"Yes. Hi."

Winona smiled at her. "Hello, Sara. It's nice to see you." She leaned over to plant a kiss on Carl's cheek. "I need to get back to work. Sara, what can I get you?"

"Shrimp sounds good."

With a nod and a wave, Winona went to turn in her order.

"Well," Sara said, sliding into the booth, "how long has this been going on?"

"A couple of weeks," he said, his cheeks flushing.

"I guess that's why I haven't seen much of you."

He shrugged. "I've been eating in here a lot and just sort of hanging around when she's not busy. She's really nice once you get past that gruff exterior. And best of all, she actually seems to like me."

"Well, I'm happy for you," Sara said. "Both of you."

"It probably won't last. I mean, she's young and pretty and... well, look at me."

"I think you're being too hard on yourself. I mean, if she didn't like you, too, she wouldn't be looking at you now, just hoping to catch your attention."

He glanced at Winona, his cheeks growing redder when she winked at him.

"See?"

"Yeah. Guess I'll stick around awhile." He shook his head. "Life's funny, isn't it?

You just never know what the future holds."

Sara thought about what Carl had said as she drove home from the cafe. She certainly never would have thought she would be in love with a vampire, that was for sure. As for the future? She couldn't begin to guess where their relationship might lead, or how long it would last.

But she loved being with Travis.

She loved Travis.

But was there any future in pursuing a relationship that, realistically, couldn't lead anywhere? Was it possible to be happy with someone so different? Someone who lived an entirely different kind of life?

Did she want to spend all of her days alone? What if they moved in together? Or got married? She would have to spend the rest of her life lying to people about why they never saw him during the day, why he didn't eat. And what about children? Could vampires even have children?

And how would she feel when she started to age and he didn't? She might be able to find excuses for everything else, but not that. The fact that he didn't age also meant they probably wouldn't be able to stay in one place too long.

By the time she pulled into the driveway, she had the mother of all headaches.

❧ ❧ ❧

Travis arrived at Sara's house soon after the sun went down. He knew something was bothering her the minute she opened the door. He didn't have to be a mind reader to know what it was. He was only surprised it had taken her so long to think of all the reasons why dating a vampire was a bad idea.

"Are we still going out?" he asked, noting her forced smile.

"Of course. Just let me grab my purse."

Stepping inside, he closed the door. "What's wrong, Sara?"

"Nothing. Are you ready? The show starts in a few minutes."

"I know something's bothering you, so you might as well tell me what it is."

She looked up at him, her expression troubled. "I..." She stared past him, her fingers holding her handbag so tightly her knuckles were white.

"Did something happen? Are you afraid to go out with me?"

"No! No. It's nothing like that. I saw Carl tonight. He's dating Winona. You know, the woman who owns the café? And I got to thinking about them. And about us. And..."

"And you started having second thoughts about dating a vampire."

Still not meeting his gaze, she nodded.

"It's all right, Sara. If you don't want to see me anymore, I'll understand."

"No! Oh, Travis, I love you!"

"Sara! I love you, too." He started to reach for her, then hesitated. She didn't sound very happy about it.

Eyes glistening with unshed tears, she gazed up at him.

"Sara?"

Tossing her handbag on the sofa, she went into his arms.

He held her close, his hand stroking up and down her back while her tears wet his shirtfront. When her tears subsided, he guided her to the sofa and pulled her down on his lap. "I know this is hard for you," he said quietly. "I know we have a lot of obstacles other couples don't. I wouldn't blame you if you don't want to deal with them."

Sniffling, she looked up at him. "Do you think we could make it work?"

"Honestly? I don't know. This whole vampire thing is still new to me." He wiped her tears away with his fingertips. "I'm still trying to figure out who I am. What I am. I can't promise that I'll never hurt you, and that scares the hell out of me."

Sara nodded. She hadn't even thought of that possibility. He always seemed to be in control.

"Maybe we shouldn't see each other for a few days," he suggested, each word like a knife in his heart. "Maybe you should spend some time alone to think things over."

Frowning, she bit down on her lower lip. And then she nodded. "If you think that's a good idea."

"I want you to be sure," he said heavily. "If I don't hear from you in a couple of days..." He eased her off his lap. Hesitated a moment. And then he pulled her into his arms and kissed her, a long, slow kiss. "Good night, Sara."

Blinking furiously, she forced a weak smile, then gasped when he vanished from her sight, something he had never done before.

Feeling more miserable than she ever had in her life, she burst into tears, thinking that his kiss good night had felt more like goodbye.

⚜ ⚜ ⚜

Filled with self-loathing for what he was, Travis stalked the dark streets. He'd finally found a woman he loved, a woman he would happily have spent the rest of his life with. But how could he expect Sara—or any woman—to tie her life to his? He looked like a man, but that man had died. And no matter how hard he tried to pretend he was human, he wasn't.

"Feeling sorry for yourself?"

"What the hell?" Travis' head snapped up when Ronan materialized in front of him.

"Good thing I'm a friend and not a hunter."

"What the hell do you want? I thought you went home."

"I did. But one of the drawbacks of being your sire is that when I let my guard down, I'm aware of everything you're doing. Or thinking."

"Everything?" Damn. That was disconcerting to know.

Travis started walking again and his sire fell in step beside him.

"A lot of changes in town," Ronan remarked, glancing right and left.

Travis grunted. The place could burn down for all he cared.

They turned a corner and Travis found himself looking at the houses they passed. Most were inhabited by the women the vampires had left behind, but a few held families now. Lights burned in the windows. He heard the sound of a child's laughter in one of the houses and it reminded him that he would never have a child of his own.

"As long as I'm here, do you have any more questions for me about what you are, what you can and can't do?"

"Gee, Dad, are you getting soft in your old age?"

"I thought I told you not to call me that," Ronan growled.

"Did you ever marry or have kids before you were turned?"

A shadow of sadness flickered behind Ronan's eyes. "I had a wife. Verity. She died giving birth to my son. The boy died, too."

"I'm sorry."

"It was a very long time ago. I scarcely remember her."

"So you never married again?"

"Not until Shannah. Three years after Verity died, I chased the wrong woman and when she caught me, she turned me. She gave me the same choice I gave you. I refused at first but, like you, I let my fear of death make the decision for me." He laughed softly. "She said I'd thank her for it one day."

"Did you?"

"Not until I met Shannah. I would have endured anything to have her in my life." They walked in silence for a time before Ronan said, "Don't give up on Sara. Not yet. And..." Ronan huffed an irritated sigh. "If you ever need me, just call my name or think it and I'll hear you."

Before Travis could come up with a reply, his sire disappeared into the night.

Chapter 23

Olivia let out a startled gasp of surprise when Jason materialized in their bedroom late that night, and then threw herself into his arms.

He held her close for several minutes, inhaling her scent.

"I missed you so much," she whispered. "Where did you go? Has the whole coven returned?"

Sitting on the edge of the bed, he pulled her onto his lap, his arm circling her waist. "I'm the only one who's here. The rest are holed up in some ghost town in Wyoming."

"Are you home to stay?"

"I don't know. Jarick found me."

"Oh, no. What does he want?"

"He wants what he's always wanted. A ready supply of humans. He has a long list of vampires who are waiting for their orders to be filled." Jason swore softly. "He let so much time go by before contacting me, I was hoping he'd moved on."

"What are you going to do? The town is different now. Some of the women have moved out and a lot of new people have moved in."

"He doesn't care."

"What are you going to do?" she asked again, her gaze searching his.

When his gaze met hers, a cold chill ran down Olivia's spine. She didn't need to hear the words to know that Jarick had threatened to kill her and the kids if Jason failed to obey. "Have you told the others?"

"I'll tell them later." He ran his tongue along the side of her neck, then pulled her down on the bed, his eyes hot with desire and need. "I don't know what the future holds for us, love, but I had to see you before I go back, even if it's just for an hour or two."

Chapter 24

Expanding his preternatural senses, Ronan cursed softly as he drifted away from Jason Bowman's house. The vampire's scent was fresh, but he was no longer at home. Or in the town.

Leaving Susandale behind, he widened his search to the surrounding areas. Three miles out of town, he found what he was looking for. He chuckled wryly when he murmured the name of the place. *Aducator de Moarte.* Romanian for Death Bringer. Apropos, he mused as he entered the dilapidated building and followed his nose to the club in the basement.

It was exactly as he had expected. Dark walls. Dim lighting. Sensuous music emanating from speakers mounted in the ceiling. The scent of blood mixed with red wine.

A lot of people clad in black. As was he, he thought with a faint grin.

Couples clung to each other on the dance floor or huddled together in high-backed booths. Others sat at the long polished black bar that spanned the back wall. A woman who appeared to be in her late fifties sat on a padded stool at the end of the bar. Not a vampire, he thought, but definitely one of those mortals who was addicted to the blood of the Undead.

He was aware of her gaze sizing him up as he walked toward the bar.

"Welcome to *Aducator de Moarte.*" Her voice was dry, like brittle leaves.

Ronan nodded in acknowledgement.

"You're new here," she said.

"And you are?"

"Zara. This is my place."

"Do you greet every newcomer?"

Zara shook her head. "Just the very old ones."

He cocked one brow. "You can tell the difference?"

She let out a cackle of laughter. "You all have that same arrogant stride, the same haughty expression that practically dares anyone to defy you."

"I had no idea."

"The blood of the old ones is always sweet." She licked her lips as she slid him a sideways glance.

"Are you asking?"

Leaning forward, she murmured, "Are you offering?"

"A taste for a little information."

"What kind of information?" she asked, eyes narrowing suspiciously.

"The kind I can compel you to give me."

She sat back, her expression suddenly wary. "What do you want to know?"

"I'm looking for information about a vampire known as Jarick."

"Never heard of him."

"What about Jason Bowman?"

Lowering her voice, she said, "He used to be a frequent visitor, but I haven't seen him lately. I heard his coven is holed up somewhere in Wyoming. I'm guessing he's with them. There's a rumor they're planning a comeback."

"Is the source of that rumor reliable?"

Zara lifted one shoulder in a negligent shrug. "I've no way of knowing for sure. But something's up. I can feel it in my bones. Can I have that taste now?"

Travis had just returned from hunting when Ronan showed up at his lair. "I thought you'd left town."

"I thought so, too, but I took a little detour to *Aducator de Moarte* and had an interesting talk with the owner."

"Zara." Travis nodded as he opened the door. "She's a piece of work, that one." He frowned and then he grinned. "You fed her!"

"In exchange for some information."

"Yeah? Must have been something juicy."

Ronan glared at him. "Do you want to hear this or not?"

"You might as well come in." Turning on his heel, Travis headed for the front room. "So?"

"She told me Bowman and his coven are hiding out somewhere in Wyoming. Apparently, they plan to go back to their old ways."

"I'm not surprised."

"No?"

Travis shook his head. "I don't know about the rest of the coven, but if they'd left for good, Bowman would have taken his family with him."

"A love match, huh?"

"So it seems."

Ronan lifted his head. "It's almost dawn. If Bowman and his bunch are coming back to Susandale, you'd best keep an eye on Sara."

"Wouldn't it be best if we all just left town?"

"No doubt."

"But?"

"I intend to put an end to Jarick and shut down Bowman's operation."

"Why? What do you care about what goes on here?"

Ronan dragged a hand over his jaw. "That's a damn good question. I only know that sooner or later what they're doing will be noticed and when that happens, it's going to cause trouble for the rest of us. I know how dangerous mortals cam be when they're on the hunt. Especially a mob of them. I lived through something like that once. I don't intend to do it again."

"So, you've decided to stay here and take on Jarick and his whole coven?"

"There's only a dozen. Thirteen counting Jarick."

"Thirteen to one," Travis muttered. "Not very good odds, especially when one of them is a master vampire."

"I was hoping for a little help from you."

Travis stared at him. "Are you kidding?"

"Not in the least."

"I had no idea you were so altruistic."

Ronan snorted. "I don't give a damn about the people in this town. I'm only looking after my own skin. And Shannah's." A vile oath escaped his lips. "And yours, too, I guess. Hell, maybe blood *is* thicker than water."

Travis shook his head. His grandmother had always claimed there was good in everyone. Maybe she'd been right.

"So, can I count on you?"

"I guess so."

"Good. I didn't want to have to compel you," his sire remarked with a laconic grin.

And vanished from sight.

Chapter 25

Sara's eyes were swollen and red in the morning, a blatant sign of a long and sleepless night. She had no appetite for breakfast, no energy to get dressed or open the shop.

Still in her PJs, she dragged herself into the living room and plopped down on the sofa. How was she supposed to decide what to do about Travis when she couldn't think straight for missing him? She knew he was still in town, that all she had to do was pick up her phone and call him, and yet it felt like there was a wide chasm between them with only one chance to cross it. And no way back if she found the courage to make the leap.

If only she had someone to talk to. Someone who would listen without judging. Someone who would understand the implications of staying with Travis.

Late that afternoon, Olivia Bowman's name popped into her mind. Olivia was married to a vampire. Surely, she would understand Sara's doubts and fears.

Infused with hope, Sara took a long shower, dressed, and brushed her hair. Suddenly hungry, she fixed a ham and cheese sandwich for lunch, added some chips and a coke.

While eating, she began to have second thoughts about going to see Olivia. She hardly knew the woman.

It was an hour until sunset when, her mind made up, Sara left the house.

Olivia's eyes widened in surprise when she opened the door and found Sara Winters standing on the porch.

Sara smiled nervously. "Could I talk to you for a few minutes?"

"Well, sure, I guess so," Olivia said. "Come on in."

Sara followed Olivia inside. A quick glance around showed a house that was cluttered with toys but not dirty. From another room came the sound of Debbie and Luke arguing about which video game to play.

"Please, sit down." Olivia indicated a flowered sofa in front of a red-brick fireplace. "What can I do for you?" she asked, taking the easy chair beside it.

"I just needed someone to talk to."

Olivia nodded. It didn't take a genius to figure out something was bothering Sara. The bags under her swollen eyes were proof of that. "Go on."

"I'm in love with Travis."

Olivia nodded, thinking that explained the misery she read in her visitor's eyes.

"I don't know what to do. Are you ever sorry you married Jason?"

"No more so than if I'd married another man. We disagree about some things, just like any other couple. Sure, there are adjustments, but that's true of any marriage." Olivia leaned forward. "The thing you have to ask yourself is, do you love him enough to make the necessary sacrifices?"

"But... what are you going to do when you grow old and he doesn't?"

"I haven't decided a hundred percent, but when my kids are old enough to look after themselves, I'll probably ask him to turn me."

"Is that what you want?"

"Not really, but it's either that or leave him. I can't tie him to an old woman. It wouldn't be fair."

"Does he ever... drink from you?"

"Of course."

Sara blinked at her. How could she admit it so calmly, as if there was nothing the least bit unusual about it? As if it was just an everyday thing, like brushing your teeth or combing your hair.

"You're shocked."

Sara shook her head vigorously.

"I know you are. I was, too, the first time Jason suggested it. I'm surprised Travis hasn't asked you. It's not bad, you know? It's actually quite pleasant."

"You must miss him. Do you think you'll ever see him again?"

Olivia clenched her hands in her lap and fell silent.

And in that moment, Sara knew Jason had been there recently. Might even now be somewhere in the house. The thought sent an icy shiver down her spine. "I should go."

"Sara." Olivia laid a hand on her arm.

"I've got to go." Yanking her arm away, Sara lurched to her feet and ran out the door.

Sara had another shock when she got home and found Ronan waiting on the front porch. "What are you doing here?" she asked tremulously.

Hearing the fear in her voice, Ronan arched one brow. "Relax. I'm not going to hurt you." He drew in a deep breath. "Let's go inside."

She hesitated, then opened the door.

The vampire closed the door, then leaned back against it. You've been with Bowman's wife."

Sara stared at him.

"I can smell her on you," he explained. "And her husband. I was about to leave town when I caught Bowman's scent. What were you doing at his house?"

"It was personal and none of your business."

"Tell me."

Something in his voice compelled her to answer. "I wanted to talk to her about…about her relationship with her husband."

Ronan nodded. "Because of Travis."

"Yes."

"He's afraid of losing you," Ronan said. "But your love life isn't why I'm here. Did you see Bowman while you were there?"

"No."

"Did Olivia tell you if he's in town? Or what he's planning?"

"No." Sara tried to look away, but she couldn't draw her gaze away from his. She felt the quick brush of his mind invading hers. And then it was gone.

"I believe Bowman is coming back to town to take up his old occupation again. I think you should ask Travis to come and stay with you."

"No!"

"It's for your own safety."

Sara stared at him. "Why do you care what happens to me? You don't even know me."

"Because Travis cares. And if you tell anyone I said that, I'll deny it. Call him, Sara. If you're honest with yourself, it's what you want."

Before she could deny it, he vanished from her sight. Maybe she should call Travis, she thought as she collapsed on the sofa. The only way to know if she wanted to spend her life with her vampire was to spend time with him, get to know him better, and see if her feelings for him grew stronger.

Sara felt better in the morning. Why had she let her doubts get the best of her?

Olivia was right. Every relationship had problems of one kind or another. If Travis was just a guy and he worked nights, he would sleep days. True, Travis would also sleep on the weekends, but they would still have a lot of time together. She could easily adjust her hours to his.

Still, she was reluctant to call him. What if he'd decided he was better off without her? Only one way to find out, she thought, reaching for her phone. And then she blew out a sigh of exasperation. It was only nine a.m. It was hours until sunset.

Muttering, "Might as well go to work," she went upstairs to get dressed.

Travis woke with the setting sun. Feeling more alone than he'd ever felt in his life, he stared up at the ceiling, thinking that without Sara, he had no reason to get up. No reason to stay in Susandale. Hell, he had no reason to go on living.

Maybe he'd just go to earth for forty or fifty years. Maybe then he would forget her.

And then, remembering Ronan's warning the night before, he paused. He couldn't leave town just yet, not when Sara might be danger. He dressed in record time.

He was on his way to her house when his phone rang. Relief washed through him when he saw her name.

"Hi, Travis. It's me."

"Sara." He closed his eyes as the sound of her voice washed over him, as welcome as warm summer rain after a drought.

"Are you busy?"

"No. I was just out for a walk. How are you?"

"Fine."

Silence fell between them, so thick it was almost tangible.

"Sara?"

"I was wondering… I mean, if you're not busy tonight…"

"I'm not."

"Ronan told me Jason Bowman might be back in town and that I should call and ask if you'd…" Her voice trailed off.

"Sure," he said, his voice cool. "I'll come over and keep the bad guys away."

"Travis, I… that's not the only reason I called. It was just a good excuse."

"Is that right?" he asked skeptically.

"It's just that everything's happened so fast between us. I'm confused and… and I miss you."

"What time do you want me to come by?"

"You don't have to come if you'd rather not," she said, stung by his seeming lack of interest.

"I'll be there, Sara." And just like that, life was worth living again. He didn't care why she wanted to see him. It was enough that she did. "As it happens, I'm almost at your house now."

Moments later, he was knocking on her door.

Sara took a deep breath. Now that Travis was here, she was having doubts—doubts that fled her heart and mind the minute she saw him. "Hi," she said breathlessly.

"Hey." She was a vision in a pair of jeans and a lavender sweater that outlined every delectable curve. The scent of her perfume wafted through the air. The music of her heartbeat, the quiet whisper of her blood flowing warm and sweet in her veins, sang in his ears. She was tempting on so many levels.

Sara didn't know who moved first, but suddenly they were locked in each other's arms, clinging together as if their lives depended on it.

Without knowing how they got there, Sara found herself stretched out on the sofa beside him, her body pressed intimately to his while his hands moved restlessly up and down her back. He rained kisses on her brow, her eyelids, the tip of her nose, the curve of her throat.

She held him close, loving the feel of his body against hers, the way they seemed to fit together so perfectly. She inhaled his scent. He wasn't wearing cologne. She didn't detect any aftershave. And yet he had a unique scent that pleased her very much.

She sighed as his mouth covered hers, his tongue dueling with hers while his hands caressed her.

"I missed you, Sara," he whispered, his voice husky. "I know it's only been a couple of days, but it seemed like forever."

"I know, I know." She traced the outline of his mouth with her fingertips and then she kissed him deeply, desperately, as if she could never get enough, while a little voice in the back of her mind warned she was playing with fire.

Travis pulled her closer, groaning softly as his desire grew blatantly evident. "Sara."

She drew back, her gaze searching his, her cheeks growing hot when she realized he was even more aroused than she'd thought. Sitting up, she murmured, "I'm sorry."

"It's all right," he said, his voice thick with need.

"I... shouldn't have... I mean, I'm just not ready," she stammered. "It's too soon and... I..."

He blew out a deep breath, then pressed a finger to her lips. "It's okay, Sara. I understand." Indeed, he understood all too well. The time might never be right.

"You're not mad?"

"No. Just horny as hell."

She laughed softly, partly in relief, partly in amusement. "I want you, too."

He nodded, though that was little comfort at the moment.

She smoothed her hand over her hair, straightened her sweater. "Maybe now would be a good time to have a glass of wine."

"Why not?" He watched her leave the room, admiring the gentle sway of her hips. And knew that, come hell or high water, he would never leave her again unless she sent him away.

After Sara went to bed, Travis called Overstreet. When there was no answer, he warded the house against intruders the way Ronan had taught him, and then went in search of Overstreet. To his surprise, the writer's scent led him to the home of a vampire. The vampire wasn't inside and hadn't been for some time.

Travis stood in the shadows for a few minutes, listening to the low hum of conversation inside the house. Overstreet and a woman were making humorous comments about the movie they were watching. After a few minutes, it was evident they were watching the old black-and-white version of "Dracula."

An interesting choice, he mused, considering the town's former occupants.

He waited another couple of minutes, then knocked on the door.

A woman's voice called, "Who's there?"

"Travis Black. I'm a friend of Overstreet's."

He heard her ask Carl if that was true, followed by the sound of a deadbolt being drawn back.

A woman with dark red hair and deep brown eyes opened the door, her expression wary. She looked him over from head to foot before inviting him in.

"Travis, what are you doing here?" Carl asked, rising from the sofa.

"I came to ask a favor."

"Yeah?"

Travis glanced at the woman, then back at Overstreet. "Let's go outside."

Carl took the woman's hand in his. "If you're worried about talking in front of Winona, don't be. She's got no love for vampires."

"Are you sure about that? She used to live with one."

"I know, but it wasn't her choice."

Travis studied the woman. "Is that right?"

She nodded. "You're a vampire, aren't you?"

"Yeah."

"But not one of Jason's."

"That's right." Travis let his mind brush hers and then Overstreet's. Neither was hiding anything. One thing was certain, Carl and the woman were already intimately acquainted. Her scent was all over him. And his on her.

"So, what's this favor?" Overstreet asked.

"I want you to start looking after Sara during the day again."

Winona looked up at Carl. "She's the one who runs the shop that sells those fancy chocolates and stuff, isn't she?"

"Yeah." Carl smiled at her. "You've got nothing to be jealous of, Winnie," he said, then looked at Travis. "If Sara needs protecting, why did you leave her home alone?"

"I warded the house. She should be safe enough while she's asleep.

"Why does Sara need protecting?" Winona asked.

"Because Ronan told me Bowman is planning a comeback."

Overstreet swore under his breath. "What? When?"

"I don't know. I'm going to talk to Sara about getting out of town, but until then, I don't want her left alone."

"Getting out of town sounds like a good idea to me," Overstreet agreed. "What do you think, Winnie?"

"The house and the café are mine. I worked hard for them and I've got nowhere else to go."

"You can come and live with me in New York City," Carl said. "I've got a place there. I'll look after you."

"I'll leave you two to hash out your future," Travis said. "Tomorrow night, I'll see if I can convince Sara to leave town before it's... damn! It's already too late! They're here!"

Chapter 26

In fear for Sara's life, Travis willed himself to her house, only to find it in flames.

Sara! Opening his senses, he got as close as he dared. Relief washed through him when he realized she wasn't inside—only to be swept away when he caught the scent of vampire, a scent that was quickly obliterated by the scent of smoke and a sudden gust of wind.

She'd been taken.

The thought no sooner crossed his mind than one of the houses down the street burst into flame. And then another. And another.

He was trying to make sense of what was happening when his sire materialized beside him.

"We waited too long," Ronan said, his voice thick with anger. "Bowman's coven went through the town and took everyone who wasn't tied to one of the vampires. And they've burned most of the houses and all the businesses."

"How did the vampires gain entry to Sara's house?" Travis asked, frowning. "She certainly wouldn't have invited them in?"

"She didn't have to. From what I can piece together, the vampires mesmerized three of the town's newcomers and commanded them to go from house to house and incapacitate anyone who wasn't involved with the coven, then they dragged them outside and handed them over to the vampires, who transported them out of town."

"Sara." Her name was a groan on his lips. Dammit! He never should have left her alone.

"We'll find her."

"How?" Travis stared at the fires that were now burning out of control. It looked like a scene from Hell. He noted that Winona's house was still standing. Was Overstreet with her? Or had they taken him, too? "How?" he asked again.

"You've taken her blood. Open the link between you."

Travis muttered an oath. Of course! Why hadn't he thought of that? But when he tried to connect with her, nothing happened. He shook his head. "I can't find her."

"She's probably been drugged. The link won't work until she's conscious again."

Impotent rage burned hot and bright within Travis. What if she was dead? What if she was alive and he couldn't find her? Could never find her? Bowman and his coven sold humans to other vampires for a number of reasons, none of them good. It tore at his heart to imagine one of his kind keeping Sara as a food source, feeding on her indiscriminately until she was so weak, they cast her aside and left her to die. Or being sold into slavery in some foreign country.

"I'll find you," he whispered hoarsely. "I swear it!"

Chapter 27

In the morning, Winona stood on the sidewalk in front of her house, unable to believe what she was seeing. Susandale looked like a scene from a disaster movie. The smell of smoke hung in the air even though the fires had burned down to embers. A brisk wind stirred the ashes, sending them spinning into the air like tiny fireflies. The only houses left standing belonged to women who had married or lived with the vampires.

The coven had abducted all the people who didn't have ties to the coven, although she had no idea where they had taken them. All she knew was what Olivia had told her earlier. Jarick had told Bowman he had decided it was too dangerous to keep the prisoners in Susandale and they were relocating. Where that might be, Olivia had no idea. All she knew was that Jarick had found a new place and those who wanted to join them there would be notified of the location at a later date.

Winona shook her head. She didn't want anything else to do with vampires. She'd had enough. But they had taken the man she loved. And she wasn't leaving town until she had him back.

Late that afternoon, the women met in Winona's café. It was the only business still standing. Winona counted heads. Of the women who had once lived in town, only a handful had remained after the vampires left, like Olivia and Merle White, who were married to members of the coven. Winona stayed because she had nowhere else to go. She suspected Deanne had stayed for the same reason. She wasn't sure why Margie Lusk and Amy Rogers were still in town. Paulina Samuels and Caryn Moody were forced to remain due to a vampiric compulsion, a hold that could only be broken by the deaths of the vampires they were bound to.

"How do we know they're coming back?" Merle asked.

"And what if they don't?" Paulina asked. "Liam said he'd come back for me, but what if he doesn't? How can I live without him?"

Winona felt sorry for the girl. Paulina was young, no more than eighteen or nineteen. She was blood-bound to Liam, although she didn't know it. Sadly, the vampire's hold on her was so strong, she wouldn't have believed it even if someone told her the truth.

"I don't even know why we're meeting," Deanna said. "I don't know about the rest of you, but I've decided to leave town as soon as I get packed."

Margie and Amy nodded in agreement.

"The sooner the better," Margie said. "Living with vampires sure isn't as romantic as the movies make it out to be."

"I don't blame you for leaving," Olivia said. In a way, she was jealous of their freedom, but she couldn't leave Jason. She was bound to him by a love that was stronger and deeper than any compulsion a vampire could conjure.

"I'm staying, too," Winona said firmly. Because if Carl managed to get away, this was the only place he knew to look for her.

Sara woke to a darkness so thick she could almost taste it. When she tried to stand, a chain around her wrist prevented her from doing so. Fear spiked through her as she settled back down on the floor. She sensed others stirring nearby. Who were they? And where was she?

Afraid to call attention to herself, she remained silent, eyes and ears straining for some hint of where she was.

"Sara?"

"Carl! Is that you?"

"Yeah. Are you all right?"

"Hardly."

He laughed, a harsh dry sound devoid of humor.

"Where do you think we are?"

"Beats the hell out of me. But if I get out of here, it's gonna make a helluva story." He paused a moment. "Is anybody else here?"

"I think they rounded up everyone in the town."

Sara recognized the voice of Robert Clary, the man who had assumed the Sheriff's job.

"What are they going to do with us?" This from Dr. Amata.

As others asked questions, Sara realized Robert Clary was wrong. The vampires hadn't kidnapped everyone in town, only those who had no ties to the coven. It sent a chill down her spine. It didn't take much imagination to figure out that the futures of those being held in this place weren't exactly bright.

She knew she wasn't the only one who had come to that same conclusion when Mary Robbins whispered, "Oh, my poor babies!" and burst into tears.

Her husband tried to comfort her, but she continued to sob uncontrollably.

Everyone else fell silent.

Sara told herself to stay calm, not to panic, not to give into despair. As soon as the sun went down, Travis would find her. But what if the sun was already down? What if no one ever found any of them?

She tried to hold onto a positive attitude, to cling to a shred of hope, but sitting in the thick darkness while listening to a mother's heartbreaking sobs made trying to cling to hope like trying to capture a moonbeam.

It just couldn't be done.

Ronan, when are you coming home? I miss you.

Shannah's voice whispered in his mind, pulling him from the dark sleep. *I miss you, too, love. I intended to come home days ago but things have changed. Bowman's coven has made off with all the humans in town except for those who have ties to the vampires.*

He felt her horror as she realized what that meant. *Sara's gone?*

Yes. And Travis is frantic with worry.

Of course he is. Should I come there?

I'd rather you didn't. I've decided to go after Jarick.

The silence that followed spoke volumes.

I have to stop him. He's a rogue and sooner or later, he's going to do something that will make people sit up and take notice and once humanity starts to believe we exist, none of us will be safe.

Why do you *have to do it?*

Ronan blew out a breath. *Because,* he said, his voice tinged with resignation. *I'm the only one who can.*

On waking, Travis immediately opened his link to Sara, blew out a soul-deep sigh of relief when he felt her at the other end. So, now what? he thought. He had never done this before. Except with his sire.

Ronan. I need you. Now.

He had barely thought the words when the man was standing beside his bed. "What?"

"Good thing I don't sleep in the raw."

Ronan snorted.

"My link to Sara is active. What do I do now?"

"If you concentrate, you should be able to follow that link to wherever they're holding her."

Sitting up, Travis focused on the thin crimson link that connected him to Sara in some mysterious way he didn't understand. As he did so, the scent of her blood was borne to him, as easy to follow as the GPS on his cell phone.

Swinging his legs over the edge of the mattress, he reached for the jeans on the foot of the bed, then looked at his sire. "Are you coming with me?"

"Sure. Unless you think you can face down a master vampire on your own."

Sara kicked and scratched and clawed at the vampire who dragged her up the stairs and out of the basement, but it was like pitting a kitten against a Rottweiler, she thought hopelessly. She didn't have a chance.

Growing weary of her pathetic struggles, the vampire struck her across the jaw, rendering her unconscious. And then he transported the two of them to his new lair, leaving Bowman and the rest of the coven to dispose of the other mortals however they saw fit.

"She's not here!"

Ronan laid a restraining hand on Travis' arm when they reached the abandoned warehouse located in a seedy part of a city some two hundred and fifty miles away from Susandale. "Calm down. We'll find her. Right now we need to look after the people still in there."

Travis fought down his frustration and as he did so, he became aware that there were vampires in the building. The hot, fresh scent of blood told him they were feeding on the adults and their children as well. Children. The thought turned his stomach. "So, what are we gonna do?"

"You're going to help me get the people out of there after I dispose of the coven."

"What about Jarick?"

"He's gone. And I think he took Sara with him."

Travis felt his inside go cold at the thought of her at the mercy of the master vampire. "And Bowman?"

"He's not here, either. Let's go."

The iron door to the building was locked. Ronan tore it from its hinges with little effort, then they followed the terrified cries and screams rising from the basement.

Travis stared at the scene before him, horrified by what he saw. The vampires were so involved in what they were doing, none of them even noticed their presence. When he would have rushed forward, Ronan grabbed his arm. "Stay behind me."

Frowning, Travis stepped behind his sire. He swore softly as a rush of preternatural power filled the room, a force that apparently only affected the vampires, who all froze in place, their expressions stunned, their eyes red and wide with alarm as they stared at the master vampire. Travis swore under his breath. What was Ronan doing to them?

"Listen to me," Ronan said, his voice as cold and implacable as death itself. "I know who you are now. It'll be no trouble at all to hunt you down. And I will do so unless you put an end to this immediately. Leave the coven. Stop trafficking in human life. Stop killing."

"If we do what you say," one of them said through clenched teeth, "Jarick will destroy us."

"No," Ronan said flatly. "He won't."

Travis grunted softly as understanding dawned in the eyes of the other vampires. Talk about being caught between a rock and a hard place, he mused.

As Ronan withdrew his preternatural power, the vampires scrambled to their feet. They glared at him as they filed toward the steps. All but one who, with a wild cry of defiance, hurled himself at Ronan.

Travis watched in amazement as his sire stood his ground and then, at the last minute, reached out with one hand and ripped the other vampire's heart from his chest.

The rest of the coven quickly transported themselves elsewhere.

Every eye in the place stared at Ronan as they waited to see what would happen next.

A murmur ran through the room, along with whispers of "Did you see that?" and the sound of retching. Mary Robbins had covered her children's eyes.

Ronan tossed the heart aside. "You start on that side and I'll start over here."

One by one, Travis moved among the people, freeing them from their shackles, speaking to them quietly, smiling at those he recognized as he assured them they had nothing to fear. Returning to Ronan's side, he asked, "What now?"

Lowering his voice so only Travis could hear, he said, "I'm going to wipe their memories of everything that's happened here and then they're free to leave."

Travis nodded. Under other circumstances, he might have suggested taking them home, but these people were safe now while his Sara still needed help.

It was only after they left the building that Travis realized Overstreet hadn't been in the basement.

But his main concern was for Sara. Where could she be? The link between them had shut down again. What if it stayed that way until sunrise? Dammit, she could be dead by tomorrow and he'd never know what happened to her.

Carl Overstreet woke to find a woman staring at him through a pair of deep-set, impossibly red eyes. Certain he was dreaming, he blinked a couple of times and pinched himself, but the woman didn't go away.

Dread stirred in his gut. He had seen eyes like that before.

"About time you woke up," the vampire remarked, licking her lips. "It's no fun dining on someone who's not fighting back."

Dread turned to panic when she smiled at him, revealing a pair of shiny white fangs. Galvanized to action, Overstreet tried to get up, only to be pushed down again by one slender hand.

"Where do you think you're going, my plump little friend?"

"Home?"

Her laughter rang off the walls. "I don't think so. You're mine now. And I'm going to drink you dry."

"No!" Adrenaline shot through him. He had never hit a woman in his life, but this wasn't a woman. And vampire or not, a good right cross to the jaw knocked her backward off the bed long enough for him to grab the bottle of holy water in his pocket. He pulled the cork as she sprang to her feet and hurled the contents in her face.

She let out a scream only heard in nightmares, her hands clawing frantically at her eyes, howling like a banshee all the while.

It gave him just enough time to get the hell out of there.

Outside, he glanced left and right, but there was nothing to see. No houses. No street lights. Nothing to tell him where he was. But the thought of what he'd left behind added wings to his feet and he ran as if the hounds of hell were snapping at his heels.

Two miles later he was wishing he was twenty years younger and thirty pounds lighter, but he kept plodding on, spurred by the memory of those hellish red eyes.

Travis and Ronan parted ways half an hour before the first rays of the sun peered over the horizon. In his lair, Travis paced the floor, fearing, with every breath, that he would never see Sara again. She was in the hands of a master vampire. How long would he keep her alive? What if he turned her?

Or violated her? Of killed her?

Each possibility was worse than the last.

Deep in despair, he sank down on the bed, his head cradled in his hands. "Sara."

His head snapped up as the link between them quickened. She was alive! He clung to that hope as the dark sleep carried him away.

CHAPTER 28

Sara woke feeling as if she had the world's worst hangover. Trying to sit up made the room spin and she fell back on the bed and closed her eyes. Only to open them again as the memory of the night past burst into her mind in living color.

She was the prisoner of a vampire. He had fed on her last night. She didn't have a hangover from drinking too much. She was suffering from being used as a blood bank.

Glancing around, she couldn't believe what she saw. She had expected to find herself in some dingy basement or locked in a windowless room. Instead, she was lying on a king-sized bed in a large room with cream-colored walls and beige drapes.

She stood slowly, then made her way to the door. It was locked, of course. Still moving cautiously, she opened the drapes of the nearest window, hoping she could open it and climb out. No such luck. The window was barred.

She paused a moment to watch the sun climb over the horizon, wondering if it would be the last sunrise she would ever see.

Thrusting that disquieting thought aside, she did a slow turn in the center of the room. There was no phone, nothing she could use to pick the lock or break it. Nothing to use as a weapon.

Resignation set in after she checked the adjoining bathroom. It was a large, square room with a bathtub, a shower, and a double sink. It also held a small refrigerator. Curious, she opened it. Inside were several bottles of water, three cans of soda, and a couple of sandwiches wrapped in plastic.

Grunting softly, she closed the door. At least he wasn't going to starve her to death, she thought. Or kill her right away, since he had provided her with something to eat. But food could wait. There were no windows in the bathroom. Cupboards and drawers yielded nothing save a couple of washrags, a half-dozen towels, and an unwrapped bar of lavender soap.

She stared at it for several moments and then burst out laughing. Was that a subtle hint from her captor to wash her neck before he fed on her the next time? Or was he some kind of undead clean freak?

She sank down on the floor as her laughter turned to hot tears of despair. She told herself Travis would find her, but she didn't believe it. Not for a minute. How could he? How could anyone?

When her tears finally subsided, she turned on the shower, not for her captor, but in hopes of washing away his touch. She washed her hair, scrubbed her neck until it felt raw. She would have liked a change of clothes, but then, she would have liked a lot of things. Like her freedom. If only she had stayed in Vermont. Right now, even marriage to Dilworth didn't seem so bad.

After dressing, she was a little surprised to discover she was starving. Considering her dire situation, she would have thought food would be the last thing on her mind. But maybe it was only natural that she was ravenous. After all, she had provided dinner for a hungry vampire the night before.

Feeling another bout of hysterical laughter coming on, she took several deep breaths, then pulled a sandwich and a coke from the fridge. She had to keep her strength up, she decided as she went into the bedroom, had to be ready to fight or get the hell out of there if the opportunity presented itself.

Travis met Ronan in front of the burned-out hospital as agreed upon the night before.

"She's alive!" Travis said. "I felt her last night."

Ronan nodded. "Let's go," he said, then placed a restraining hand on Travis' arm. "Wait a minute."

"Like hell!"

"Overstreet's here."

"Here?"

"In the hospital. Come on."

Treading cautiously, they went inside. Made of brick, the outer walls were scorched but still standing. Inside, anything not made of brick or metal had been destroyed. Here and there, small fires still burned.

They found Overstreet in one of the labs in the basement, asleep on the floor, his head pillowed on his coat, one bloody hand wrapped in his handkerchief. He was snoring softly.

"I wonder how he escaped," Travis said.

"Just dumb luck, I'd say." Bending down, Ronan shook the writer's shoulder.

Overstreet let out a startled yelp as he rolled to his feet, his eyes wild. He stared at Ronan and Travis a moment, then steadied himself against the wall with his uninjured hand, only to jerk it away. "Damn! That's still hot."

"What happened to you?" Travis asked.

"Some female vampire carried me away." Carl shook his head. "She couldn't have weighed more than ninety-eight pounds soaking wet, but she picked me up like I wasn't any heavier than a sack of potatoes and carried me out of the place. When she told me she was going to drain me dry, I went crazy and slugged her as hard as I could, then I threw a vial of holy water in her face and got the hell out of there. I hitched a ride with a trucker to get here." He shook his head again. "Where' Sara? Is she all right?"

"We're on our way to find her," Travis said.

"You're not going to leave me here alone, are you? What if that crazy vampire comes after me?"

"Go stay with Winona," Ronan said. "You'll be safe there."

"Are you sure?"

"Trust me."

Carl nodded, but he didn't look convinced.

"We're wasting time," Travis said impatiently.

Ronan nodded. "Go to Winona's and get cleaned up, Carl. We'll meet you there later."

Once Travis got the hang of tracking the blood link between himself and Sara, it didn't take long to locate where she was being held. He was surprised to find that Jarick's lair was located about thirty miles from Susandale. Unfortunately, there was no way to get into the place. The house was warded against humans and vampires alike, the windows and front door barred and reinforced with steel. There was no sign of life save for Sara's heartbeat.

He sent a glance at Ronan. "Now what? How do we get in?"

"I'm working on it."

Travis paced back and forth, his agitation growing with every step. They were so close!

"We need Bowman."

"Why?"

"He's Jarick's number two."

"Why would he help us?"

"To quote a line from a famous movie, I'll make him an offer he can't refuse."

⚜ ⚜ ⚜

It took only minutes to transport themselves to Bowman's house in Susandale. Olivia's eyes grew wide when she saw Ronan on the front porch, whether from fear or surprise or both, Travis couldn't say.

Ronan got right to the point. "Tell your husband I need to see him. Now!"

"He isn't…"

"Forget it. I know he's inside."

Face pale, she said, "Wait here," and closed the door.

Several minutes passed before Bowman opened up. He didn't step outside. "What do you want?"

"I want you to take me to Jarick's lair."

"No way!"

Ronan didn't argue. Merely unleashed his preternatural power.

Travis watched, fascinated, as Bowman's whole body tensed and then began to shake uncontrollably.

"I'm not going to ask again," Ronan said, his voice razor-sharp. "If you refuse, your wife will be a widow and you'll be a dark stain on the floor."

"All right." Jason forced the words through clenched teeth, grabbed hold of the door to steady himself when Ronan released him. "What do you want me to do?"

"I need you to either get me inside or get him outside."

"He'll kill me if I do what you want."

Ronan twitched one shoulder. "I'll kill you if you don't."

"Just let me tell Olivia where I'm going."

Ronan nodded. "I trust you won't do anything stupid."

"I won't," Jason replied sullenly.

"Dammit!" Travis hissed. "This is taking too long!"

"Patience, fledgling," Ronan said.

"Easy for you to say. It isn't Shannah's life in danger. I can feel Jarick feeding on Sara! Dammit, I think she's drying!"

When Jason stepped outside, Ronan grabbed his arm. "Let's go."

With a wary glance over his shoulder, Bowman knocked on Jarick's door. Several minutes passed and when there was no answer, he looked over his shoulder to where Ronan and Travis waited and shrugged. At a signal from Ronan, he knocked again. And again.

Finally, the door opened.

Jarick stared at Bowman. "What the hell are you going here? You're supposed to be retaking the town."

"We did that. Mind if I come in?"

"Why?"

"I think I was followed."

"Make it short," Jarick said with a feral grin. "I'm in the middle of a seven-course meal."

Bowman forced a laugh. Took a deep breath. Grabbed Jarick's arm and yanked him across the threshold.

Ronan immediately sprang forward, hands reaching for the vampire.

Travis growled low in his throat as waves of preternatural power washed over him, driving him backward so that he skidded across the driveway. He saw Bowman go flying through the air and crash into the block wall separating Jarick's house from the vacant lot next door.

Travis struggled to regain his footing but to no avail. He seemed frozen in place. Unable to move, he could only watch as the two master vampires came together in a rush, fangs and claws ripping and tearing into preternatural flesh that healed almost instantly. In all his life, he had never seen anything so brutal or so vicious.

He looked up at the house as a movement caught his eye, let out a wordless cry of rage when he saw Sara dragging herself across the threshold toward the porch steps, her breath coming in labored gasps. But it was the two bloody puncture wounds in her neck that held his attention.

"Sara!"

She looked in his direction, her face as pale as the clouds scudding across the sky, her eyes dark holes of pain as she struggled toward the steps, only to lose her balance and tumble down the stairs to the cement walkway.

He cried her name again, every fiber of his being fighting against the power that held him immobile. With a last, desperate effort of will he freed himself and ran toward her. "Sara. Sara." Just her name as he lifted her into his arms.

"You ... came."

He nodded, afraid they were too late, that she would die in his arms. Her cheeks were sunken, her lips bloodless.

A high-pitched scream of denial drew his attention toward the struggle between Ronan and Jarick. As the scream died away, Ronan raised his arm over his head.

Travis stared at the bloody object in his hand. It took a moment to realize it was Jarick's heart. There was no sign of Jason Bowman. Apparently, he had taken off sometime during the fight. Not that Travis gave a damn. "Ronan!"

The urgency in Travis' voice brought the vampire to his side.

"She's dying," Ronan said dispassionately.

"No!" But it was true. Her eyes were closed, her heartbeat so faint Travis could scarcely hear it.

"You have two choices. You can bring her across. Or I can give her my blood and hope it's not too late to save her."

Travis stared at him. How could he make a decision like that? Making her a vampire would save her life without a doubt. Did he dare take a chance that she wasn't too far gone for Ronan's blood to save her? Would she hate him if he stole her life to save it? How would he live with himself if he let her die?

Ronan laid his hand on Travis' shoulder. "You need to make a decision. Now."

"I can't turn her," he said, anguish thick in his voice. "Give her your blood." And if that didn't work? He thrust the disquieting thought aside.

"As you will." Ronan took Sara in his arms, then sat on the porch step. "Open her mouth for me."

Travis did as asked. Ronan bit into his own wrist. Dark red blood welled in the shallow gash. Turning his arm over, he held it over Sara's mouth.

Travis watched, repulsed and fascinated, as the crimson drops fell on her tongue. She swallowed convulsively, once, twice, three times. Slowly, faint color returned to her cheeks. He knew a moment of relief as the beat of her heart grew stronger.

Another few minutes and Ronan ran his tongue over his wrist, sealing the wound. "She should be fine in the morning. Take her to Winona's house. I'll clean up this mess. And then I'm going home."

Winona was more than willing to let Sara stay as long as necessary. She led the way to a guestroom at the back of the house.

Carl trailed behind them, looking anxious. "Is she going to be all right?"

"I don't know," Travis said. "I sure as hell hope so."

Winona pulled the covers back and Travis laid Sara, ever so gently, on the mattress, then drew the blankets over her.

"You're welcome to stay with her, if you like," Winona offered.

"Thanks. I will, at least until sunrise."

Winona nodded and left the room.

"What are you going to do now?" Overstreet asked.

Travis smoothed a lock of Sara's hair from her brow. "I don't know. How about you?"

"It's up to Winona." Carl glanced at Sara. "I hope she'll be all right."

"Thanks. You take of yourself."

"Don't worry. No more vampires for me." He gave Travis' shoulder a squeeze and left the room, quietly closing the door behind him.

Travis sat on the edge of the bed, watching Sara sleep. He hadn't prayed in years, but he prayed now, begging Heaven to restore her to full health, to watch over her when he couldn't be with her, to keep her safe, to grant her a long and happy life.

It wasn't until Travis ended his prayer that he realized he'd been saying goodbye.

Chapter 29

For the second time in her life, Sara woke in a strange bedroom with no memory of how she'd gotten there. For a moment, she simply lay there staring up at the ceiling. She felt odd but couldn't pinpoint why. She didn't hurt anywhere. She didn't have a headache or feel sick to her stomach. She just felt... different.

Rising, she padded to the door, then stood there, listening. She breathed a sigh of relief when she heard Carl Overstreet's voice, followed by Winona's laughter.

She found the two the them sitting in the kitchen, their breakfast dishes pushed aside.

Carl smiled when he saw her. "Hey, girl, how are you feeling?"

Sara shrugged. "I'm not sure. All right, I guess."

"Would you like some breakfast?" Winona asked. "A cup of coffee?"

"Breakfast sounds wonderful, thank you."

"Sure, sit down, hon. Bacon and eggs okay?"

"Whatever's easiest."

Nodding, Winona moved to the stove where she put some bacon and eggs in a pan, then poured Sara a cup of coffee.

Sara smiled her thanks. "Is everything all right here?" she asked. "I mean, now that the vampires are gone? They are all gone, aren't they?"

Overstreet cleared his throat. "Yeah."

"What is it?" she asked, fear for Travis' life spiraling through her. "What's wrong?"

"The vampires, uh, pretty much destroyed the town before they left. I'm afraid your house and your store are gone."

She stared at him blankly. "Gone?"

"They torched your car, too. Damned vampires burned everything except the houses that belonged to members of the coven or their women."

Sara stared into her cup. Everything she had brought with her was gone. All her clothes. Her handbag. Her checkbook and wallet and driver's license. Her cell phone.

"Sara?"

Blinking rapidly to hold back her tears, she looked at Carl.

"What can I do?" He reached for her hand and gave it a squeeze. "I've got a little cash if that'll help."

"Thank you. Is Travis all right?"

"He was fine when I saw him last night."

She nodded, then murmured her thanks again as Winona set a plate in front of her.

"What are you going to do now?" Winona asked, resuming her place at the table.

What, indeed? she thought. And then she squared her shoulders. "Carl, will you lend me enough money to buy a plane ticket?"

"Are you sure you want to leave?"

She nodded. "I can't afford to stay, nor do I want to. There are too many bad memories here." *And too many good ones.* She would miss Travis dreadfully, but she'd had enough of vampires to last a lifetime. Her lifetime. She was going home. Back to Vermont where people weren't afraid to go out at night. A place where no one believed in vampires. "Can you drive me to the airport in Langston?"

Overstreet nodded. "Sure. Whenever you're ready to go."

Sara stood on the sidewalk in front of her parents' home. It was a lovely old place, two-stories high, set on half an acre. A wide verandah spanned the front of the house. Ancient maple trees grew on both sides, providing shade in the summer.

Feet dragging, she walked up the winding pathway to the front porch, reluctant to ring the bell. Defeat weighed heavily on her shoulders even though she hadn't technically failed to succeed. After all, it wasn't her fault vampires had destroyed her business, her rental house and most of the town.

She smoothed the wrinkles from the dress Winona had been kind enough to lend her. Took a deep breath. And knocked on the door.

It was opened moments later by the Winters' housekeeper, Gracie. "Miss Sara!" she exclaimed. "Landsakes, child, I'm that surprised to see you. Your folks didn't say anything about your coming home."

"I didn't tell them," she said.

"Well, it'll be a nice surprise, won't it? They just sat down to lunch. Where's your luggage?"

"I'm afraid I don't have any." Moving past the housekeeper, Sara took another deep breath, forced a smile she was far from feeling, and walked briskly into the dining room.

Her mother and father glanced up.

"Sara!" Her mother sprang to her feet and hurried forward to give her daughter a hug. "Why didn't you tell us you were coming? Lucy," she called, "fix a plate for Sara."

Her father rose more slowly, his brow furrowed. "Is everything all right?" he asked, stepping in to give her a hug.

"I had a bit of a problem," she said when he released her.

"Well, sit down and tell us all about it," her mother said.

Sara took her customary place at the table, smiled her thanks as Lucy set a plate and a glass of iced tea in front of her. "I don't know where to start."

"The beginning is usually a good place," her father suggested.

"I was doing really well," she said, choosing her words carefully. "It was a small town, but the tourist trade helped. But a few days ago a gang of… of ruffians invaded Susandale. They burned the town to the ground, including my shop and the house I was renting. They torched my car." She lifted one shoulder and let it fall. "So I came home."

"I'm so sorry," her mother said. "At least you weren't hurt."

Sara nodded.

"The things you lost are easy enough to replace," her father said.

"Yes." Sara looked down at her plate. Dresses and shoes, even her wallet and her phone, they were just things with little sentimental value. She could buy dozens of new clothes to replace what the vampires had destroyed. If only it would be as easy to fill the empty place in her heart.

Pleading a headache, Sara excused herself from the table after lunch and went up to her room. She had to admit, she had missed it. Built-in bookcases stood on both sides of an antique four-poster bed. A matching dresser stood against one wall. A large window looked out over the backyard, which was lush and green. A white gazebo stood in one corner of the yard. Her mother's rose garden took up a good portion of the east side. A number of wrought iron benches were placed here and there inside the garden.

Kicking off her shoes, Sara sat on the edge of her bed, her thoughts on Travis.

Had she made a mistake in leaving him without a word? And yet, what was there to say?

He was a vampire and as much as she cared for him, as much as she already missed him, she just didn't see how they could possibly have any kind of a lasting future together.

She thought about Shannah and Ronan. They seemed happy, but how long would that relationship have lasted if Ronan hadn't turned her?

And then there was Olivia Bowman, hiding out in a small town with her children and vampire husband. That was no kind of life, either, always living in fear that hunters would find your husband or that your kids would let the truth about Jason slip. She didn't understand how Olivia had stayed with Jason, knowing what he was doing to the innocent men, women, and children who passed through Susandale.

Her tears came them, stinging her eyes, burning her throat, as she wept for Travis and what might have been if he had never hunted Ronan.

She dried her eyes with the corner of her bedspread when someone knocked at the door.

"Sara? Honey? It's Mom. Can I come in?"

"Sure."

"What is it, hon?" Donna Winters asked, sitting beside her daughter. "I was on my way to my room when I heard you crying."

"Just feeling sorry for myself, I guess," Sara said, dabbing at her eyes again.

"You're not crying because of losing the store, are you?"

"No," she said, sniffling. "I met a man in Susandale."

Donna Winters nodded as she handed Sara one of the small white handkerchiefs she always carried. "And you liked him?"

Sara nodded as she wiped her eyes.

"Tell me about him."

What to say? Sara wondered. The truth was out of the question. "He was just a really nice guy. Easy to talk to. He had a crooked smile and... and he needed me."

"I see. Does he have a name?"

"Travis." Sara looked out the window. A wayward breeze moved among the leaves of the trees. She heard the distant hum of a lawnmower, the slam of a car door, the exuberant laughter of a child. Ordinary sounds in an ordinary town. Every day background noises that had been missing in Susandale.

"And does he care for you, too?"

"Yes."

"So...?"

"He's not the kind of man I want to marry." Fresh tears flooded her eyes and spilled down her cheeks. "He's a wanderer, with no home and no job."

"But you love him anyway."

And that was the problem, Sara thought. She did love him.

Chapter 30

Travis woke with the setting of the sun. Knowing that Ronan had gone home left him with a peculiar emptiness inside, which he thought was almighty strange considering there was no love lost between them. And yet… it had felt right to be with his sire. It was a feeling he intended to examine more closely at some other time. Right now, he needed to see Sara, to know she was safe.

He had spent the night in the hospital morgue. Located in the basement, it had escaped the worst of the fire. He washed in one of the sinks, then willed himself to Winona's house.

At his knock, she answered the door. "Come on in, Travis."

He puzzled over the blank expression on her face as he followed her into the living room.

Overstreet sat on the sofa wearing the same impassive expression.

Travis was about to ask what was wrong, but it wasn't necessary. Without asking, he knew that Sara wasn't in the house. Nor was she anywhere in town.

"She went home," Carl said. "I drove her to the airport this morning. Lucky for me, when the vamps were burning everything, they missed my truck."

Travis dropped into an easy chair covered in a blue-and-brown plaid. "Did she leave anything for me? A note? A message?"

Overstreet shook his head. "I'm sorry."

Travis nodded. When he'd left Sara last night, he had fully intended to walk out of her life and never look back. They had no future together. Apparently, she had come to the same conclusion. He couldn't blame her for leaving town. There was nothing for her here now. No doubt she had gone back home to settle down with Dilmount or whatever the hell his name was.

Jealousy rose inside him like bile, leaving a nasty taste in his mouth and the urge to kill any other man who would dare touch her.

"Travis?" Carl shot a worried glance at Winona as a wave of preternatural power flooded the room. "Hey, Travis? You okay?"

Hands clenched, he nodded. She was better off without him. He wished he could say he was better off without her, but he feared that, without her sweet influence in his life, he might someday become the kind of remorseless monster he had once hunted.

Sara spent her first two days at home shopping for new clothes, shoes, a handbag, and a new cell phone. She went to the DMV and reported that her driver's license had been lost and requested a new one, then spent two hours on the phone with the company she had leased her car from trying to explain what had happened to it. They seemed reluctant to believe someone had set it on fire but said they would send someone to pick it up. She learned her house in Susandale had belonged to the vampire community, so she didn't have to worry about notifying anyone about its loss.

She spent her evenings at home with her mom and dad.

Her parents didn't waste any time spreading the word that their daughter was home again. By the end of the week, her mother had put together a welcome home party for the following Saturday night and invited all of Sara's friends. It wasn't something she was looking forward to. Her mother seemed to think a party was just what Sara needed to chase the blues away. She huffed a sigh. Why couldn't her mother understand that she just wanted some time alone?

Time to think.

Time to forget.

It was only at night, when Sara was alone in her room, that she let herself think about Travis, remembering the color of his eyes, the sound of his voice, the way it had felt so right to be in his arms, the touch of his lips on hers. She hadn't known him very long, or very well. How could she miss him so desperately when so much of their time together had been anything but normal?

Going to her bedroom window, she stared out into the darkness. Had Travis stayed in Susandale? Had she done the right thing in leaving him without a word? Would saying goodbye have made it easier for both of them?

Harder?

Or just impossible?

Saturday night came all too soon. The backyard looked like a fairyland. Colorful paper lanterns were strung around the yard. Her mother had hired her favorite caterer, along with a DJ. Round tables covered with crisp white linen cloths had been set up on the patio. A long table held drinks–everything from lemonade and soda, to mixed drinks and champagne. Another table held finger foods and desserts—individual pies, cupcakes, cream puffs, strawberry tarts, various meats and cheese.

Sara stood in front of the mirror in her room, trying to summon a modicum of excitement and failing badly. She brushed her hair, applied a bit of blush and her lipstick, took a deep breath and went downstairs to help greet her guests.

Travis stood in the deep shadows in a far corner of Sara's backyard. Perhaps fifty people of various ages milled around the covered patio. Dinner was over and couples danced on the patio, or clustered in small groups, talking and laughing.

But he had eyes only for Sara. Wearing a yellow and white sundress, her hair falling in loose waves over her shoulders, she looked more beautiful than ever. And so at home. She stood in the center of a group of young adults, mostly male, all vying for her attention. He had no trouble picking out Dilworth. Tall, blond, and athletic, the man stuck to Sara's side like a cocklebur.

When the DJ pulled up a ballad, Dilworth led Sara onto the patio. Travis' hands knotted at his sides when the man took her in his arms. They looked good together, both young and glowing with good health, their whole lives ahead of them.

For a moment he hated them. Both of them. Hated Ronan for stealing his mortality. Hated himself for falling in love with Sara, for letting himself hope they could have a life together when he had known from the start that it was impossible.

Sick at heart, he murmured her name. As if she had heard him, she glanced over her shoulder in his direction. And then, to his astonishment, he heard her voice in his mind, whispering his name.

He frowned, wondering how that was possible. He had taken her blood and that enabled him to read her thoughts, but she had never taken his. He hadn't been reading her mind and yet she had sent her thoughts to him. His frown deepened. She had taken Ronan's blood. And Ronan was his sire. Had that somehow created a two-way link between himself and Sara?

"Did you say something?" Dilworth asked.

"What?" Sara pulled her gaze from the far corner of the yard. She must be losing her mind, she thought, imagining that Travis was nearby. And yet she had heard his voice in her mind as clearly as if he had whispered in her ear. She hadn't imagined that.

"I asked if you said something."

"Oh, it was nothing. I'm thirsty. Let's go get a drink, shall we?"

It was after midnight when the party broke up. As Sara had feared, Dilworth was the last to leave. They sat on the front porch swing watching the last of the guests drive away.

"Alone at last," he murmured, slipping his arm around her shoulders.

She forced a smile as she tried desperately to think of a tactful way to tell him to go home. Sadly, nothing came to mind.

"You know I'm crazy about you, don't you?" His hand cupped her nape, gently drawing her toward him. "It would make our families very happy if you'd say yes."

Their families had been friends since before she was born. Her parents had always expected her to marry him. She looked up at Dil, searching for the right words, when his mouth descended on hers.

It was a very nice kiss. Proof, she supposed, that he had done it many times. She didn't know how it affected the others, but she found herself thinking of Travis and how his kisses made her insides curl with pleasure.

Dilworth lifted his head, his gaze searching hers. "There's no hope for us, is there?"

"I'm sorry."

"Is there someone else?"

"Yes. No."

"What is it? Yes or no?"

"There's someone else, but it doesn't matter. We can't be together."

"Then don't shut me out, Sara. I know I could make you happy if you'd just give me half a chance."

Sighing, she gazed into the darkness. Why not? she thought. Dilworth was pleasant company. They had the same background, the same friends. She could think of worse ways to spend her life. And who knew? Maybe, given enough time, she might even learn to love him.

Swearing under his breath, Travis transported himself to another part of the city, afraid if he stayed in the shadows beside the porch any longer, he might do something rash, like throw himself at Sara's feet and beg her to love him.

Chapter 31

Jason Bowman left his lair, his thoughts churning, his anger rising as he viewed the destruction of the town. They'd had a good thing going here, until Travis and that nosey writer showed up. Now the town was in ruins, Jarick was dead, his coven had scattered, and he was alone. True, Ronan had destroyed Jarick, but it was Travis and the writer who had set everything else in motion. He should have killed them both long ago.

Olivia had told him in no uncertain terms that she'd had enough. She wanted to pack up their belongings and re-locate to the West Coast to be near her parents.

Jason snorted. He had no intention of moving closer to her family. Living among humans was exhausting, always pretending to be what he wasn't, always fighting the urge to sink his fangs into warm, tender flesh. Here, in Susandale, he hadn't had to hide what he was. He'd been free to feed when and how he pleased.

With the need for revenge burning hot within him, he stormed out into the night. He didn't know where to find Ronan or Travis or that troublesome woman who'd run the bath shop, but the writer was right down the street, tucked into bed with Winona.

Carl Overstreet bolted upright as the bedroom door swung open.

"What is it?" Winona asked, her voice thick with sleep.

Frozen with fear, Carl couldn't answer. He could only stare at the ominous shape stalking toward him, eyes glowing red in the darkness.

Sensing his alarm, Winona sat up, only to let out a terrified cry as the intruder picked her up and threw her across the room.

"No!" Carl screamed the word, but it emerged from his throat as a hoarse whisper as the vampire pushed him down on the mattress and sank his fangs into the side of his neck.

Carl pummeled the creature's back as he writhed beneath the vampire. In a dim part of his mind, he thought, so, this is what it's like to be prey.

He knew a moment of relief when the vampire lifted his head, watched in horror as the vampire bit into his own wrist. Bowman's next words quickly killed that brief moment of hope.

"Drink!"

Sheer terror engulfed Overstreet as the vampire forced his mouth open and compelled him to drink. And drink. And drink.

"You think you have a right to judge me and the way I live?" the vampire snarled. "Let's see how you like it."

Carl stared at the creature that was now his sire until a wave of darkness swallowed him whole.

He woke with a start, something he rarely did. The room was pitch black, yet he saw everything clearly. He knew he was in Winona's bedroom and that she was in the house. The pounding of her heart rang loud and clear in his ears, giving rise to an excruciating pain that exploded inside him. For a moment, he thought he was dying.

And then he remembered he had died last night. And the agony burning in his veins was a need for blood.

He found Winona in the living room. She had turned on every light in the house and now she sat in a chair, her back to the wall, a stout wooden stake in one hand, a bottle he suspected held holy water in the other.

Carl stood in the doorway, well out of reach. "I thought you'd be gone."

"I don't have anywhere to go."

"How'd Bowman get in last night? I thought vampires needed an invitation?"

"Usually. But all the houses belong to the vampires."

His nostrils flared as the scent of her blood called to him. "You aren't safe with me."

"Maybe you aren't safe with me."

"You've given me many a meal since first we met," he said with a wry grin. "But I've never been hungrier than I am now. Or more in need."

Head tilted to one side, she regarded him through narrowed eyes. "How do I know you'll stop feeding before my heart stops beating?

"You don't trust me?"

"Do I look crazy to you? I've been living among vampires for years. There's nothing more unpredictable than a hungry fledgling."

Carl groaned low in his throat. "Winona, please."

"All right. But I'm holding the stake against your heart and if you don't stop when I tell you to, you'll be a dead fledgling."

He groaned again. "Anything you want."

She held out her arm, palm up. "Not my neck."

He dropped to his knees in front of her, too desperate to argue. The scent of her blood called to him, over-riding his disgust at what he was doing. But he wasn't human anymore and one taste quickly changed disgust into pleasure. He closed his eyes, savoring the warm, salty taste on his tongue as if it was the sweetest nectar.

Which it was.

Only the slight pain of the stake's point piercing his skin made him stop. He ran his tongue over the wounds in her wrist, watched in amazement as the tiny punctures healed in seconds.

Muttering, "I'm sorry," he stood and backed away from her.

For the first time, he noticed the bruise on her cheek, the swelling on the side of her head. Only then did he remember that Bowman had thrown her against the bedroom wall.

She flinched when he reached out to run his fingers over the bruise. "Does it hurt?"

"A little. It knocked me out. He was gone when I came to. And you were ... I thought you were dead."

He nodded. "I guess I am. Technically." He sat down on the sofa, head bowed, hands dangling between his knees. "Where do I go from here? I've got no family. No friends except Travis." He barked a laugh. "He'll get a kick out of this."

"You can stay here."

At the touch of Winona's hand on his shoulder, he looked up. "You mean it?"

She shrugged, a faint grin teasing her lips. "Why not? I've gotten used to having you around."

Chapter 32

During the next three weeks, Sara fell back into her usual routine. She jogged in the morning, spent her afternoons with her girlfriends. Mondays they played tennis. Tuesdays they relaxed at the spa. They played bridge on Wednesdays, did charity work at the hospital on Thursdays, went to lunch on Fridays.

Her weekends were spent with Dil.

The only fly in the ointment was that he was no longer content to be friends. Had he been less of a gentleman it might have caused a problem. But he was a well-bred young man and when she said no, he reluctantly put on the brakes.

Many nights, lying alone in her bed, Sara wished desperately that she had let Travis make love to her. He was rarely out of her thoughts, never out of her heart. Time and again, she thought of calling him. Probably a good thing she'd lost her phone and couldn't remember his number, she mused, or she probably would have called him by now. And said what?

Sometimes, when she was thinking of him, she had the feeling he was nearby, that if she just called his name, he would come to her.

Late one night she awoke, certain that he had been in her room, that she had felt his fingers in her hair, his lips on hers.

Now, as she dressed to go out with Dil, she wished it was Travis coming to call, because she had a terrible feeling that Dil was going to propose—and an even worse feeling that if he asked, she would say yes just to get out of the rut she seemed to be in.

Hands shoved into his pockets, Travis wandered through the town. For the last three weeks, he'd been trying to work up the nerve to knock at Sara's door, but every time he got close, he chickened out. She lived in a luxurious home he could never afford, drove a baby-blue Corvette. Her friends were all young and beautiful and rich. They wore the latest styles, drove expensive cars. Men and women alike were filled with a kind of innate self-confidence he'd never had. Would never have.

He had been a fool to think they could have a future together. He had nothing to offer her. Nothing at all. Even if he hadn't been a vampire, they were worlds apart.

And still he lingered, just to catch a glimpse of her from time to time, to see her smile, if only from a distance, hear her laughter, the sound of her voice.

He was a vampire, the most powerful creature on earth, and he was acting like some love-sick teenager. But then, he had never been in love before. And hoped like hell this would be the first time and the last.

Travis had just decided to take in a movie since he had nothing better to do when his phone rang. He frowned when he looked at the display, then hit Answer. "Overstreet, how's it going?"

"Are you sitting down?" Carl asked.

"No, why?"

"Our old friend, Bowman, turned me three and a half weeks ago."

"Are you shittin' me?" Try as he might, Travis couldn't imagine Overstreet as a vampire, but then, he had never imagined himself as one, either.

"I wish."

"Hey, man. I'm sorry."

"Split milk, I guess. It's sure as hell nothing like I thought it would be. Even after all the research I've done on the Undead, there's still a lot I don't know."

"I hear ya. Been there, done that, and I'm still learning. I'd be glad to help you in any way I can. Are you still in Susandale?"

"Yeah, but I was thinking of leaving here. I was wondering if I might come and hang out with you for a while until I get a handle on things. I'm afraid for Winona. Afraid I'm going to hurt her. Or worse."

"I hear ya. I'd be glad for a little company. I'll text you my address."

"Thanks, Travis. I really appreciate it. See you soon."

"Nicely done." Jason said, releasing his choke hold on Winona's neck. "I trust you won't call him back and let him know I'm on my way?"

Overstreet shook his head, his gaze on Winona's pale face. She looked scared to death, but who could blame her?

"I'll know if you do." Jason tightened his hold again. "And she'll pay the price."

"I believe you!" Overstreet exclaimed. "I won't say anything, I swear it! Just let her go."

"I'm glad we understand each other." Easing his hold again, Jason said, "You won't mind if I have a little drink for the road, will you?"

Hands clenched at his sides, Overstreet shook his head. Winona gasped with pain, hands flailing, as Bowman sank his fangs into her neck.

Unable to watch, Carl looked away.

After what seemed like forever but was only a few moments, Bowman lifted his head and licked the blood from his lips. He fixed Overstreet with a last warning look, and then vanished from sight.

"I'm sorry, love!" Carl said, pulling a trembling Winona into his arms. "Some day I swear I'll kill him for this."

Travis trailed behind Sara and Dilworth as they strolled hand-in-hand through the City Mall. It made his gut clench with jealousy every time Sara laughed at something the man said. He'd told himself he wanted her to go on with her life, to be happy, but it was killing him inside. He told himself he should leave town and try to forget her, but so far, he hadn't been able to make himself go. He made excuses, saying he was waiting for Overstreet, but the truth was, he just couldn't bear to leave her.

It was nine o'clock when they left the mall. He watched them get into Dilworth's Maserati and drive away before he went in search of prey.

He fed on a young woman he found waiting alone at a Bus Stop, then, with nothing better to do, he walked the ten miles to his lair.

He was about a block away when he caught the scent of vampire. But it wasn't Carl Overstreet. It was Jason Bowman. What the hell! How had Bowman found him?

Frowning, he dissolved into mist and drifted down the sidewalk. When he reached the house he was renting, he circled it twice. When there was no sign of the other vampire, he resumed his own form. Bowman's scent was stronger now, proof that he had been there recently.

Inside, Travis gathered his few belongings, stuffed them in a duffel bag, and went in search of a new lair.

He found a suitable place to spend the day in a house with a *Sold* sign out front, figuring the odds of the buyers taking possession the next day were pretty slim.

Once inside, he pulled his phone out of his pocket and called Ronan.

His sire answered on the second ring. "What do you want now?"

"I've got a problem."

Ronan snorted. "So, what else is new?"

"I followed Sara to Vermont."

"And that's my problem because?"

"That's not the problem," Travis said impatiently. "Bowman followed me."

"Interesting."

"Not as interesting as the phone call I had from Overstreet last night. He told me Bowman turned him."

Ronan grunted softly. "The plot thickens."

"Yeah. Carl asked if he could come and stay at my place until he got things figured out."

"So what do you want me to do?"

"I'm not sure."

"How are you and Sara getting along?"

"We're not. She's dating the guy her dad wants her to marry."

"Get rid of him and your second problem is solved."

"Yeah," Travis muttered. "But what am I gonna do about the first one?"

"Bowman? Take him out."

"I'm not sure I'm strong enough to do that on my own."

"Are you asking me to come to Vermont and back you up?"

"Not exactly. I'd just like to know I can count on you if I need you."

"Sure, kid."

"Thanks, Dad."

A low growl sounded in Travis' ear before his sire muttered an oath and ended the call.

⚜ ⚜ ⚜

Shannah looked up from the magazine she had been reading. "What are you going to do?"

"Do?" Ronan shrugged. "Nothing right now."

She laid the magazine across her lap, her head cocked to one side. "If you wait until Travis actually needs your help, you might get there too late."

Ronan shrugged again. "That's his problem."

The magazine in Shannah's lap slid to the floor when she stood. "Don't you ever get tired of playing the tough guy?" she asked as she sat down beside her husband, her thigh tight against his.

"Hey, woman, I'm not playing," he said sternly, his eyes blazing. "I *am* a tough guy."

"I know you are," she said with mock horror. "And I'm terrified of the big bad monster. But seriously, Ronan, what are you going to do?"

"You think I should go now?"

"You don't have to tell Travis you're there. But I'd feel better if you were close by."

"I'm beginning to think you've got the hots for guy," he muttered irritably.

"Oh, baby, you've gotta be kidding! He's just a boy." She cupped his face in her hands and kissed him deeply. "I gave up boys a long time ago. I like men."

A low rumble of laughter emerged from Ronan's throat as he slid off the sofa and onto the floor, carrying her with him so that she landed on top of him, chest to chest and thigh to thigh. His hand slid into the heavy fall of her hair, drawing her head down. "Show me," he whispered, his voice husky with desire as his other hand glided suggestively up and down her back. "Show me how much you like men."

"Not men," she corrected, nipping his lower lip. "Just one man."

"Show me," he said for the third time.

"My pleasure." Straddling his hips, she teased and tormented him until he was on fire for her. "More?" she purred.

"I'll take all you've got, darlin'."

"And then we'll go to Vermont?"

"Anywhere the hell you want." He growled low in his throat as her hands caressed him. "Just finish what you started."

Chapter 33

Sara woke with a start. Sitting up, she turned on the bedside lamp, her gaze darting nervously around the room. She had been dreaming of Travis, reveling in the touch of his hands, the pleasure of his kisses, the way he said her name, almost like a prayer. He had needed her in a way no one else ever had and although she didn't understand it, she had found his need extremely sexy until, suddenly, he didn't want her any more because she was human and puny and he was strong and immortal. His words of rejection had brought tears to her eyes until she was sobbing because she wasn't good enough for him. And then, abruptly, something had awakened her. An unshakeable feeling that she was being watched.

Throwing back the covers, Sara went to close the curtains, only to let out a soft shriek when she saw a figure in the window. She laughed out loud when she realized it was only her reflection in the glass.

After quickly closing the curtains, she let out a long sigh of relief. She'd been having trouble sleeping for the last week or so. Trouble concentrating on what was going on around her. Lost in her own thoughts, she kept reliving the time she had spent with Travis, daydreaming about the future they would never have, missing him more with every passing day.

She was tired of endless parties. Tired of pretending she was having a good time, that she was interested in the latest gossip. Tired of pretending to be thrilled when one friend got engaged and another got married and a third had her first baby. She was bored out of her mind. Bored with living back home. Bored with her friends. Bored with Dil.

Hard as it was to believe, she missed the excitement of being with Travis, of living on the edge of danger, which made her wonder if there was something wrong with her. She had been terrified when Jarick kidnapped her, knew she could have been killed.

Surely there must be some happy medium between being utterly bored and moments away from a hideous death!

Padding across the floor, she slid into bed.

Just before she drifted off, she thought she heard Travis' voice whispering her name.

⚜ ⚜ ⚜

A phone call from Dil woke Sara the next morning. She glanced, bleary-eyed, at the clock, wondering what was so urgent that he'd called before nine. "Hello?"

"What are you doing, sugarplum?" he asked.

"I was sleeping," she said, yawning. "What are you doing?"

"I'm parked out front. I thought we'd go for an early breakfast."

"Now?"

"Come on, sleepy head. It's a beautiful day."

"Oh, all right. Knock on the back door and ask Lucy to give you a cup of coffee. I'll be down in twenty minutes."

Throwing back the covers, Sara went into the bathroom. After a quick shower, she brushed her teeth, tied her hair back into a ponytail, then pulled on a pair of white shorts and a red tank top, stepped into a pair of sandals, and hurried downstairs.

Dil was waiting for her in the kitchen. "Gee, hon, you didn't have to dress up on my account," he said with a laugh.

"This is what you get when you come calling before ten," she said with a shrug. "Where are we going for breakfast?"

"It's a surprise."

"Lucy, please tell my folks where I've gone."

"Yes, Miss Sara," the cook said with a broad smile. "Have a good time now, hear?"

Sara wondered what had put Lucy in such a jovial mood as she followed Dil out the front door.

As Dil had said, it was a lovely day. He had the top down on his Maserati and she sat back in her seat, enjoying the beauty of the countryside as it flashed by.

She frowned when Dil pulled turned off the highway and drove into a wooded area some distance off the road.

"I don't recall any restaurants out here," Sara remarked, glancing around.

"It's new." He parked the car, got out, and opened her door. "Come on." Taking her hand, he led her toward a patch of lush green grass surrounded by tall trees.

Sara's eyes widened when she saw the white wicker picnic basket sitting on a blanket beside a chilled bottle of champagne. She felt suddenly apprehensive as he indicated she should sit down. Dil had always been a romantic at heart and she had a horrible feeling in the pit of her stomach when he sat across from her and opened the basket.

"You know how I feel about you, Sara," he said as he withdrew a single red rose and handed it to her. "I'm hoping you feel the same." He reached into the basket again. This time, he pulled out a small, black velvet box. "I love you." He lifted the lid, revealing a large diamond set in a platinum band. "Will you marry me, Sara?"

She stared at him. Not long ago, she had told herself she might as well marry Dil and settle down. What difference did it make, now that Travis was gone?

"Sara?"

"Dil, I..." She shook her head. "I love you, but I'm not *in* love with, not in the way you deserve. I didn't mean to lead you on."

He closed the box with a snap. "Still in love with that other guy?"

"Yes." Even as she said it, she wondered if she was making a horrible mistake. She would probably never see Travis again. Did she want to spend the rest of her life alone? She could be content with Dil. They got along well. They could have a comfortable life together. Their parents were good friends. But even as she considered accepting, she knew it would be a mistake. Dil deserved a wife who loved him the way she loved Travis. And that would never be her. "I'm sorry."

"Good thing I didn't follow your mom's advice and ask you at the dance tonight," he said, forcing a wan smile. "At least this way no will ever know you turned me down."

Sara nodded.

"So, who is this guy you're so crazy about?"

"I met him in Susandale."

"Is he in love with you, too?"

"I think so."

"You *think* so? Well, dang, maybe there's still hope for me."

"I'll always love you, Dil. But only as a friend."

"I guess I'll have to live with that," he said, glumly. "But I won't like it. And I won't give up hope."

Leaning forward, Sara kissed him on the cheek. "I hope you find a wonderful girl who'll love you as you deserve."

"Yeah, me, too. I mean, I'm a pretty good catch."

"Yes, you are," she said, grateful that he was taking her refusal so well. "Did you pack any food in that basket?"

If Sara had thought it was hard refusing Dil's proposal, it was even harder to tell her parents about it before the dance that night.

Donna Winters stared at her daughter as if she couldn't believe her ears. "But why? Why would you say no?"

George Winters shook his head, obviously disappointed. "I trust you have a good reason."

"The best there is. I'm not in love with him. Dil understands. Why can't you?"

"We just always expected the two of you to marry," her mother said. "But of course your happiness is what matters."

Sara nodded, thinking it was too bad her mother's tone didn't match her words.

"You'd best go get ready," her father said. "We don't want to be late."

The last thing Sara wanted to do was go to another dance at the country club. Dil would be there, as would all of their friends. At least she knew Dil hadn't told anyone of his plans to propose. Going to the club would have been unbearable if everyone knew.

She dressed with care. Tonight, she would be the perfect daughter. She would would speak to all of her parents' friends, dance with old Mr. Blumberg, laugh at Mr.

Bowers' jokes, listen to Aunt Dorothy's endless stories about her Siamese cat, Tigger.

Pasting a smile on her face, Sara went downstairs, determined to be in a good mood and have a good time. Determined not to waiver from the decision she had made that morning.

Travis stood in the shadows outside the country club. Although the building was packed with people, he had no trouble locating Sara or reading her thoughts. She was biding her time until the dance was over, trying to find an easy way to tell her parents she was leaving home.

Filled with a need to see her, he willed himself to a men's shop and helped himself to a change of clothes—black trousers, white shirt, black jacket, black tie, black shoes.

Five minutes later, he slipped through the kitchen door of the country club and made his way up a winding staircase to the second floor.

He spied Sara dancing with an elderly gent. She looked lovely in a gauzy, pale- blue dress. Unlike most of the women, she wore her hair down so that it fell over her shoulders in silken waves. Never had she looked more beautiful.

Moving across the floor, he tapped the elderly man on the shoulder. "Do you mind if I cut in?"

The old man inclined his head as he surrendered the field.

"Travis, what are you doing here?" Sara asked, eyes wide with astonishment as he took her in his arms.

"Dancing with you."

"How did you get here? How did you find me?"

"How do you think?"

Her lips twitched in a knowing smile. "Oh."

"I couldn't stay away any longer," he said. "I had to make sure you were all right. Just one dance and I'll go."

"No! No. Please stay."

"Does that mean you missed me, too?"

"You have no idea how much. Let's go some place where we can talk."

"Whatever you want."

When the song ended, Sara took his hand and led him to a winding stairway that led to the third floor. French doors opened onto a balcony that overlooked a flower garden. The air was warm, fragrant with the scent of roses and lilacs. Music drifted on the breeze, punctuated by the sound of laughter and the faint hum of conversation from the floor below.

"How have you been?" she asked, stepping out onto the balcony.

"Never better than now, when I'm here with you."

She smiled as his words sank deep into her heart. "What happened in Susandale after I left?"

"The place is pretty much a ghost town now. Bowman turned Overstreet."

"Oh, no! Poor Carl."

"Yeah. Listen, Sara, I never should have come here. I think Bowman threatened Overstreet and Carl told him where I am. Which means you might be in danger."

"I don't care." Cupping his face in her palms, she kissed him. "You're here and that's all that matters."

"I can't stay. You're not safe as long as you're near me. As soon as Bowman's no longer a threat, I'll come back for you."

Soft laughter came from the doorway.

Muttering an oath, Travis put Sara behind him then pivoted to confront Jason Bowman. Travis swore again when he saw that Bowman hadn't come alone. Four vampires Travis didn't recognize stood behind him.

"Afraid to face me by yourself?" Travis taunted.

"This time we finish it," Bowman snapped.

Murmuring, "Stay here, Sara," Travis stepped into the room and closed the balcony doors behind him. "Let the girl go. She's got no part in this."

"She knows too much. And I want her."

"No way in hell!"

With a shake of his head, Bowman jerked his chin at one of the other vampires, then stepped back while the vampire flew across the room, claw-like hands aiming for Travis' throat.

Sara glanced around, looking for a way off the balcony so she could go find help, but the only exit was going back the way they'd come.

Looking through the door, Sara pressed a hand to her heart as Travis and the other vampire came together in a silent, bloody battle. Faces impassive, Bowman and his three companions watched until, in one swift move, Travis ripped the heart from the other vampire's chest and tossed it aside. The vampire collapsed like a rag doll and disintegrated.

Sara looked away, her hand covering her mouth as she fought down the urge to vomit.

The other three vampires were on Travis before the dead man hit the floor.

Filled with despair, Sara closed her eyes, certain Travis would be killed. She risked a peek, let out a startled cry when Bowman materialized beside her. Terror trapped the scream in her throat as he grabbed her by the shoulders and sank his fangs into her throat.

Travis let out a harsh cry of denial when he saw Bowman bending over Sara's neck. Fighting for his life and for hers, he managed to tear the throat from another of Bowman's henchmen. It made the other two wary and they backed off.

Panting, Travis faced them across three feet of blood-stained oak floor. He needed to end this now, before it was too late.

His head jerked up when he felt a stir of preternatural power in the room and suddenly Ronan was there. And he wasn't alone. Overstreet was with him.

"I want Bowman," Overstreet said,

Travis snorted. "Get in line."

"No way! Damned bloodsucker turned me and threatened Winona. He's mine!" Carl declared and darted past Travis out to the balcony.

Travis turned to follow him, let out a cry of denial when he saw Sara sprawled on the balcony floor. He ran toward her, only to be stopped when the two remaining vampires flung themselves at him.

Desperate to get to Sara, Travis was trying to fight them off when his sire's power tore them to shreds.

"Get Sara," Ronan said. "I'll clean up the mess.

Travis raced toward the balcony, eyes burning with tears as he knelt beside Sara and lifted her into his arms. Bowman hadn't been gentle. Her neck had been cruelly savaged. Her face was fish-belly white, her breathing shallow, her heartbeat so faint he could scarcely hear it.

"Sara? Sara! What should I do?"

"Travis..."

"I'm here!" He held her close, one hand lightly stroking her cheek. "Tell me what to do."

"I don't... want... to... leave..." Her voice trailed off as her eyelids fluttered down.

"Sara!" He looked up as Ronan came to stand beside him. "What should I do?"

"That's your decision. But whatever you decide, you'd better do it quick. She's almost gone and even I can't bring back the dead."

Travis shook his head. How could he make a decision as life changing as this for someone else? He glanced at Overstreet, who had come to stand beside Ronan. The writer's clothes were splattered with blood. The fact that he was still alive meant Bowman was dead.

"She said she didn't want to leave," Ronan remarked. "I can only surmise it's you she didn't want to leave."

"I've never turned anyone. What if I do it wrong? Can't you...?

"If I turn her, I'll be her sire."

"No!" He glanced at Sara. "What if I do it and she hates me for it?"

Ronan shrugged. "Then you'll have centuries to apologize."

Travis scowled at him. "I can't do it here. What if someone comes?"

"Don't worry. No one will come up here until you're through."

Travis drew in a deep breath and blew it out in a long, slow sigh. He had never turned anyone before, but he discovered that he knew instinctively what to do. Because her neck had been savaged, he bit gently into her arm and drank as much of her blood as he dared take. And then, praying she wouldn't hate him for what he was about to do, he bit into his own wrist and held it over her mouth. "Drink, love," he whispered. "Drink and be mine forever."

When it was over, Travis wrapped his arms around Sara and transported them to his lair, leaving Ronan and Overstreet to clean up the mess.

After removing Sara's clothes down to her underwear, he washed the blood from her neck and face, then carried her to his room and put her to bed. He watched in amazement as the torn flesh in her neck knit together. A hint of color returned to her cheeks. Her breathing grew less labored, her heartbeat stronger, although it beat less often than when she was human. Her hair took on an added luster.

He sat at her side all through the night, praying that she wouldn't hate him, that he had made the right decision.

Two hours before dawn, Ronan materialized beside the bed. "You doing all right?"

"I'm okay. It's her I'm worried about."

Power swirled through the air as Ronan placed his hand on Sara's brow. "She'll finish healing while she sleeps. When she wakes tomorrow night, she'll be as good as new."

"She'll be a vampire," Travis said dryly. "I don't call that as good as new."

"Well, if you look at it from my perspective, she'll be better than new."

"Somehow I doubt if she'll think of it like that."

"She might surprise you once she's had time to think about it. After all, being forever young and beautiful and healthy isn't such a bad thing."

Hewitt grunted softly. "Where's Overstreet?"

"He went back to Winona's place. The guy's got guts, I'll give him that. He intends to write about his experiences in Susandale and how he was turned."

"What? Are you kiddin' me?"

"Nope. Only this time, he's writing a book of fiction instead of a series of articles."

Travis chuckled. "Looks like he's going to give you some competition in the publishing game."

"More power to him." A faint grin twitched at his sire's lips. "Maybe he can get Winona to pretend to be him if he gets the thing published and his editor wants him to go on tour."

"And there is nothing new thing under the sun," Travis said, grinning as he remembered how Shannah had posed as Ronan.

"Are you quoting the Bible now?"

Travis shrugged. "It seemed appropriate."

"Seriously, are you going to be all right?"

Travis glanced at Sara. "I won't know that until she wakes up."

"Well, you know where to find me."

Nodding, Travis said, "Thanks, Dad."

Ronan glowered at him, then was gone as quickly as he'd arrived.

As the sun climbed over the horizon, Travis brushed a kiss across Sara's lips, then stretched out on the floor beside the bed.

Murmuring, "I hope you can find it in your heart to forgive me, love," he closed his eyes and let the darkness carry him away.

CHAPTER 34

Sara woke to the sound of rain drumming on the roof, so loud, it sounded like horses' hooves pounding on the tile.

Where was she? The room was dark and unfamiliar, yet she could see everything clearly. When the light came on, she closed her eyes against the brightness. When she opened them again, cautiously, she saw Travis standing at the foot of the bed, a peculiar, almost fearful look in his eyes.

"How are you?" he asked, his voice guarded.

Sitting up, she said, "I had the most horrible nightmare."

Something in his expression told her it hadn't been a dream.

"Sara..."

"Why are you looking at me like that? What's wrong?" Fear's icy tentacles slithered down her spine. "Where am I? What have you done?"

Clearing his throat, he shoved his hands into his pockets. "What do you remember?"

"Remember? About what?" she asked. And then she frowned as snatches of the previous night returned—Travis fighting with another vampire, ripping out his heart. Bowman grabbing her... biting her... Eyes wide, she stared at Travis. "Did he turn me? Is that why I feel so peculiar?"

"No."

She stared at him. Waiting.

"You were dying," he said, his voice ragged. "I couldn't let you go."

Her gaze searched his. "*You* turned me."

He nodded, his eyes dark with guilt and regret and something that looked like fear.

He had turned her into a vampire. One of the Undead. A creature of the night. It was incomprehensible. Unbelievable.

"Sara, are you all right?"

"All right? All right!" she exclaimed, her voice rising with every word. "How can I be all right? I'm dead!"

"You don't look dead."

She scowled at him, then burst into uncontrollable laughter. *Welcome to the club,* she thought hysterically. *First Travis. Then Overstreet. And now me.* Just one big happy family of ghouls. Maybe she should change her name to Morticia.

"Sara?" He looked worried now.

When he took her in his arms, her laughter dissolved into tears.

He held her close while she cried, his hand lightly stroking her back. "I'm sorry," he murmured, his own tears dripping onto her hair. "So damn sorry. But I couldn't lose you. Hate me for all eternity if you want, but I just couldn't live in a world without you in it. I love you, Sara."

I love you, Sara. Four simple words that healed the hurt and banished her fears. She recalled her grandmother saying there could only be happiness in a relationship when like married like. Well, she and Travis were alike now, that was for sure. And, in reality, this was the only way they could ever realistically have been together. After all, a turtle might love an owl, but where would they live?

"Sara? Say something."

"I love you."

He drew away a little so he could see her face. "You mean it?"

"Of course."

"So, you don't hate me?"

"Have your ears stopped working? Didn't I just say I loved you?"

"I know, but…"

"But what?"

"I thought you'd be angry, despise me, say you never wanted to see me again."

She blew out a sigh. "I guess I should be more outraged, but what's the point? What's done is done. And you did save my life, after all. How can I hate you for that? Am I upset? Of course. I never wanted this," she said with a wry grin. "But, like you once told me, it's done and can't be undone. So I've decided to accept it. I'm sure there will be days when I regret it, when I *will* hate you, but for now, I'm just glad to be alive." She looked at him intently. "*Are* we alive?"

Travis nodded. "We're alive, just in a different way. We still breathe, our hearts still beat." He raked his fingers through his hair. "So, since you don't hate me, would you consider being my wife?"

"I'll have to think about it," she said, her brow furrowing. "Okay, I thought about it. I'd love to marry you."

"Sara!" Pulling her back into his arms, he held her tight. She loved him. It was a miracle.

"What am I going to tell my parents?" she asked at length.

"Anything but the truth," he muttered dryly.

"I don't… oh!" Hit by a sudden pain unlike anything she'd ever known, Sara doubled over. She groaned deep in her throat as agony spread through every nerve and fiber of her being. "What's happening to me?"

"You need to feed."

Feed! Wide-eyed, she looked up at him. "I can't do that."

"Yes, you can." He bit into his wrist and held it out to her.

Sara licked her lips as she stared at the dark crimson blood oozing from the shallow punctures, closed her eyes as the scent of it seemed to infuse her very pores. When had anything ever smelled so good?

"Drink, Sara. It will ease the pain."

Feeling horribly self-conscious, she took hold of his arm and lapped at the blood like a kitten with a bowl of fresh cream. The taste was intoxicating, and she let out a soft cry of protest when he drew his arm away.

"That will hold you for a short time, but sooner or later, you'll have to hunt, because you can't survive on my blood."

Hunt. The very thought sent a shudder through her. It sounded so primitive, so barbaric. How could she feed on other people? She certainly loved the taste of vampire blood, but would she like the taste of human blood as much? What was it Travis had said? *Once you taste it, you really don't want anything else.* Would she feel that way, too?

"Would you like to go for a walk?"

She blinked at him. "A walk?"

He shrugged. "It will help clear your mind." He gestured at the chair in the corner. "I brought you a change of clothes and some other stuff." Rising, he moved away from the bed. "I'll wait out here," he said, and closed the door behind him.

Sara stared after him. She was a vampire. She knew it. She felt the difference—the other-worldliness of it—with every breath. And still it seemed impossible. A distant part of her mind held to the hope that she was in bed, dreaming. Even though she knew she wasn't.

Blowing out a sigh, she stood and began to dress.

⚜ ⚜ ⚜

Sara's gaze moved quickly through the darkness. It was like seeing the world for the first time. Her vision was amazing. Colors appeared as bright in the night as they did in the light of the sun. She could make out the numbers on a license plate a mile away. Her hearing was just as acute. She heard a leaf fall to the earth, the beating of a moth's wings, the cry of a baby two blocks away, the mother's lullaby as she comforted the child. And, over all, the incessant beating of human hearts—a siren call she was reluctant to answer.

Walking beside her, Travis squeezed her hand. "You're going to have to give in sooner or later."

"I know." She could feel the hunger like a living thing inside her, gnawing at her vitals, demanding to be fed. Travis' blood had eased the pain but did nothing to ease her thirst.

"Travis, what happened to Jason Bowman?"

"Overstreet killed him."

"And the other vampires?"

"They're dead, too."

"Poor Olivia," Sara murmured. "She loved him so much. I wonder what she'll do now."

"Get out of that town, if she's smart. Make a new life for herself and her kids."

Sara nodded.

They walked for an hour. Sara was aware of Travis watching her. He knew what she was going through. It hadn't been that long ago that he'd been turned. Even knowing that didn't really make her feel any better. She could only help herself. Her decision made, she said, "All right, let's get it over with."

Holding tight to her hand, he willed the two of them to a town some miles away. Although it was late, it was Saturday night and the sidewalks were crowded with couples and families.

When they came to a nightclub, Travis guided her inside. "See anyone that looks good to you?" he asked as they headed toward the bar.

"What do you mean?"

He twitched one shoulder. "Sometimes you're drawn to a particular person. I'm not sure why."

Sara glanced around. Couples and small groups occupied the booths that lined the walls. Several men and women sat at the bar. Most of them seemed to be alone. How was she supposed to choose one? And if she did, how was she to get him alone so she could —she grimaced—bite him?

"It's easy. Just concentrate on your choice, then speak to his mind and he'll come to you."

"He will?"

"Trust me."

She focused on the man sitting on the last stool. He was well-dressed, in his late twenties, with long black hair. She stared at the back of his head, willing him to come to her, but nothing happened. "I must be doing it wrong."

"It takes a little practice." Travis spoke to the man's mind. A moment later, he slid off the bar stool and walked toward them. Taking Sara's arm, Travis said, "Come on. He'll follow us."

Once outside, they walked to the end of the block and turned left into a parking lot. Travis led the way to the far corner, away from the streetlights. When he stopped, the man stopped beside him, his expression blank, his arms at his sides.

Sara stared at Travis. "I don't think I can do this." But even as she spoke the words, the scent of the man's blood was calling to her, over-riding her revulsion. Taking hold of his shoulders, she rose on her tiptoes and sank her fangs—oh, lordy, she had fangs—into his neck.

She closed her eyes as she tasted human blood for the first time.

Once you taste it, you really don't want anything else.

Oh, Travis, she thought, feeling almost giddy. *You were so right!* It took her a moment to realize Travis was tugging on her arm.

"Sara! Sara! That's enough."

"Just a little more."

"You don't want to kill him, do you?"

Alarmed, she pushed the man away, then grabbed a fistful of his shirt to keep him from falling face down on the pavement. "Is he going to be all right?" she asked anxiously.

"He'll be fine." Focusing on the man, Travis wiped the memory of what had transpired from his mind and sent him on his way.

Sara licked the last traces of blood from her lips as she watched her prey hurry across the parking lot toward the street. *Prey*. Not a man. Not a human being. Just prey. She shook her head as she gained a new respect for Travis. If not for him, she might have killed the guy. It would have been so easy, so satisfying, to take it all, to feel his heart beating in time with hers. She would have to be more careful in the future.

"You doing okay?" Travis asked.

Sara nodded. She felt elated, jubilant, better than she ever had in her whole life. Travis might not be happy to be a vampire, but it gave her a sense of power, of freedom, that she had never known before. Who wouldn't want this? "What?" she asked, feeling suddenly uncomfortable under his gaze.

"Nothing."

"Tell me."

"I'm just a little surprised at how easily you've accepted all this. It doesn't bother you at all, does it?"

The way he looked at her made her feel ashamed, as if she'd done something wrong. "What's done is done," she said with a shrug. "There's no going back."

He grimaced. Once, he'd said that very thing to her. "I guess it's time I stopped wishing for my old life and started enjoying the new one," he muttered. Pulling her into his arms, he kissed her. "I think it'll be a lot easier now that I've got you to share it with."

"We'll help each other," she said, smiling. "We've got a long time to figure things out."

"So, what about that wedding?"

"The sooner the better. We should ask Carl and Winona to stand up with us."

Travis nodded. And then he grinned. "I guess we should invite Ronan and Shannah, too."

"Of course!"

Pulling out his cell phone, Travis called his sire.

Ronan answered on the first ring. "Don't tell me you're in trouble again?"

"No, Dad. I've got good news. Sara's agreed to marry me. I hope you and Mom will come to the wedding."

"I wouldn't miss it, son," Ronan said gruffly. "Just let us know where and when."

⚜ ⚜ ⚜

Shannah looked at Ronan, one brow arched, as he put his phone away. "Dad?"

He grunted softly. "His juvenile idea of humor."

"I'll need a new dress," she said. "And you'll need a new suit."

Ronan shook his head. Just like every other woman, she jumped at the chance to buy a new gown. Not that he minded. He would gladly buy her a hundred dresses—and shoes to match—just to see her smile.

Overstreet grinned as he tossed his phone on the sofa.

"What's so funny?" Winona asked.

"Travis and Sara are tying the knot."

"Sounds like a good idea to me."

"Does it?" Carl smiled at her as he pulled her into his arms. "Maybe we should be thinking about doing the same thing."

"Do you mean it?" she asked.

"If you'll have me."

"There's no one else I'd rather be with."

"If Sara doesn't object, maybe we could tie the knot at the same time?"

"Our guests have accepted," Travis said. "All we need to do now is find a venue and set the date. Oh, Carl wants to know if you'd mind making it a double wedding?"

"I don't mind if they don't."

"I'll let him know."

Sara found an old Gothic church in upstate Vermont that she thought looked perfect for a vampire wedding. Built of white stone, it had a tall spire, ancient oak doors, and the most beautiful stained-glass windows she had ever seen. She made the arrangements with the priest and set the date for October 31st.

"Halloween?" Travis said, grinning. "Perfect. How do you feel about a double wedding?"

"With who?"

"Overstreet and Winona."

"The more, the merrier!"

"Are you sure you're okay with this? You could invite your parents."

Sara shook her head. "They'd insist on a big wedding with a sit-down dinner and all their country club friends in attendance. I just can't handle all that, or trying to explain why it has to be at night, or..." She shook her head again. "I'll send them a telegram and tell them we eloped."

"All right, if you're sure."

"I am. It'll be just us and our new family."

Taking her in his arms, Travis swung her around and around. "I love you, Sara Ann Winters. For now and always!" he exclaimed. "And day after tomorrow, I'll show you how much!"

Chapter 35

Sara woke abruptly, instantly aware of what day it was and where she was. Sitting up, she brushed a wisp of hair away from her face, wondering if she would ever get used to sleeping without dreaming and emerging from nothingness to wakefulness the minute the sun slid behind the horizon.

And then she smiled. She was getting married in two hours. When she went to bed tonight, she would be—who? Mrs. Travis Black? Or Mrs. Jim Hewitt? She laughed softly. A rose by any other name, she mused, as long as her Mr. Right was there.

She had sent a telegram to her parents the night before, informing them that she was eloping with Travis and that they would visit them as soon as they returned from their honeymoon.

She swung her legs over the side of the mattress, anticipation bubbling inside her like champagne as she went into the bathroom to shower.

Travis had contacted Ronan and Overstreet with the details, and they had all agreed to meet at the church at the appointed time.

If she didn't hurry, she was going to be late!

⚜ ⚜ ⚜

Sara and Travis were the last to arrive at the church.

"We thought you'd changed your mind," Overstreet remarked.

"No chance of that," Travis said, holding tight to Sara's hand.

Sara's heart skipped a beat when she saw the minister enter through a side door and take his place in front of the altar. It was really happening. She was getting married!

"Shall we begin?" The cleric glanced at Travis, who nodded. "Very well then." Motioning to Carl and Winona. "If you'll two will stand here on my right," the minister instructed. "Mr. Hewitt, you and your bride will please stand beside them."

The minister glanced at Ronan and Shannah. "And if you two will take a place on my right, we'll get started." He waited while everyone took their proper place.

The ceremony was brief. Sara scarcely remembered the words she spoke, until the minister said, "Do you, Sara Winters, take James Hewitt to be your lawfully wedded husband, to have and to hold, to love and to cherish, so long as you both shall live?"

As she murmured, "I do," the stark reality hit her.

She and Travis were vampires. They might be married for centuries. When she met his gaze, he smiled, and she knew he was thinking the same thing.

When the ceremony was over, they gathered in front of the church to congratulate each other. Winona and Carl left shortly thereafter, headed for a honeymoon at the Plaza Hotel in New York City.

"How about you two?" Ronan asked. "Got a big honeymoon planned?"

"We're going to Alaska for a while until we decide where we want to settle," Travis replied. "We're leaving tomorrow night."

"Good choice this time of the year," Ronan said. "Take care of each other."

"Thanks, Dad," Travis said, stifling a grin.

Ronan glared at him. "Stay out trouble, kid. I'm tired of saving your butt."

Shannah hugged Sara. "I hope you two will be as happy as we are."

"Me, too," Sara said.

Shannah took Sara's hands in hers. "Come see us when you get back. We're family now."

"We will," Sara promised as Shannah and Ronan took their leave.

"Well, Mrs. Hewitt, are you ready to go home?"

Feeling suddenly shy, she nodded, then let out a gasp as her husband swung her up into his arms and transported them to a luxury hotel in Vermont.

Sara's nerves were humming with excitement as they checked in, then took the elevator to their room.

Inside, she stepped out of her heels and looked around. It was a lovely suite, all done in mauve and green and white.

She shivered with anticipation as Travis moved up behind her. Leaning forward, he nuzzled her neck. "I love you, Mrs. Hewitt."

"And I adore you, Mr. Hewitt."

"Remember, you're only Mrs. Hewitt when we're alone," he cautioned as he rained butterfly kisses along the side of her neck.

"I feel like a secret agent," Sara said with a grin. "The respectable Mrs. Black in public, the mysterious Mrs. Hewitt in private."

"And both of us love you more than life itself," he murmured, as his hands cupped her breasts.

Turning to face him, she crooned, "Stop talking, my husband, and show me."

"My pleasure." His hands were moving as he spoke, removing her veil, unfastening the long row of button down the back of her gown, his gaze devouring her as she turned and stepped out of her dress.

When he reached for her, she slapped his hands away.

Purring, "My turn," Sara removed his shirt, her fingertips sliding seductively over his chest and down to his waist. She unfastened his belt, waited while he kicked off his shoes, unzipped his fly, and stepped out of his trousers.

With a low growl, he carried her to bed and stretched out beside her. "You're beautiful," he whispered, his voice thick with desire as he rained kisses on her lips, her breasts, her belly. "I want to explore every delectable inch of you, every hill, every valley. Every hidden place."

Sara closed her eyes as his words and his clever hands aroused her until she was on fire for him.

She cried out as his body melded with hers, making her feel whole and complete for the first time in her life. She was his at last, she thought. Always and everlastingly his.

As he was hers.

As he would be from this night forward and forever.

~ finis ~

Excerpt from Night's Illusion

8th book in the Children of the Night series
Coming August 2021

Father Giovanni Lanzoni strolled through the city park's narrow, deserted, twisting paths. A brilliant yellow moon hung low in the sky, illuminating his way, though he needed no light to guide his feet. He was Nosferatu, one of the oldest of his kind. As such, he was blessed—or cursed—with supernatural senses and preternatural strength.

Like all vampires who had survived more than a century or two, he had grown to love and appreciate the quiet beauty of the night. He enjoyed being able to see clearly in the dark, to hear the flutter of a moth's wings, to be able to move from place to place with astonishing speed, to think himself across great distances, to move faster than mortal eyes could follow, to dissolve into mist. So many amazing supernatural powers, all his to command.

He had never expected to survive so long. He had always been a pacifist—given to contemplation rather than conflict. As a child, he had dreamed of dedicating his life to the Church. It had proved to be all he had hoped for and more. He had loved the discipline, the interior silence, the sense of inner peace born of service and self-sacrifice. Hearing confessions…

He grinned inwardly. His most recent confession – heard only a few years ago—had come from Nick Desanto. Nick had been born a slave in Egypt and had been turned by the infamous Queen of the Vampires—Mara, herself.

Giovanni had known Mara for centuries. They had met when he was still mortal. He had been a young priest at the time, hoping to render aid and comfort on a battlefield in Tuscany. She had been in search of prey. The only thing that had saved him that night had been her surprising reluctance— or perhaps it had been some ancient superstition about harming a man of the cloth.

They had met again when he was a young vampire in the streets of Paris. He had been badly injured and close to death when she found him. She had generously offered him a little of her ancient blood and it had revived him. And then, for reasons unknown, she had tasted his. They had both undergone some amazing changes since that long-ago night.

In the years since then, he had made a few friends and an enemy or two—both mortal and immortal—in countries around the globe. As a priest, he had willingly given up all thought of home and family. But now, having lived like a monk for so long, he thought he would gladly give up immortality to know the simple joys of one mortal lifetime. To experience a woman's love. To father a child. To watch his sons and daughters grow and have children of their own. What good was living a dozen lifetimes when you had no one to share it with?

Leaving the park, he ambled down the street toward his lair.

The DeLongpre/Cordova coven was the closest thing he had to a family. He considered himself blessed indeed to be a part of their lives and to have officiated at their weddings.

His steps slowed as he gazed at the vast expanse of the sky. Worlds without end, he mused. Times changed, the world itself changed, but he remained forever the same. In mortality, he had been an ordained priest. As such, he had made vows of chastity, poverty, and obedience. He had been celibate in mortality.

And in death.

Lately, he had begun to rethink his vow to remain chaste. Though he was, at least in his own eyes, still a priest, he was no longer recognized as such by the Church that doubtless thought him dead long ago. He had no parish, no superior. Why did he cling to a vow that, after so many centuries, were very likely no longer binding? He had broken the others without a second thought.

Why now, after so many centuries, did he suddenly feel so alone? So lonely?

He thought of Mara again. She had spent centuries refusing to be tied down. Yet, she had been married twice—once to a mortal, and now to Logan Blackwood, the man she had loved for centuries. She had been blessed with a son.

Others of his kind had found companions. Roshan DeLongpre. Vince Cordova and his twin sons, Rane and Rafe. Mara's son, Derek. Nick Desanto. Vampires one and all. Yet each had found love. Even feisty ex-vampire hunters Edna Mae Turner and Pearl Jackson—both turned far past their prime—had found life mates.

Why not him? Perhaps it was time to remember that, in addition to being a priest, he was first and foremost a man.

He chuckled softly. He was, undoubtedly, the world's oldest male virgin.

The oldest male virgin *vampire,* he amended.

He had been turned on his thirty-ninth birthday. He recalled the event as clearly as if it had happened only last night instead of centuries ago.

He had been on his way back to the rectory after giving last rites to an aged nun when he was attacked. It had happened so fast, he'd had no chance to defend himself, although he knew now that would have been impossible. He was floating, drifting away into darkness, when the vampire suddenly reared back. Giovanni remembered staring up into a pair of blood-red eyes that somehow managed to look surprised.

"You're a priest!" the creature hissed. "I can't kill a priest! Heaven forgive me," he murmured, and sinking his fangs into his own wrist, he held the bleeding wound to Giovanni's lips. "Drink!"

Giovanni wanted to refuse but something in the monster's voice compelled him to obey. The blood had been thick and hot, unlike anything he had ever tasted. He gagged with the first swallow and then, to his horror, he grabbed hold of the vampire's arm and suckled as if the blood was as sweet as mother's milk.

He had cried out in protest when the vampire jerked his wrist away.

"We have to find you a place to rest," the vampire muttered, yanking Giovanni to his feet. "And there are things you must know before you rise tomorrow night."

The vampire had dragged him to a cave in the Apennine Mountains and tossed him into it with a warning to stay inside until he returned.

Giovanni had had no intention of doing as he was told, but minutes after entering the cave he had collapsed on the floor. As his vision narrowed and the world went black, he knew he was dying. Sinking into oblivion, he had uttered a prayer begging for mercy and forgiveness with his last breath.

When awareness returned, it was dark again. Lurching to his feet, he had stumbled toward the cave's entrance, his gaze searching for the creature who had warned him to wait for his return.

Hours passed and there was no sign of the vampire.

As the hours dragged by, what started as discomfort gradually turned to agony.

Afraid he was really dying this time, he staggered out of the cave and made his way to the city in search of a doctor.

Ignorant as he was, he had no idea what was happening to him. He stopped abruptly, nostrils flaring. He didn't recognize the scent, knew only that whatever it was, he needed it. Veering down a narrow alley, he came upon two men engaged in a knife fight.

Giovanni took a deep breath. *Blood,* he thought. The enticing smell was blood.

Hardly aware of what he was doing, he stepped between the two men. It took no effort at all to control them. One was bleeding from a cut on his neck. As though mesmerized, Giovanni leaned forward to lick it up and then, to his horror, he bit the man. Overcome with euphoria at the taste of fresh hot blood, he hadn't stopped to wonder at how effortlessly his teeth had bitten through flesh. It was only later that he discovered he had fangs, and that blood was the only thing that could ease the awful hunger that clawed at his insides.

And later still that he found the courage to admit he was no longer human, but Nosferatu.

The transformation had not been easy. To his shame, he had taken human lives before he learned it wasn't necessary to kill his prey to survive. Stricken with guilt, he had gone to confession time and again in hopes of finding forgiveness for the lives he had taken, but he had found none.

Thrusting his past behind him, Giovanni willed himself to his lair in the bowels of an abandoned church. He had another, more comfortable place where he occasionally passed the daylight hours, but resting here, among the dead, seemed more appropriate for one of his kind.

Stretching out on the cold stone floor between a pair of ancient coffins, he closed his eyes, and surrendered to the death-like sleep that swallowed him whole.

Cassie ran headlong through the darkness. Heart pounding with terror, lungs burning, she plunged through the thick hedge that bordered the east side of the park. She whimpered as sharp thorns raked her arms and tore at her clothing.

She never should have let Darla talk her into attending that party. Something had warned her not to go, but she hadn't listened. It was Friday night, after all. Time to forget about her boring life. Time to stop wondering if she was going to get fired. Time to have a little fun for a change.

She darted a glance over her shoulder. Had she lost her pursuers?

But no, she could hear them clamoring through the hedges, their drunken laughter as they called back and forth, their threats of what they would do to her when they caught her.

Her legs were trembling when she reached the concrete walkway that meandered through the gardens.

Gasping for breath, sides heaving, she glanced over her shoulder again. They were gaining on her.

She was doomed.

A startled cry erupted from her throat when she slammed into something solid. Only it wasn't some*thing*, but some*one.*

The man took a step back, his arms darting out to grab hold of her to keep her from falling.

Cassie stared up at him, but it was too dark to see his face clearly. Had she run away from one predator only to fall into the arms of another?

And then Lynx and four of his buddies were there, circling her and the stranger. Moonlight glinted on the wicked-looking knife Lynx held in front of him.

The stranger's arms tightened around her waist. "Easy, girl," he murmured. "There's no need to be afraid."

No need to be afraid, she thought. Was he blind? Didn't he see Lynx and the others surrounding them like hungry wolves around a wounded animal? The knife blades glinting in their hands?

"Give us the chick, old man," Lynx demanded. "And we might let you go."

Cassie closed her eyes and buried her face against the stranger's side. She felt an odd tremor in the air. It made the fine hairs at her nape stand at attention. Gathering her courage, she dared open her eyes to see what was happening, only to find that Lynx and his buddies were nowhere in sight. "What? Where ...?"

"They've gone." Her rescuer's voice rumbled in her ear, deep and kind. "What are you doing out here, child, wandering in the park alone at this time of the night?"

Child? She was over twenty-one. "It wasn't my idea," she said, taking a step away. "My girlfriend took me to a party. I didn't know what I was getting into. When I said I was leaving, Lynx said I couldn't go until I... until I'd paid the toll."

It took him a moment to comprehend her meaning. "He's a friend of yours?"

"No! I just met him tonight." He had seemed so nice when she was first introduced to him.

"If he's smart, he won't bother you again." Feeling suddenly protective of her, he asked, "Where do you live? I'll walk you home."

"That's not necessary."

"Maybe not, but I'm still taking you home."

Shoulders slumped, Cassie muttered, "Whatever," and started walking.

"What's your name?" he asked, falling in step beside her.

"Why?"

"Suspicious, much?" he asked.

She glanced up at him. In the glow of a nearby street light, she saw his face clearly for the first time. His eyes were light—hazel, perhaps—his shoulder-length hair black and wavy and edged with silver. He seemed awfully young to have gray hair. "Sorry, but you *are* a stranger."

He nodded, a faint smile lifting the corners of his mouth. It was, she thought, a very nice mouth.

"Perhaps I should introduce myself first. My name is Giovanni Lanzoni, but please, call me Johnny." It was what his mother had called him, though he'd given the girl the English translation.

"Hi, Johnny."

"I'm very pleased to meet you, Miss ...?"

"Douglas. Cassandra, but everyone calls me Cassie." She frowned, thinking she had never known a man with such nice manners. Not that she'd known that many men.

They walked in silence for a time. Cassie was acutely aware of the man beside her. Though he was not big and bulky and stood only a few inches taller than she, there was an air of power and authority about him that was both comforting and unsettling. With a shake of her head, she dismissed it as nothing more than the after effects of the night's events.

She felt drawn to him in a way she didn't understand. But what was even stranger, she felt safe with him, and that was really odd, because she hadn't trusted anyone since her parents abandoned her when she was fifteen.

"What happened back there?" she asked as they left the park. "Why did they leave without a fight?"

"I merely advised them that it would be in their best interest to leave you alone."

Cassie frowned. "I didn't hear you say anything."

He shrugged. "Perhaps you were too frightened to pay attention."

Cassie shook her head. She had been scared, sure, but too scared to hear whatever threat had sent Lynx and the others hurrying away without an argument? She didn't think so. She shook her head again. Why was she always drawn to the wrong guys? First her ex, and then Lynx? Not that she ever wanted to see *him* again.

She felt a sudden spark of attraction when Johnny's hand accidentally brushed hers.

His gaze jumped to hers, leaving Cassie to wonder if he had felt it, too. She stopped at the end of the concrete path that led to the door of her apartment complex. "We're here."

Giovani glanced at the rundown building. It was in desperate need of a coat of paint. Some of the roof tiles were missing. A few of the windows were patched with tape. "You live here?"

She bit down on her lower lip, suddenly embarrassed as she looked at the place through his eyes. "It's a dump, I know, but it's all I can afford."

"What is it you do?"

"I serve drinks at the Winchester Lounge five nights a week." The place was a dive. Tips were lousy. But it paid the rent. Barely. "Do you know it?"

"Yeah." He had gone hunting there a time or two. "I live alone," he said, weighing each word carefully. "In a rather large house with five bedrooms. It's nothing fancy, but certainly better than this. And in a safer neighborhood."

She blinked up at him. "Are you asking me to move in with you?" she exclaimed. "Are you crazy? I've only known you, what? Ten minutes?"

"I'm not suggesting anything immoral," he said, obviously insulted that she would think otherwise. "I'm gone all day, and a good deal of the night, so you would have the place to yourself most of the time. The house is paid for, so there's no need to pay rent. I've been alone a very long time and I've grown weary of my own company. I merely thought... Forgive my impertinence. It was a bad idea."

Cassie shrugged it off. Had she known him better, she might have jumped at the chance to live rent-free in a decent house. "Thanks for walking me home."

"Please accept my apology," he said stiffly. "I didn't mean to offend you. I was merely trying to help. Good evening."

She stared at him a moment. Perhaps she *had* misjudged his intentions, she thought as she walked swiftly up the stairs to the front door. She paused, her hand on the latch. Maybe she owed him an apology. She turned to tell him she was sorry, but he had already gone.

What a strange man. He had seemed harmless, enough. A gentleman. And yet... she shivered as her mind replayed what had happened in the park. There was something about him, although she couldn't put her finger on it. Something she'd felt on some primal level but couldn't explain.

With a shake of her head, she went inside and closed the door behind her, thinking that perhaps she had escaped two predators that night, even though one had rescued her from the other.

She laughed softly as she went into the bedroom, bemused by her fanciful thoughts.

Giovanni's first thought when the sun went down was for the young, golden-haired, brown-eyed woman he had met the night before. Cassie Douglas. No woman had ever affected him quite like she had. Even now, hours later, he clearly remembered the flowery fragrance of her hair. The warmth of her skin.

The tantalizing aroma of her life's blood.

When she'd looked at him, his whole body had responded. That, too, was unusual. He was, after all, a priest. Years of abstinence and rigid self-discipline had left him immune to the temptations of the fairer sex.

Or so he'd thought.

Her scent, the sound of her voice, had awakened feelings and desires he'd not felt since Maria Elena.

Leaving his lair, he went to his lonely house where he showered, dressed and ran a comb through his hair. And all the while, the memory of his meeting with the young woman played in the forefront of his mind. He told himself he was centuries too old for him. She was barely more than a child. But try as he might, he couldn't stop thinking about her.

Cassie. She worked five nights a week at the Winchester Lounge, he thought. Was tonight one of those nights? Before he could talk himself out of it, he was on his way out the door.

Cassie glanced at the clock, willing the hands to move more quickly. It never worked, of course. Tonight, more than usual, she hated her job. Hated the lustful stares of the men, their furtive snickers, their lewd attempts at humor. She was tired of fighting off their unwanted advances, tired of forcing herself to laugh at their vulgar jokes. Heck, she was just plain tired.

Waiting at the bar for an order to be filled, she found herself thinking of the man who had come to her rescue the night before. What was his name? Johnny something. A real gentleman, he was. Then again, maybe he wasn't. After knowing her for only a few minutes, he had hinted that she should move in with him. Though he seemed nice enough, she could only imagine what might have happened if she had agreed. No doubt she would have become one of those women you read about in the paper who vanished without a trace, never to be seen or heard from again. *Suspicious, much?* She grinned inwardly as his words from the night before replayed in her mind. *Always*, she thought.

And with good reason.

She slapped the hand of one of the regular patrons when he tried to pat her behind as she passed by, more annoyed than usual. She needed a vacation from this place, but that wasn't going to happen any time soon. Not if she wanted to continue eating.

Maybe she should have taken Johnny what's-his-name up on his offer, she thought, then shook her head. Definitely not a good idea. She was just tired and edgy. She tensed every time a new customer arrived, always afraid Lynx and his buddies might come swaggering through the door.

Where had Darla found a loser like that anyway? Cassie wondered. And why was she always attracted to the wrong kind of guy? Maybe it was in her blood. Her mother had certainly picked a loser.

She felt a startling sizzle of awareness when the door opened and Johnny stepped inside. Had he come looking for her? Filled with a nervous sense of excitement and apprehension, she licked her lips and ran her fingers through her hair.

He smiled when he saw her.

She lifted her hand in acknowledgement, then delivered her drink order to a booth in the back. When she turned around, Johnny was sitting at one of the small tables near the front window. One of her tables.

"I didn't expect to see *you* here tonight," she said, her order pad at the ready. He looked quite handsome in a pair of dark slacks, a white shirt and a thigh-length black coat.

"I was out for a walk and ..." He shrugged. "I thought I'd stop by for a drink. I hope you don't mind."

"It's a free country. What can I get you?"

"A glass of red wine, please."

Nodding, she made her way to the bar, conscious of his gaze on her back.

Giovanni glanced around the room. He rarely frequented nightclubs, preferring to hunt in less crowded venues. He had spent far too much of his existence alone, he thought ruefully. Perhaps it was time to change that.

He murmured his thanks when she returned with his drink.

"I didn't think I'd ever see you again," Cassie remarked.

"I was hoping I might walk you home."

She hesitated a moment, then said, "I get off at two a.m."

"I'll meet you at the door."

With a nod, she moved to another table.

Giovanni sipped his wine, content to sit and watch her as she took orders and served drinks. Twice, he was tempted to interfere – once when a man tried to place his hands on her and a second time when another man made a lewd suggestion – but she seemed capable of fending both of them off without causing a scene.

When he finished his drink, he left her a hefty tip, lifted his hand in farewell and took his leave. He had plenty of time to hunt before he was meet her.

Cassie applied fresh lipstick, tucked a lock of hair behind her hear, took a deep breath and stepped outside, wondering if Johnny would really show up. Most people, working or otherwise, were in bed by now, she thought, but maybe he didn't work. Maybe he was a bored, retired millionaire who'd grown weary of dating wealthy socialites and had decided to go slumming. She shook her head. He didn't seem like the millionaire type, but then, how was she to know? She had certainly never met one, nor was she likely to.

She smiled shyly when she saw him waiting for her. "Hope I didn't keep you waiting."

"Not at all." Drawing his hand from behind his back, he offered her a bouquet of red roses.

Cassie stared at the bouquet, momentarily speechless. "Why?"

"Why not?"

"No one's ever given me flowers before."

"Then I'm glad to be the first."

"They're beautiful."

As are you, he thought, but he lacked the courage to say the words out loud.

"How was your day?" she asked.

"Long," he murmured. "And quiet."

"Oh? Are you retired?"

"In a manner of speaking," he said, stifling a grin.

"What did you do before you quit?"

"I was a priest."

She stared at him, eyes wide. "A priest!"

"Guilty as charged."

"I didn't know priests left the church. I thought it was a lifetime calling. You know, like being a Supreme Court Justice."

He shrugged. "It happens."

"You seem awfully young to be retired. How old are you, if you don't mind me asking?"

"I was thirty-nine on my last birthday. Might I ask how old are you?"

"Twenty-six. You're not married or anything, are you?"

"Of course not!" he exclaimed, obviously offended by the question. "Would I be here with you now if I were?"

She shrugged. "I don't know. Lots of men cheat on their wives."

"Well, *I* would never!"

She laughed at the horrified expression on his face. "I believe you."

Suddenly at a loss for words, his steps slowed. What was he doing here with her? In mortal years, he was thirteen years her senior. But as a vampire, he had existed hundreds of years longer. Yet he feared she was far more worldly-wise than was he. He knew nothing of women, of intimacy—sexual or otherwise. Of dating. Or marriage.

He was relieved when her apartment building came into view.

She paused at the foot of the stairs. "Thanks for walking me home."

"I was happy to. You shouldn't be walking the streets at this hour."

Frowning, Cassie looked up at him. *Walking the streets!*

"Is something wrong?"

"Are you implying that I'm a whore?"

"What? No, of course not! What makes you think that?"

"You practically called me a street walker."

He stared at her in confusion for a moment, then with growing horror as he realized what he had unthinkingly implied. *Street-walker. Doxy. Lightskirt.* "Cassie, please forgive me. That's not what I meant at all."

She found herself grinning at his stricken expression, and then she laughed. "Don't worry about it. I've been called that and worse at the Winchester."

He was surprised to find himself laughing with her. And even more surprised when she went up on her tiptoes and kissed his cheek.

Murmuring, "Good night, Johnny," she ran up the stairs. She stopped at the door and glanced over her shoulder. "Thank you again for the flowers," she called before going inside and closing the door behind her.

Whistling softly, Giovanni strolled down the sidewalk. Maybe she would agree to let him walk her home again tomorrow night.

Excerpt from Dead Perfect, 2013

Chapter 1

Shannah had followed him every night for the last four months. At first, she hadn't been sure why, other than the fact that she was dying and out of a job and had nothing better to do.

She remembered the first time she had seen him. She had been sitting by the back window in the Pot Pourri Café across the street from the town's only movie theater. She had been sipping a cup of hot chocolate when she saw him emerge from the theater. It had been late October, near Halloween, and the theater had been running classic vampire movies all month, showing a different film each night of the week. The old Bela Lugosi version of *Dracula* had been playing that night.

The stranger had been wearing a long black duster over snug black jeans and a black shirt. With his long black hair, her first thought was that he could have been a vampire himself except that his skin was a dusky brown instead of deathly pale. A wannabe vampire, obviously. She knew there was a whole cult of them in the city, men and women who frequented Goth clubs. They wore black clothes and capes.

Some of them wore fake fangs and pretended to drink blood. She had heard that some didn't pretend, but actually drank blood. Others role-played on the Internet in vampire and Goth chat rooms.

Shannah had been sitting by the window in that same café when she saw the stranger the second time. He hadn't been coming out of the movie theater that night, merely strolling down the street, his hands thrust into the pockets of his jeans, which were black again. During the next few weeks, she saw him walking down the same street at about the same time almost every night, which she supposed wasn't really all that strange. After all, she went to the same café and sat at the same booth in the back at about the same time every night.

One evening, simply for something to do, she left the café and followed him, curious to see where he went. She followed him the next night, and the next. And suddenly it was a habit, a way to spend the long, lonely nights when she couldn't sleep. Sometimes he merely walked through the park across from City Hall. Sometimes he sat on one of the benches, as unmoving and silent as the bronze statue of the town's founding father that was located near the center of the park.

While following the man in the long black duster, she learned that he went to the movies every Wednesday evening and always sat in the last row. He wandered through the mall on Friday nights. He spent Saturday nights in the local pub, invariably sitting in the shadows in the far corner. He always ordered a glass of red wine, which he never finished. Other than the wine, she never saw him eat or drink anything. He never bought popcorn or candy at the movies. He never bought a soda or a cup of coffee or a hot dog in the mall.

When she followed him home, she learned that he lived in an old but elegant two-story house at the edge of town. The house had bars on the windows and a security screen door, and was surrounded by a block wall that must have been twelve feet high, complete with an impressive wrought-iron gate. She wondered what he was hiding in there and spent untold hours pondering who and what he might be. A drug lord? An arms dealer? Some sort of international spy? A reclusive millionaire? A serial killer? A mad scientist? A terrorist? Her imagination knew no bounds.

The holidays came and went. He didn't go to visit family for Thanksgiving, and no one came to visit him. As far as she could see, he didn't celebrate Christmas. No tinsel-laden tree appeared in the large front window. No colorful lights adorned his house. He didn't go out to celebrate the New Year. But then, neither did she. As far as she knew, he didn't buy flowers or candy on Valentine's Day, nor did he go to visit a lady friend. He was a handsome man – tall, dark and handsome – which begged the question, why wasn't he married, or at least dating? Perhaps he was in mourning. Perhaps that was why he always wore black. Then again, maybe he wore it because it looked so good on him.

She camped out in the woods across from his house three or four times a week, weather permitting, but she never saw him emerge during the day. He took a daily newspaper, but he never picked it up until after the sun went down. The same with his mail. He never had any visitors. He never had pizza delivered. No repairmen ever came to call.

She wasn't sure when she started to think he really was a vampire, but the more she thought about it, the more convinced she became. He only came out at night. He lived alone. He didn't eat. He always wore black. He never had any visitors. She never saw him with anyone else because...

He was a vampire.

Vampires lived forever and were supposed to be able to pass immortality on to others.

Ergo, he was the only one who could help her.

All she needed now was the courage to approach him. But how? And when? And what would she say?

It was the first of March before she finally worked up enough courage to put intention into action. Tomorrow night, she decided resolutely. She would ask him tomorrow night.

But, just in case he refused her or she changed her mind at the last minute, she armed herself with a small bottle of holy water stolen from the Catholic Church on the corner of Main Street, wondering, briefly, if stolen holy water would retain its effectiveness. She found a small gold crucifix and chain that had belonged to her favorite aunt. She fashioned a wooden stake out of the handle of an old broom. She filled the pockets of her coat and jeans with cloves of garlic.

That should do it, she thought, patting her coat pocket. If he was agreeable, by this time tomorrow night she would be Undead. If he decided to make a meal of her instead of transforming her, she would just be dead a few weeks earlier than the doctors had predicted.

Chapter 2

Ronan didn't have to glance over his shoulder to know that the slender girl with the long black hair and big blue eyes was following him again. She had drifted in his wake like a pale shadow for the last five months or so. She followed him to the park. She followed him to the movies, to the local pub, to the mall, to his post office box when he picked up his mail. She followed him home. Sometimes she spent the night in the wooded area across from his house.

He wondered when she slept.

He wondered why her complexion was so ashen.

He wondered who she was.

He wondered why in blue blazes she was following him.

One thing was certain. He didn't like her trailing after him one damn bit. He could have lost her easily enough. He could have destroyed her. He could have hypnotized her and made her forget he existed.

So, why hadn't he?

It was a question he had asked himself every night for the last five months.

It was a question for which he had no answer, and that annoyed the living hell out of him. But just now, he had other, more important things on his mind than a skinny mortal female.

Lifting his head, he caught the scent of prey on the evening breeze. With a thought, he vanished from her sight.

Shannah blinked and blinked again. Where had he gone? One minute he had been a few yards ahead of her and the next he was gone as if he had never been there at all.

Pausing, she rubbed her eyes. Had she started to imagine things? Maybe it was just one more symptom of her illness, like the fever that burned through her. Or maybe he really was a vampire. She giggled. Or the Invisible Man.

Feeling suddenly light-headed, she reached out, bracing one hand against the wall of a tall brick building. Her time was running out. She felt it in the deepest part of her being, knew it was only a matter of weeks, perhaps days, before she lapsed into a coma, never to awake again. And then what? The endless nothingness that she feared, or the heavenly paradise that her grandmother had promised awaited all those who believed?

Shannah took a deep breath. Before she left this world, she had to know if the man she had been following was truly a vampire.

On legs that wobbled with every step, she walked to the woods across from his house and settled down in her usual place to keep watch. It was quite cozy, all things considered. She had a couple of warm quilts, a small pillow, an ice chest filled with water and soft drinks, another chest filled with potato chips and her favorite candy bars. Not exactly a healthy diet, but what difference did it make now? It was only a matter of time as to which ran out first, the money her grandfather had left her, or her life. She giggled as she reached for a soda. At least she didn't have to worry about high cholesterol or getting fat. Or catching some horrible fatal disease, she thought with morbid amusement, since she already had one.

Tonight, she didn't have to wait long for the stranger to appear. He emerged out of the darkness a short time later and entered his house. The lights came on. Plumes of blue-gray smoke drifted from the chimney to be blown away by an itinerant breeze.

She had promised herself that she would approach him tonight but her courage suddenly deserted her. She would keep watch here again tonight, she decided, and knock on his door tomorrow afternoon. If he answered, she would know he wasn't a vampire. If he didn't... somehow she would have to work up the nerve to approach him after the sun went down.

But for now... her eyelids fluttered down. For now she needed sleep.

⚜ ⚜ ⚜

She woke late in the afternoon with the sun in her face and the usual cramping in her stomach. Sitting up, she folded her arms around her middle and rocked back and forth. When the worst of the pain was over, she drank some water, then splashed some on her face. Though she wasn't really hungry, she knew she needed to eat to keep her strength up and she forced herself to eat one of the bran muffins she had bought the day before, and to drink some orange juice.

Finally, with one hand propped against a tree, she gained her feet, her gaze moving to the house across the way. It looked like the kind of house you saw in movies, the kind inhabited by witches or haunted by unfriendly ghosts.

She had planned to approach the mysterious stranger that afternoon but now that the time had come, she found her courage failing her once more. Even though she was convinced he was the only answer to her problem, she wasn't sure she was ready to meet a vampire face to face.

"Oh, for goodness sakes, stop being such a coward," she muttered. "What have you got to lose? A few days at most."

Still, she wanted those days. In the last few months, she had learned that each new day, each hour of life, was a precious gift from God, a gift that was meant to be savored and cherished. She only wished she had realized that sooner.

She dusted off her jeans, straightened her blouse, ran her hands through the tangles in her hair. Glancing at her watch, she saw that it was a little after five. Too early for a vampire to be up and about. So, if he answered the door, that would prove he wasn't a vampire. And if he didn't answer, well if he didn't, it could mean one of two things. Either he had left the house while she slept, proving that he was just a man, or he was stretched out in his coffin somewhere, sleeping the sleep of the Undead.

Taking a deep breath, she squared her shoulders and marched resolutely across the grassy field and the road beyond. She pushed on the heavy gate, blew out a sigh of exasperation when it didn't open. She should have known that it would be locked.

Well, she wasn't going to let a little thing like a locked gate deter her now that she had finally found the courage to approach him. Turning to the left, she followed the block wall along the property line and there, at the back of the house, she found a tree with branches that extended over the wall.

Taking another deep breath, she reached for the lowest branch. It had been years since she had climbed a tree and now she knew why. She hadn't worried about falling and breaking a leg or, worse, her neck, when she'd been a little girl, but the possibility of either or both occurred to her now. And then she shrugged. A broken neck would be a quick, reasonably painless way to go.

Shaking the thought from her mind, she gained the top of the wall, swung her legs over the other side, and dropped to the ground in the back yard.

The house looked as forbidding from the back as it did from the front. The grounds were in dire need of attention. The lawn hadn't been mowed in weeks, perhaps months. There were weeds that needed pulling, trees that hadn't been pruned in a long time, a wrought-iron bench in need of paint. It was a big yard, one that could have been beautiful. It seemed a shame to let it get so overgrown. If she lived here, she would plant flowers along the walkway and rose bushes in the weed-infested gardens. She'd put a covered swing in the corner, maybe a gazebo near the gardens.

But it wasn't her house. With a shake of her head, she walked around to the front porch. Her palms were damp, her mouth as dry as the Sahara in mid-summer when she finally summoned the courage to knock on the door.

Minutes passed.

She knocked again, harder. And then once more.

So, was he sleeping in his coffin, or just not at home?

She was about to turn away when the door opened and she found herself staring up into the face of the man she had been following. She had never been close enough to see the color of his eyes. Now she saw that they were black. *As black as death.* The words whispered through the corridors of her mind even as she felt the warmth of the late afternoon sun on her back. Danger emanated from him like heat rising from summer-hot pavement.

He couldn't be a vampire.

He couldn't help her.

She was going to die.

Tears burned the backs of her eyes and dampened her cheeks. She didn't want to die, not now. She was only twenty-four. There was so much she wanted to do, so many places she wanted to go, so much of life she had yet to experience. And she was afraid. Afraid of the pain, afraid of dying.

His hooded gaze met hers, cool and direct. "What are you doing here?"

"Nothing. I'm sorry. I thought you were someone else."

"Who are you looking for?"

"It doesn't matter."

"Have you a name?"

"Shannah." She wiped her tear-damp cheeks with the back of her hand. "I'm sorry I bothered you. Goodbye."

She tried to turn away but her legs refused to obey. Caught in the dark web of his gaze, she could only stand there, her arms limp at her sides, staring up at him while hot tears trickled down her cheeks. She had never really noticed how handsome he was. Not in the way that the blond, bland young men in Hollywood were handsome, but in a dark, mysterious and forbidding sort of way. He had short thick eyelashes, a fine straight nose, a strong jaw line. He looked like a man who knew what he wanted in life and wouldn't hesitate to take it by fair means or foul.

"You've been following me for the last five months," he said brusquely. "Who did you think I was?" He glanced past her to the wrought-iron gate. "And how the hell did you get in here?"

She felt a rush of heat climb up the back of her neck as she searched her mind for a convincing lie but his gaze continued to hold hers captive and she suddenly lacked the will to lie to him.

"I thought you were a vampire," she said, thinking how foolish the words sounded when spoken out loud.

One dark brow lifted. "A vampire?" he murmured. "Indeed?"

She nodded, embarrassed now. "But it's still daylight, you know, and you're awake instead of closed up in your coffin so I guess I was wrong..." She bit down on her lower lip, aware that she was babbling like an idiot. "I'll be going now. I'm sorry I bothered you."

Shoulders drooping with discouragement, she turned away, took a few wobbly steps and with a small moan, tumbled down the porch stairs.

Ronan stared at the girl sprawled at the bottom of the steps, at the thin trickle of crimson oozing from a shallow cut in her forehead. He took a deep breath as the intoxicating scent of her blood was carried to him on an errant breeze. Was there anything in the world that smelled as sweet?

Muttering an oath, he turned on his heel and went back inside the house, only to emerge a moment later swathed in a heavy black hooded cloak that covered him from head to heel.

Bracing himself for the pain to come, he flew down the stairs, swept the girl into his arms, and darted back into the house, kicking the door shut behind him.

Eyes closed, he stood in the entryway for a moment, panting heavily, his skin tingling and tightening in a most unpleasant way. When the worst of the pain receded, he glanced down at the girl in his arms. She was unconscious, her breathing labored, her cheeks ashen. She was far too thin. Her skin was feverishly warm. There were dark purple shadows, like bruises, beneath her eyes, hollows in her pale cheeks. He could hear the beat of her heart, slow and heavy, smell the life-giving blood that flowed sluggishly through her veins and oozed in thick red drops from the shallow cut in her brow.

The crimson droplets beckoned him. His hold on her tightened. He licked his lips as the hunger stirred deep within, searing his insides, demanding to be fed.

Unable to resist either the pain of his hunger or the temptation of her blood, he lowered his head and licked the blood from the wound.

And tasted death.

Chapter 3

Shannah woke slowly. Her eyelids felt heavy and it was an effort to open her eyes. For a moment, she stared blankly at her surroundings. The walls were painted taupe with white trim. The ceiling was white. A fire burned in the hearth across from the canopied bed on which she lay. A thick white carpet covered the floor. Heavy draperies the same color as the walls covered the room's single window. The dresser against the far wall looked like an antique, as did the high-backed oak rocking chair in the corner. Large, expensive-looking paintings hung on the walls—one was of a stately park where people in eighteenth century clothing strolled along tree-lined lanes; one was of a Paris cathedral; the third depicted a quiet lake beneath a full moon. The fourth painting was of a dark castle set upon a windswept hill. Where was she?

Where was he?

Her head ached and when she touched her fingertips to her forehead, she made two discoveries—her fever was gone and there was a rather large bandage taped above her left eye. She didn't remember being injured. Frowning made her head hurt worse.

It wasn't until she slid her legs over the edge of the bed that she realized she wasn't wearing anything save for her bra, panties, and a dark blue velvet robe with a black satin collar.

When she stood, the robe's hem dragged on the floor and the sleeves fell past her hands. She glanced around the room, looking for her clothes, but they were nowhere in sight. She checked the closet and the chest of drawers. Both were empty.

She walked across the floor, her bare feet making no sound on the soft thick carpet. Putting her ear to the door, she listened for a moment before she opened it and stepped out into the hallway.

A glance up and down the narrow corridor showed several doors. None of them were open.

Clutching the collar of the robe in one hand, she tip-toed along the hallway, her footsteps muffled by the thick carpet beneath her feet.

She paused at the top of the landing, listening, and when she heard nothing, she padded quietly down the staircase.

At the bottom, she paused again.

Was she in *his* house? And if she was, where was he, and why were there no clothes in the closet? She had come here looking for a vampire. Now that her fever was gone and she was thinking more clearly, she knew how foolish that had been. Vampires were creatures of myth and legend.

But what if he was something even worse?

Where had he put her clothing? She could hardly walk back to her apartment in her bare feet, wearing nothing but a too large bathrobe, nice and comfy as it was.

Moving as quietly as she could, she made her way into the kitchen, thinking to fortify herself with a cup of strong black coffee.

No such luck. The cupboards were empty. The stove and the refrigerator looked new and unused. The fridge was empty. There was no table. Odd, that there was no food in the house but then, maybe he never ate at home. Still, it was mighty strange that he didn't at least have the basics. Or a few dishes.

She couldn't remember the last time she had been truly hungry. She rarely ate a full meal any more. Doing so made her sick to her stomach and yet, for the first time in months, she was famished.

She was standing in the middle of the floor, her stomach growling, when there was a knock at the back door. She hesitated a moment before opening it.

A cute young man with curly brown hair stood at the door holding a large box of groceries. "Miss Shannah?"

"Yes?"

"Where do you want this?"

She glanced at the cardboard box in his hand. "I'm not sure. I didn't..."

"It was a phone order from Mr. Dark."

"Oh." Was that the stranger's name? Mr. Dark? She took a step backward. "Just put it on the counter, I guess."

The young man did as bidden. He handed her a receipt and a pen. "Just sign here."

She signed the receipt and handed the slip of paper and the pen back to the young man. "I'm afraid I don't have any cash for a tip."

"Don't worry about it," he said, grinning. "Mr. Dark took care of it. Have a good day, ma'am."

"Thank you."

She closed the door, then went to look through the box. It held a jar of instant coffee, a half-gallon of milk, a box of assorted individual servings of cereal, a small box of sugar, a loaf of bread, lunch meat and cheese, eggs, bacon, a box of pancake mix, syrup, a jar of peanut butter, another of jelly, a six-pack of soda, butter, salt and pepper, a small jar of mayonnaise, mustard, and ketchup, as well as paper plates and a package of plastic knives, forks, and spoons, some plastic cups, as well as a toothbrush and toothpaste. At the bottom of the box she found two frying pans and a toaster.

Her stomach growled loudly as she stared at the bounty before her. With a shake of her head, she put everything away, then set about making French toast and bacon for breakfast.

Mr. Dark, indeed, she mused. She didn't know if that was his real name or not, but it fit perfectly.

She carried her breakfast into the living room and sat on the sofa since there was no place to sit in the kitchen.

When she finished eating, she sat back, waiting for her stomach to cramp, for the food to come back up again, as it always did when she ate too much too fast. But nothing happened. Rising, she carried her dishes into the kitchen and put them in the sink. She would wash them later, she decided, for now she wanted to see the rest of the house.

The living room, done in shades of blue and gray, was roomy and comfortable, with a high-backed sofa, an overstuffed chair, a glass-topped coffee table, and a big screen plasma TV with surround sound. Heavy draperies covered the big picture window and the smaller windows located on either side of the front door.

The dining room was bare save for a large oil painting of a tall-masted ship adrift on a storm-tossed sea.

Continuing down the hallway, she looked in every room. There was a bathroom with a large shower, a marble sink, and a sunken tub. A large walk-in linen closet was located across from the bathroom. The bedroom next to the bathroom was decorated in shades of forest green and gold. The furniture was country oak. The walls were beige, all hung with large paintings—a stag in the midst of a sun-drenched meadow; a wolf posed on the edge of a craggy hill; a shepherd cradling a lamb to his chest; a herd of wild horses running across a moonlit prairie. He seemed to have a taste for art, she mused, moving on down the hallway. She was no expert, but all the paintings looked extremely expensive.

It was the last room that drew her inside. The walls on either side of the door were lined with floor-to-ceiling bookshelves; heavy wine-red velvet drapes covered a large window in the third wall. An enormous desk stood in front of the fourth wall. It held a computer, a large LCD flat screen monitor, a cordless mouse and keyboard, a combination printer/scanner/copier, and nothing else. She was tempted to turn on the computer but something held her back.

The bookshelves held a wide variety of books, everything from encyclopedias to mysteries to romance novels. One shelf held a dozen paperback books by the same author, Eva Black. Shannah had never read a romance novel in her life but the author's name sounded vaguely familiar.

Another shelf held mysteries written by Claire Ebon. Still another shelf held several hardback contemporary novels written by Stella Raven.

Shannah frowned. Black, Ebon, Raven. Odd, that they all had last names so similar in meaning. Odder still that her host's name was Mr. Dark. She puzzled over that for several minutes, then shrugged. It was probably just a coincidence.

Leaving the computer room, she went upstairs to explore the second floor. She wasn't surprised when she discovered that all the rooms except the one she had awakened in were empty. Bare floors, blank walls, all painted the same shade of off-white. Perhaps he had moved in recently, she thought. Maybe it was his first house. That would explain the lack of furniture, knickknacks, and the other odds and ends that people tended to collect when they had lived in the same house for a long time.

She should go home, she thought, before he came back from wherever he had gone. He hadn't been happy to see her on his doorstep. She was certain he wouldn't be happy to know she had been snooping around his house while he was away. She was surprised he had taken her in and let her spend the night.

Yes, she should go home, but not now. Feeling suddenly weary, she made her way back into the taupe-colored bedroom and climbed up on the bed. Pulling the covers up to her chin, she closed her eyes. She was tired, so very, very tired. The doctors had warned her that she would feel that way when the end was near, though how they knew that was beyond her. They didn't even know what was wrong with her. At first, they had thought she had some rare form of leukemia, then they'd thought it might be some sexually transmitted disease similar to AIDS, only she didn't do drugs and she had never had sexual intercourse. Though the doctors couldn't decide what was wrong with her, they had all agreed on one thing. She was dying, and she didn't have much time left, perhaps six months. And now five of them were gone.

But she wouldn't think of that, not now. She would just close her eyes for a few minutes and then she would call for a cab and go home.

He rose at dusk, his nostrils assailed by the faint, lingering odors of eggs and milk and bacon. And over the stink of food he detected the tantalizing scent of the woman. So, she was still here. He had expected she would be long gone by now.

He moved through the house until he reached the bedroom, his senses quickening when he saw her lying in his bed, her hair spread across the white pillowcase like a splash of black ink. Her face was very nearly as pale as the pillowcase beneath her head. Her eyelashes lay like dark fans upon her cheeks.

She was dying. A rare disease of the blood, something so rare even her doctor wasn't sure what it was or what had caused it. Perhaps that explained why she had come looking for a vampire.

He had known many people in the course of his existence. Most came and went without making any noticeable impact on his life. Only a few had been memorable. She would be one of them, though he couldn't say why. He hardly knew her. If he were still capable of human feelings, he might have shed tears for her.

She moaned softly, her fingers worrying the covers. "No! No, I'm afraid. Oh, please, no..."

She began to thrash around under the covers. And then she screamed.

He had heard countless cries of terror throughout his long existence but this one cut through his heart and soul like a knife.

"Shannah." Murmuring her name, he sat on the edge of the mattress and drew her into his arms. "Wake up, child."

Her eyelids fluttered open. For a moment, she stared at him, her eyes wide and frightened. And then, with a strangled sob, she collapsed in his arms, her body trembling.

"It's all right, Shannah," he whispered. "There's nothing for you to be afraid of. You're safe here, with me."

It was a lie, of course, but she didn't know that.

When she continued to shiver, he pulled the blanket from the bed and draped it around her, and then he rocked her back and forth as if she were, indeed, a child.

Gradually, her trembling ceased and she lay quiet in his arms.

He brushed a lock of hair from her brow. "How do you feel?"

"I'm dying."

"Is that why you were looking for a vampire?"

She nodded. "I thought..."

"That I would bring you across?"

"Yes."

He smiled faintly. "You came well-armed." He had smelled the garlic she carried when he opened the door and saw her standing on the porch, had noted the cross she wore on a fine gold chain around her neck. When he put her to bed, he had been amused to find a crudely fashioned wooden stake tucked inside the waistband of her jeans, cloves of garlic and a small vial of holy water in the pockets of her jacket. He had disposed of all but the cross and chain. "And do you want to be a vampire?"

"No!" she exclaimed softly, and then, softer still, "but I don't want to die, either."

"Perhaps the doctors were wrong."

"They can't all be wrong," she said wearily. Pushing away from him, she sat up, her shoulders slumped, defeat evident in every line of her body. "I should go home."

"You should rest a little longer. Why don't you go back to sleep?"

"No." She had only a short time left; she didn't want to waste any of it by sleeping more than was absolutely necessary. She wanted to live every minute while she could. "Anyway," she said, throwing the covers aside. "I can't stay here."

He gazed deep into her eyes. "Of course you can." He tucked her under the covers once more, then stood beside the bed, looking down at her. "Go to sleep, Shannah. Everything will be better tomorrow."

"Yes," she said, yawning behind her hand. "Tomorrow." Her eyelids fluttered down. A moment later, she was asleep.

He watched her for a moment more, then knelt beside the bed. Brushing a lock of hair away from her neck, he ran his tongue lightly over her skin, felt his fangs lengthen in quick response to the scent of her blood, the pulse beating slow and regular in the hollow of her throat.

He closed his eyes as the hunger rose up within him, demanding to be fed. As gently as possible, he buried his fangs in the soft skin beneath her ear. In spite of the ravening hunger that clawed at him, he drank only a little. In spite of the impurity in her blood, it was sweet, sweeter than anything he had ever tasted.

Drawing away, he made a gash in his wrist with his teeth. Dark red blood bubbled from the ragged incision.

"Hear me, Shannah," he said, holding the bleeding wound to her lips, "you must open your mouth and drink."

Obediently, she opened her mouth and swallowed a few drops of his blood.

A flick of his tongue closed the wound in his wrist.

"Sleep now, my sweet Shannah," he murmured. "Sleep and dream of a long and healthy life."

About the Author

Amanda Ashley started writing for the fun of it. Her first book, a historical romance written as Madeline Baker, was published in 1985. Since then, she has published numerous historical and paranormal romances and novellas, many of which have appeared on various bestseller lists, including the *New York Times* Bestseller List and *USA Today*.

Amanda makes her home in Southern California, where she and her husband share their house with a Pomeranian named Lady, a cat named Kitty, and a tortoise named Buddy.

For more information on her books, please visit her websites at www.amandaashley.net and www.madelinebaker.net

Email: darkwritr@aol.com

About the Publisher

This book is published on behalf of the author by the Ethan Ellenberg Literary Agency.

https://ethanellenberg.com

Email: agent@ethanellenberg.com

Made in the USA
Middletown, DE
15 October 2020

22005796R00166